Maurice

A Thousand Years

Maurice H. Harris

A Thousand Years

1st Edition | ISBN: 978-3-75233-895-9

Place of Publication: Frankfurt am Main, Germany

Year of Publication: 2020

Outlook Verlag GmbH, Germany.

A Thousand Years of Jewish History

BY THE
REV. MAURICE H. HARRIS

INTRODUCTION

"Wenn es eine Stufenleiter von Leiden giebt, so hat Israel die höchste Staffel erstiegen; wenn die Dauer der Schmerzen und die Geduld, mit welcher sie ertragen werden, adeln, so nehmen es die Juden mit den Hochgeborenen aller Länder auf; wenn eine Literatur reich genannt wird, die wenige klassische Trauerspiele besitzt, welcher Platz gebührt dann einer Tragödie, die anderthalb Jahrtausende währt gedichtet und dargestellt von den Helden selber?"

—ZUNZ: *Die Synagogale Poesie des Mittelalters.*

When the impatient youth demands, like the heathen from Hillel, a definition of Judaism, bid him "go and learn" the history of the Jew. Let him follow the fascinating story from hoar antiquity, when the obscure Hebrews, "leaving kindred and father's house," took a bold and new departure for the land that God would show—the land that would show God.

Point to the colossal figure of Moses on Sinai, "greatest of the prophets," who gave the first uplifting impulse with his Ten Words of Faith and Duty. Trace with him the soul struggle of this "fewest of all peoples" to reach the truth of divinity—beginning with a crude conception that became steadily more exalted and more clarified with each successive age, until, at last, the idea is realized of an all-pervading Spirit, with "righteousness and justice as the pillars of His throne," the "refuge of all generations."

Make clear to him how the revelation of the divine will came to be expressed in Law. And, how the preservation and development of this Law, in the interpreting hands of prophets, scribes, rabbis, poets and philosophers, became henceforth the controlling motif of the history of the Jew, his *modus vivendi*, whether under Babylonians, Persians, Greeks, Romans, Arabians or Franks. Help him to see that through it the Jew held in his keeping the religious fate of Orient and Occident, that took from him their respective impressions of Islamism and Christianity.

Let him see the "God-intoxicated" teaching his message by living it; the Suffering Servant whose martyrdom brought healing to his smiters.

Then, perhaps, he may understand that no one definition can completely express the Faith of the Jew and his place in the divine economy. But with this glimpse of his history the grandeur of his inheritance will sink into his consciousness, becoming part of himself, and he will be thrilled with the tremendous responsibility devolving upon him as a member of the priest-people, the witnesses of God, whose mission was and is to "bring light to the Gentiles—that salvation may reach to the ends of the earth."

BOOK I.

JUDEA, A VASSAL STATE.

CHAPTER I.

UNDER PERSIAN SWAY.

PERSIA		JUDEA		FAMOUS CONTEMPORARIES	
	B.C.E.		B.C.E.		B.C.E
Cyrus conquers the Babylonians	538	Return of Judah from Exile	536		
Cambyses	529	Haggai and			
Darius	522	Zechariah,			
defeated at		prophets	520-516		
Marathon	490	Second Temple		FLOURISHED	
Xerxes	485	rebuilt	516		
Artaxerxes I		Esther and		Gautama Buddha	500
(Longimanus)	465	Mordecai	485	Confucius	500
		Ezra goes to Jerusalem with second group of exiles	458		
		Nehemiah's first visit	444		
		Nehemiah Governor of Judah	432	Socrates	430
		Malachi the prophet about	430		
Darius II	424			Xenophon	400
Artaxerxes II					
Artaxerxes III				Plato d.	347
(Mnemon)	404				

The story covered by the early dates in this table is not yet post-Biblical. It is already told in the later Books of Ezra, Nehemiah, Haggai and Zechariah i-viii. The history of this volume begins with the close of the life-work of these men.

The restoration of the Jews to Judea did not materialize as gloriously as Isaiah of Babylon had prefigured in his sublime addresses (Isaiah xl-xlvi.) Life's realizations very often disappoint their anticipations. Cyrus, the Persian king, opened the door; but only a poor remnant returned to a poor land. Even then, enemies made their appearance, envious of the royal grant, and plotted against their welfare. So it took many years to rebuild the Temple and many more to rebuild Jerusalem and to reorganize a new community. This service we owe to Nehemiah.

Political Silence.

After the chronicle of Nehemiah's service in placing the Jewish settlement on a working basis, we are told hardly anything more of the doings of Israel in this epoch. Either there was no further historic incident of the Jews under Persian sway, or it has never been told. There is a silence of about a hundred years after the last chapter of Nehemiah, which is, roughly speaking, the last chapter of Jewish history in the Bible. One reason for this silence of course, is that the Jews had no separate political life. They were a subject people; their State was gone. What there is to tell can be disposed of in a few sentences.

We perhaps infer from the sixty-third chapter of Isaiah that they suffered during the campaigns of the two Artaxerxes against Egypt. We know that some were banished to the Caspian Sea because they were implicated in a wide-spread insurrection against the fast declining Persia, instigated by the different peoples settled around the Mediterranean shore. We are told further that an upstart named Bagoas heavily taxed the Jews and made a quarrel over the priesthood an excuse to desecrate their Temple.

That is really all. When this intriguer attempted to place his own candidate on the Persian throne the knell had been rung. Persia's days were numbered. Like its Babylonian predecessor, it had been "weighed in the balance and found wanting." The Greek forces of Alexander were advancing and about the year 332 the Persian dynasty, founded by Cyrus—let us say "The Great"—passed away.

7

Religious Activity.

But silent though the period was in external doings, it was a stirring time in Israel for what we might call the experience of the soul. When we turn to the religious life of the Jews, the epoch, apparently so barren, is full of significance. Great achievements are here disclosed behind the historian's silence.

To tell the religious story, we must go back to Ezra again—the Ezra who came to Judea with the second group of Babylonian exiles and who revived the religious life of the community (*People of the Book*, vol. iii, ch. xxxiv), was the father of the *Scribes*. A scribe was not merely, as the name might imply, one who copied the writings of others, but one who expounded them. The Pentateuch, which contains many codes of law in Exodus, Leviticus, Numbers and Deuteronomy, came to be called "the Law" as a whole. (Torah.) We shall learn how this term later came to include the vaster code that was gradually deduced from these Biblical books. In fact, from now on, *Judaism is interpreted as law.*

How did it happen that the Jewish religion was accepted by its observers as a Law? In ancient times Religion and State were one. There was not that division between sacred affairs and secular that we are familiar with to-day. Duty to God and the King were allied; patriotism merged into piety. Hence the Pentateuch contains laws touching civil as well as spiritual relations, and regulates affairs both secular and sacred. For example, it contains laws about kings, servants, agriculture, war, food, dress, courts of justice, loans, inheritance, in fact every need that arose in the civilization of the time. It contains the Decalogue, regulations for festivals and sacrificial worship, duties to the poor, the stranger, the dumb animal, the code of Holiness (Levit. xvii-xxvii), and exhortations to noble living. It is beautiful to notice how the moral pervades the secular and gives to all a sanctifying touch.

Thus the scribes of this latter day had to interpret Scripture for the daily affairs of public life as well as for the regulation of the holy seasons and the religious ceremonial in Israel's semi-independent state. So the Sanhedrin (a Greek word), a body of seventy members, was both a House of Legislature and an ecclesiastical council. It numbered 70 like the Council of Elders appointed by Moses (Exodus xxiv, 1).

Thus it happened when all political power was taken, from the Jews, the presentation of religion through the forms of law very naturally survived.

There is yet another reason for Judaism being interpreted as Law, which touches the genius of Judaism. Judaism has always been less a faith to be confessed than a life to be lived. The emphasis was laid on deed rather than on dogma, on law rather than creed. We shall later see (p. 133) that it was on this very distinction that Christianity broke away from the parent religion to become a separate Faith.

The reduction of religion to law had its abuses as well as its excellences. It led to the multiplication of ceremonials. The laws of ritual cleanliness, especially for the priests and of Sabbath observance, were very voluminous and very minute. Perhaps too much importance was laid on minor detail; there was little room for voluntary and spontaneous action. On the other hand, too much freedom in religious observance has its dangers and pitfalls too. At its best the Jewish Law tended to sanctify every act of life and to bring the humblest obligation into relationship with God. But whenever a religion crystallizes into an institution, as it inevitably must, the spirit occasionally gets lost in the form. Then it becomes the function of the prophet to bring back the emphasis to religion's vital issues.

Priest and Synagogue.

A further word on the religious life of post-exilic Israel. We must remember at the start that Judea was a colony subject to Persia, but enjoyed complete autonomy in the management of its internal affairs. The head of the community was the High Priest. He not only regulated all functions in the Temple (the religious centre), but because religion and government could not be entirely separated, as explained above, he exercised secular power too. As the high-priesthood became a hereditary office it acquired quite a royal distinction. This regal splendor and "temporal" power in the High Priest's hands were to cause Israel much woe later and became one of the causes of its downfall.

Distinct from the Temple, Houses of Prayer were springing up, called Synagogues. The Synagogue gradually developed a distinct ritual, and Sabbath readings from the Pentateuch and the Prophets became a permanent institution. This is treated in fuller detail in chapter xxv.

The religious activities and conditions here described were not limited to the Persian era, but continued in the Greek period that immediately followed.

A word about the literature of this Second-Temple or post-exilic epoch. The most important of the later Biblical books are ascribed to it, notably the Holy

Writings, specified below.

It was further the time of literary activity in editing Bible books already written and deducing new law from Scripture. But nothing of the Prophetic style of writing appeared. Haggai, Zechariah and Malachi were the last, and already we miss in them the earlier Prophetic grandeur. Ah, the days of prophecy were over! There were no more great names. But there was a general body called "Men of the Great Synagogue." "Synagogue" does not here mean House of Worship, but a Council of Scholars, consisting of 120 members. Under this title some noble masters of the Law contributed splendid literary service, satisfied to sink their identity in this general term.

The Bible Canon.

A sacred collection of writings, accepted as books of authority on religious life is called a *Canon*, a Greek word meaning rule. The task of deciding what was worthy to be admitted into the Canon of the Hebrew Scripture was a task of great responsibility. Nor was it completed at one time. Begun by the Men of the Great Synagogue, its final completion was postponed until nearly a century after the Christian era.

The Bible Books were placed in three groups, namely: *Law*, *Prophets*, *Holy Writings*. This sequence marked both the order of their importance in rabbinic estimate and to some extent, the sequence of their production. 1st, The Law consists of the five books of the Pentateuch, Genesis, Exodus, Leviticus, Numbers, Deuteronomy. 2d, The Prophets fall into two groups: (a) the Former Prophets, comprising the historical books—Joshua, Judges, First and Second Samuel, First and Second Kings, illustrative of the divine guidance of Israel; (b) the Later Prophets, the Prophetic Books proper: the three largest, Isaiah, Jeremiah, Ezekiel; the twelve smaller Prophets, Hosea, Joel, Amos, Obadiah, Jonah, Micah, Nahum, Habakkuk, Zephaniah, Haggai, Zechariah and Malachi. 3rd, The Hagiographa (Holy Writings), was a miscellaneous collections of Scriptures, some written very late indeed. It included Psalms, Proverbs, Job; five little books called Megilloth (Scrolls): Song of Songs, Ruth, Lamentations, Ecclesiastes and Esther; Daniel, Ezra, Nehemiah and First and Second Chronicles.

These were doubtless selected from the larger library of Jewish literature only after long discussion. All were well weighed before being admitted into this sacred Canon. Some of those not chosen are doubtless lost. Some found their way into another collection, known as the Apocrypha, to be considered later.

Enough is assuredly indicated here to show that the post-exilic epoch was not a time of empty silence, but one of tremendous activity—one of the most fruitful literary periods in our history.

NOTES AND REFERENCES.

Persian Influence:

Persian ideas unconsciously exercised their influence on Jews living under Persian rule. As a result, conceptions of the future life and retribution beyond the grave became more definite than in their earlier Biblical presentation; the belief in angels and evil spirits received further development.

Judaism as Law:

That Israel laid small stress on creed is further proved by the late date of the formulation of any articles of faith. Even the thirteen creeds of Maimonides (see *History Medieval Jews*, p. 157), were drawn up rather to differentiate Judaism from Christianity and Mohammedanism, than to explain its teachings to Jews.

Israel's detractors say that Judaism interpreted as Law tended to blur moral distinctions. This is a superficial and erroneous inference, for it quite as often re-inforced them and prevented temporizing with duty.

Read "The Law and Recent Criticism," in the eleventh volume of the *Jewish Quarterly Review* (London, Macmillan) in reply to a criticism against Judaism as Law; Montefiore, "*Bible for Home Reading*," vol. ii, pages 12-18, on the Law; *Hibbert Lectures*, 1892, Montefiore, parts of chapters vi and ix on the Scriptures. *Introduction Literature of the Old Testament.* Driver, (Scribner.)

Bible Books:

The order of the Bible Books in the Septuagint, which order is followed by all Church translations of the Bible, differs from the Hebrew order, as follows: 1st, the Writings precede the Prophets. 2d, Ruth, Lamentations, Daniel and Chronicles are taken from the Writings and placed as follows: Ruth after Judges, Lamentations after Jeremiah, Daniel after Ezekiel, Chronicles after Kings. 3d, Job precedes Psalms.

Theme for discussion:

Discuss the relation between *Judaism as law*, and Mendelssohn's statement that "Judaism is not a revealed religion, but a revealed legislation." See *Modern Jewish History*, p. 78.

Chronological Table.

CHAPTER II.

GREEK AND JEW.

Alexander the Great.

The Greeks and the Jews have been the greatest contributors toward the higher civilization of mankind, the Greek in the intellectual and artistic realm, the Jew in the religious and moral. Therefore we discern the hand of Providence in bringing them together for they influenced each other. The meeting of Greek and Jew is one of the great events of history, greater than many of the battles that have decided the fates of empires. Greece had already lived her most thrilling epoch when the meeting began, but Plato, disciple of the moral philosopher, Socrates, had but recently passed away and Aristotle, profoundest philosopher of antiquity, still lived.

Macedonia had absorbed other Greek principalities and Alexander, now sole master, carried his army eastward in the hope of founding a universal empire. Whenever he conquered a land, he colonized it with Greeks and thus spread Greek civilization. Egypt, Asia Minor, Syria, Phoenicia, and ultimately Ethiopia and India fell successively before his triumphant approach.

The Persian empire that had been fast decaying, was included in the great array of conquests. Tired of the intriguing adventurer placed over them in the last years, the Jews gladly welcomed the conqueror. Legend weaves a pretty story of the Jewish High Priest, Onias, going forth with a company clad in white to meet Alexander, and that in this picture Alexander saw the fulfilment of a dream. It is certain that the Jews hailed this change of masters and many settled in several of the new Greek colonies he founded. In this rise and fall of empires a new grouping of the countries took place. The rebellious Samaritans were quelled and Alexander gave their land to the Judeans, to whom he further showed his favor by freeing them from taxation during the Sabbatic year. (see Lev. xxv.)

Another reason for Alexander's kindness to our ancestors may be the fact that some Jews already settled in many places outside Judea became his guides and interpreters when he entered the unfamiliar realm of Asia. Indeed, this broad-minded conqueror was a second Cyrus to the Jews; but there was no Isaiah now to immortalize his advent in the grandeur of prophetic address, or to interpret his triumphant advance in terms of divine purpose.

Judea Part of Greco-Egypt.

All too soon, in the midst of his ambitions, Alexander died. Conflict among his generals followed, and the great empire was dismembered. In one of the many wars which followed, the Jews showed their religious fidelity by submitting to slaughter rather than defend themselves on the Sabbath day. Finally, the empire was divided into the following four kingdoms: The Greco-Syrian, the Greco-Egyptian, the Thracian and the Macedonian. Greco-Syria, including the greater part of Western Asia, with Persia as its centre, was claimed by one of Alexander's generals named Seleucus. He introduced the Seleucidan era named after him beginning with the year 312. This calendar was used by the Jews when they later came under Seleucidan sway; for this name, too, came to be applied to the kingdom itself. Many Jews were invited to settle in the new capital—Antioch, on its Mediterranean border. The next kingdom fell to Ptolemy Lagos and included Egypt and the adjoining Asiatic lands, one of which was Cælo-Syria, with boundaries from Lebanon to Egypt, really corresponding to Palestine. Thus the Jews first came under the Ptolemaic regime. It will be well to keep these geographical divisions distinctly in mind. The remaining two divisions of the empire, Thrace and Macedonia, hardly enter into this history.

The Jews did not suffer in the change of rule. They were as free as before to live their own life, and with even greater political independence than under Persian rule. The High Priest continued as the head of the Jewish community, the centre of which was still Jerusalem. Alexandria, a seaport named after the conqueror, was made the capital of Greco-Egyptian kingdom. Many Jews settled there, and it gradually became the most important Jewish community outside of Palestine, both intellectually and religiously. If there were Jews in Greek towns, so also were there Greeks in Jewish towns. This meant a mingling of the two races and a lessening of Jewish isolation. Alexander had brought the Greek tongue to the East; it became the international language; and even the commercial interchange of commodities brought necessarily with it an interchange of ideas. The Orient was becoming Hellenized (p. 31).

The first man of achievement to hear from in this epoch was the High Priest, Simon the Just. That he was called "The Just" tells much in a word. Like Aristides the Good he really earned his title. He rebuilt the walls of Jerusalem, ravaged by war, and improved the water supply. Ben Sirach (one of the writers of the Apocrypha) speaks of Simon in these words of exalted praise:

> How was he honored in the midst of the people
> In his coming out of the sanctuary!

15

He was as the morning star in the midst of a cloud,
And as the moon at the full;
As the sun shining upon the temple of the Most High
And as the rainbow giving light in the bright clouds:
And as the flower of roses in the spring of the year,
As lilies by the rivers of waters,
And as the branches of the frankincense tree in the time of
    summer;
As fire and incense in the censer,
And as a vessel of beaten gold set with all manner of precious
    stones;
And as a fair olive tree budding forth fruit,
And as a cypress tree which groweth up to the clouds.
When he put on the robe of honour,
And was clothed with the perfection of glory,
When he went up to the holy altar,
He made glorious the precincts of the Sanctuary.

Here is one of his maxims: "The world rests on three pillars, on the Law, on worship, and on Charity." He took a broad and moderate view of life. When over-zealous souls would wish to impose upon themselves the abnegations of the Nazarite (see Numbers vi) he discouraged such extremes. "Why voluntarily renounce gifts that God in his love has bestowed for our joy?" That voices the spirit of Judaism. It is said that certain wondrous manifestations of Divine grace ceased with his death. These are but legends, but they show how much he was revered and loved.

Joseph the Satrap

Joseph, the nephew of Onias, a man of resources, was appointed tax-gatherer of the Palestinian lands. A tax-gatherer was given a military retinue to enforce his claims. It was a position of great importance, and made him practically governor of all Palestine with title of Satrap. He exercised his power with severity. Still he brought wealth and improvement to Judea and awakened in the Jews a greater confidence in themselves.

Certainly contact with the Greeks widened the horizon of the Jews, furthered their culture, and gave them a taste for the arts of architecture and sculpture. The Greeks also inculcated love of freedom, the dignity of man, and intellectual research in the realms of science and philosophy. But Greek civilization had perils as well as advantages. Nor was it transplanted to the East in its noblest form. The best of Greek thought was evolved in Athens, not in Alexandria. Then too, the Greeks everywhere were fond of conviviality, so often the stepping-stone to immorality. That was why the prophets, from Samuel on so frowned upon Canaanitish revelries. Some Jews quickly imitated this pagan frivolity and dissipation. Joseph, the satrap, in order to please Ptolemy Philopater, the Greco-Egyptian monarch, introduced the festivities of Dionysus (Bacchus) into Jerusalem; these really meant drunken orgies. Next he imported to the Jewish capital dissolute dancing-women. These associations began to loosen the adherence of the people to Judaism's strictly moral code. Epicureanism, that had become a sanction for indulgence, was beginning to take its place.

Judea Part of Greco-Syria.

In the meantime the greed and ambition of kings changed the map once more. Antiochus the Great, of Syria, seized Egypt and its Asiatic possessions in 203. This transferred Judea from the Egyptian to the Seleucidan rule. Warring nations had played battledore and shuttlecock with the land of our ancestors since the year 600. Antiochus was checked by the newly rising power of Rome from retaining all the Greco-Egyptian dominions, but Celo-Syria including Judea remained under his sway. In the struggle some Jews sided with the Egyptian and some with the Seleucidan party.

For Jews were beginning to differentiate; they were not any more all of one mind either politically or religiously. Led by the unfortunate example of Joseph and his successors, some Jews began cultivating Hellenistic (from Hellas, Greece) habits to win favor with their surroundings. A Jewish leader of the Greek faction was one Joshua, who Grecized his name to Jason. This worldly man encouraged his people to neglect their Jewish ideals in favor of pagan standards of life. The safeguards built around the Jewish Law by the teachers of old were ruthlessly overthrown. But these traitorous extremes brought their own reaction. A pious party sprang up to counteract them and it zealously determined to fulfil the Jewish Law in its strictest interpretation. These were the *Chassidim* (Greek, Assidean), meaning the pious.

Here then were two extreme parties in Israel—one, the Hellenists, whose mania for everything Greek made them almost traitors to the Jewish cause; and on the other hand the Chassidim, who observed the law with a rigidity greater than its own demands; and in the midst the great bulk of the people, who tried to avoid the extremes of both.

NOTES AND REFERENCES.

Greek and Jew:

17

Read "Hebraism and Hellenism" in Matthew Arnold's *Culture and Anarchy.*

Someone remarks, "The Greek praised the holiness of beauty: the Jew the beauty of holiness." Heine writes: "The Greeks were only beautiful youths, the Jews strong and steadfast men."

Theme for discussion:

What was the significance of the defeat of Persia by Greece for civilization in general and for the Jew in particular?

─────────────

CHAPTER III.

JUDEA FIGHTS FOR ITS FAITH.

	B.C.E.		B.C.E.
Seleucidan Era begins	312	Judea under Greco-Syrian rule	203
		Uprising under Mattathias	168
Antiochus III, the Great	223	Judas Maccabee	167
Antiochus IV Epiphanes	175	Book of Daniel written, about	166
		Temple re-dedicated—Hanukkah	165
Antiochus V, Eupater	164		

High Priest's Office Sold.

Antiochus was succeeded by his son of the same name, an eccentric despot who claimed the title of Epiphanes, the "illustrious," though styled by his enemies Epimanes "the madman," and in rabbinic literature *Harasha*, the "wicked." The rule of this ill-balanced tyrant was to bring woe to Judea, for which their own internal troubles were in a measure responsible. Indeed, it was these discords that drew his attention to this particular province. The Hellenists, who had grown to quite a party, sought his interference in their behalf. Jason offered the king a bribe to make him High Priest and depose Onias, his own brother. What a blasphemy on the holy office to fight for its material powers! The pity was that material power should be vested in a spiritual office, so the system was wrong as well as the man.

Imitation of Greek life went on apace. Olympic games, *gymnasia*, were now introduced into Judea. These games named from Olympia in Macedonia, Greece, where they first took place, were also religious festivals and were accompanied by sacrifices to the Greek god Zeus. Yet they involved immoralities, so contradictory were some ancient conceptions of religion.

Menelaus, another unscrupulous character, offered to Antiochus a still higher bribe for the priesthood and thus obtained it, regardless of the fact that it had already been sold to Jason. Like master, like man.

Led from crime to crime, Menelaus became a traitor to his people. He robbed the Temple of some of its treasures to pay his bribe and then slew the deposed but worthy Onias because he had denounced the sin. The outraged people rose against Menelaus, but an armed guard provided by the king enabled him to hold his office by force, and saved him for the time being.

At about this time (170) Antiochus IV, like his predecessor, attempted to seize Egypt. Some patriotic Jews in Alexandria showed active sympathy for the endangered nation. Therefore Antiochus on his return from the expedition seized Jerusalem, aided by the traitor Menelaus. This attack meant the slaughter of many souls and the desecration and plunder of the Temple. Not content with this, Antiochus spread slanders against Judaism to justify his excesses. The rumor went forth, for example, that a golden headed ass was found in the Temple.

Religious Persecution.

Next year his further attack on Egypt was checked by Rome, rapidly becoming a great power. Again he vented his rage on the Jews and determined to exterminate the Jewish religion by attacking their most revered institutions, as the most complete means of erasing their distinct individuality. The predecessors of Antiochus Epiphanes had encouraged the spread of paganism among the Jews; but he, less intelligent and more despotic, tried to force it upon them. He did not realize that where persuasion may succeed, tyranny often fails. Apollonius, his general, cowardly attacked Jerusalem on the Sabbath day, when he knew religious scruples would prevent the Jews defending themselves. So it proved. Many more were slain and the women and children sold in slavery. A general plunder followed. The paganizing of Judea became now his avowed policy. Therefore a decree went forth forbidding the recognition of the God of Israel and His Law and commanding the worship of Greek divinities—"gods that were nothings," to quote Psalm xcvi. The Law was burned and the statue of Jupiter set up in the Temple. Jewish ceremonial, Sabbath, festivals, the Abrahamic rite, were replaced by the sacrifice of unclean animals. At the same time other methods were employed completely to subdue the people.

The same policy was applied against Jews in Higher Syria and Phoenicia. But if some were weak enough to surrender their Faith, many were prepared to remain staunch to it. Eleazar in Antioch met a martyr's death. Hannah, a mother in Israel, taught her sons how to die for conscience's sake. Here are the words with which she exhorted them: "Doubtless the Creator of the world who formed the generations of man will also of His own mercy give you breath and life again as ye now regard not your own selves for His law's sake." Martyrdom such as that found its counterpart in many scattered places. Not succeeding by threats and persecutions Antiochus once more resorted to arms. Again followed an unresisted Sabbath slaughter. The walls of Jerusalem were leveled and Zion made a fortress with a Syrian garrison. Greek colonists were transplanted to Palestine for the purpose of Hellenizing Judea. The country was placed under rigid surveillance. If a copy of the Law was found on the monthly inspection the punishment was death. Participation in the festivals of Dionysius was now a compulsion.

Yet many dared resist. From the worldly point of view, opposition seemed madness, but religious zeal counts not the material cost.

In Modin, a town eighteen miles northwest of Palestine, lived Mattathias, with his five sons, John, Simon, Judas, Eleazar and Jonathan. Hither in the year 168 came officials of the tyrant with promises of a large bribe to Mattathias if he would make offering to an idol and with threats of punishment if he declined. Mattathias was a leading townsman and his example would bring many followers. Not only did he scorn the infamous proposal, but slew a coward who prepared to obey. That act was casting down the gauntlet to Antiochus; it was a declaration of war. With his brave sons around him, the aged hero sent this message to the people: "Whoever is zealous for the Lord and whosoever wishes to support the Covenant, follow me." That became the rallying cry. The little band deposed the Syrian overseer and the guard. Once more when attacked on the Sabbath, the Jews submitted to slaughter. Then they came to the realization that self-defense was their duty, even on that holy day. Were they not fighting for a holy cause? They began at first guerilla warfare on apostates and heathens. Avoiding regular attacks, they would swoop down with a bold clash on a town to punish and reform.

Judas Maccabeus.

Next year Mattathias died. Simon became the counselor and Judas was chosen commander of the trusty band of revolutionists. He was Israel's greatest warrior since David. The title given him was transmitted to his party —*Maccabeus*, the Hammer. But a something more than generalship was to decide this contest—*faith*. Judged by material standards, resistance seemed like a forlorn hope, but the intrepid bravery of this staunch band fighting *pro aris et focis*, "for their altars and their hearths," increased the number of their adherents and even won back the allegiance of some who had almost drifted from the fold.

The first victory over the Syrians was small, but Appolonius, the general who had been entrusted with carrying out the persecuting laws, was slain. In a second engagement the "rebels" were attacked at Beth Horon, north of Jerusalem, and Judas won here a still more decided success over an army much larger than his own. Antiochus became alarmed. He had not the means to raise a large army to meet this unexpected opposition, because all his resources were taxed to meet troubles in other quarters—Parthia, Armenia, Phoenicia.

Angered at the rebellion of this petty people, he now determined on their extermination, Hellenists and all. He sent Lysias with full power to Jerusalem to raze the city to the ground. To the Syrians the Jewish defeat seemed so certain that slave-dealers with money and chains followed the army, sure of a harvest in their repulsive trade. A horror like unto that of Shushan in Esther's days spread through the doomed city. But it raised champions, even among the Hellenistic Jews, who were still attached to their Faith when the decisive test came.

It was in the year 166 that Lysias, the viceroy of Antiochus, sent an army of four thousand men into Judea under the generals Ptolemy, Nicanor and Gorgias. But Judas Maccabeus had now a well organized force, although it consisted of but six thousand men. Before the struggle began he called a solemn assembly at Mizpah, where Samuel had gathered Israel nine hundred years earlier, ordered a fast, conducted a service of prayer and read the Law. In reading the story of the Puritan war against Charles I of England and their singing hymns before the battle, we are reminded of the religious earnestness of these Maccabees. "When they saw the host coming to meet them, they said to Judas, how shall we be able, being so few, to fight against so great a multitude and so strong.... Judas answered: with the God of heaven it is all one to deliver with a great multitude or a small company." The usual proclamation of the Mosaic Law (Deuteronomy xx), was now read, excusing certain classes from the ranks; this reduced the army still more. Then the struggle once more began. By a clever stratagem Judas Maccabeus met the Syrian army on a plain near Emmaus, not far from the capital. With the words of the Law on his lips and with an encouraging appeal to fight for the holy cause, he gave the signal to advance. Defeating the first contingent of the enemy before the main army came up, the next battalion fled without fighting.

The moral effect of this decisive victory was most valuable, apart from the fact that the booty obtained supplied arms to the Maccabees—the "sinews of war" both in a literal and metaphoric sense. But Lysias dared not be beaten. He therefore sent a big army against Judas, whose force had meanwhile increased to some ten thousand, proving again that nothing succeeds like success. The Syrians chose a new route to Beth Horon, but only to meet the old defeat. This was the turning point in the war. The struggle was not over, but confidence was restored and a respite gained.

Feast of Hanukkah.

Judas Maccabeus marched to the capital and a sorry picture of desolation met his gaze. His first work was to remove all signs of idolatry and desecration. A new altar was built, the Temple was repaired and cleaned and on Kislev the 25th in the year 165, it was reconsecrated. The ceremony recalls Solomon's consecration of the first Temple; not as splendid a ceremonial perhaps, but it meant far more. Solomon's Temple had cost treasure, but this had cost blood. It was more than a civil victory; it was that least, it was a triumph of the divine cause expressed in Israel's mission. They fought for Zion as an idea rather than Zion as a city—the "Zion from which goeth forth the law." They proved again that ideals can conquer battalions. This great lesson is always brought home to us when we celebrate our festival of Hanukkah (re-dedication) instituted by the Great Council—the successor of the "Great Synagogue"—to celebrate the victory. The Syrian had been defeated. He was the enemy without. But a greater foe had to be conquered, the enemy within—religious indifference, that lurked among the Hellenist worldlings and many faint-hearted souls throughout the land.

The legend runs that when Judas Maccabeus wished to consecrate the Temple, but one flask of pure oil bearing the priestly seal had been left after the enemy's ravage. It was a measure that would last for a day, but— marvelous to tell—it served for eight, by which time new oil was prepared. The story is immortalized in the second name "Feast of Lights," given to the Hanukkah festival. The ceremony of kindling lights begins with one on the first night, continues with two lights on the second and thus progresses till the eighth and last night is reached. What is the meaning of the ceremonial and the story? It is the Maccabean victory told in symbol; for it was a story of advance from strength to strength. First, Mattathias stood alone for Judaism's cause, a solitary light. Next came his sons; then a tiny army growing instead of lessening with each conflict, from two thousand to six thousand, from six to ten, then victory crowned their efforts; and with the conquest on the field rose the faith in the hearts of the people in the same progressive way. The tiny embers became a flame, and the flame burst into a conflagration. This miracle is often found repeated in Israel's history.

The Feast of Lights is called a Minor Festival in our calendar, for reasons accidental rather than intrinsic. It is hard to institute a new observance after a religion is crystallized. It is still harder to give it the old sanction. So the rabbis did not venture then to place Hanukkah or Purim on a par with Passover, Pentecost and Tabernacles. Yet in very truth Hanukkah is a great festival. None question its authority—all are thrilled by its stirring story.

The Book of Daniel.

In seeking to realize this critical time of "storm and stress," we shall be aided somewhat by taking a glimpse at its literature. For here we see pictured the struggles and sufferings experienced and the alternate hopes and fears that swayed the heart of the nation, far better than in the record of the historian.

A work reflecting these times, the Book of Daniel, is perhaps the latest of the Bible books. The book throws light on the epoch and the epoch is the key to the book. Daniel is written in the form of a revelation of events that were to happen centuries later, made known through dream and vision to the God-fearing Daniel, one of the Babylonian exiles. These visions are presented as foretelling the main incidents after the exile. The pictures grow in detail as they reach the Maccabean uprising (168 B.C.E.), showing that the author probably belonged to this time.

The first picture is the dream of King Nebuchadrezzar, which Daniel—who is as wise as he is good—is able to interpret. The dream presented an image with a head of gold, breast and arms of silver, the lower limbs of brass and iron mixed with clay. A stone cut without hands destroyed the image and then grew to a mountain that filled the earth. In the light of later events, it is thus explained: The golden head was Babylon, the silver breast and arms the kingdom of Media, the bronze trunk Persia, the lower limbs of baser metal and clay represented the Greek empire, split up into many principalities, thus bringing the picture down to the rule of Antiochus Epiphanes. What did the "stone" represent? It expresses the faith of the writer in Israel's eventual triumph and the spread of Judaism over the world. But it was doubtless written when the outcome was still uncertain, perhaps in the very height and heat of the struggle.

The same march of events is later repeated in visions to Daniel himself. The four empires are depicted in the figures of beasts that give the same assurance of Israel's ultimate victory. "The greatness of the kingdoms under the whole heaven shall be given to the people of the saints of the Most High; his kingdom is an everlasting kingdom and all dominions shall serve and obey Him."

In another vision our attention is focused on the events nearer the Maccabean time. First a ram with two horns is the Medo-Persian empire. Next a he-goat represents Greece, its horn Alexander the Great. Four horns that uprose in its place are the four kingdoms into which his empire was split —Macedonia, Thrace, Syria and Egypt, while a little horn that overthrows Judah's sanctuary is none other than Antiochus Epiphanes.

A last vision drops metaphor and mentions the kingdoms by actual name. The persecutions under Antiochus are vividly depicted:

"They shall profane the Sanctuary, even the fortress, and shall take away the continual burnt offering; and they shall set up the abomination that maketh desolate. And such as do wickedly against the covenant shall he pervert by flatteries; but the people that know their God shall be strong and do exploits. They that be wise among the people shall instruct many. Yet they shall fall by the sword and by flame, by captivity and by spoil many days. Now when they shall fall they shall be helped with a little help (the Maccabees).... And some of them that be wise shall fall, to refine them and to purge and to make them white."

ANTIOCHUS
EPIPHANES.

The last reference indicates the ennobling influence of martyrdom touchingly depicted also in the fifty-third chapter of Isaiah.

The death of these noble souls deepened the belief of this writer in the future life, as demanded by divine justice:

"Many of them that sleep in the dust of the earth shall awake, some to everlasting life, and some to shame and everlasting contempt. They that be wise shall shine as the brightness of the firmament and they that turn many to righteousness, as the stars for ever and ever."

The book was certainly written by a patriotic and pious author to inspire his brethren during that dark struggle, to urge them to be loyal to God and His Law with the staunch conviction that all would come right in the end. It is an appeal to the faith and courage of Israel, with Daniel held up as a thrilling exemplar. He is portrayed as unswerving in his determination to be steadfast to the God of his fathers; on one occasion daring a fiery furnace and on another a lion's den, and his faith saves him from both perils.

Who can say how many may have been nerved to be loyal and to "wait for God's salvation" by these impassioned pictures? So, next to Judas Maccabeus, the hero of the Hanukkah story, let us enshrine in our hearts and memories the unknown author of the Book of Daniel who fed the faith and the courage of Israel in their days of sorrow and darkness.

NOTES AND REFERENCES.

Birthday of the Maccabees:

This was the title of a special day set aside by the Church to commemorate the martyrdom of the Jewish mother and her seven sons.

Daniel:

Immortality. In addition to the quotation from Daniel on immortality, here are appended further Biblical quotations that express this belief: Isaiah xxvi, 19; xxv, 8; Ezekiel xxxvii, 1-14; Psalm xvi, 10, 11; xvii, 15; Proverbs xii, 28; Ecclesiastes xii, 7. Montefiore, *The Bible for Home Reading*, Part II, section v, chapter ii. Driver, "Daniel," *Cambridge Bible*, (Cambridge University Press.)

CHAPTER IV.

JUDEA FIGHTS FOR ITS INDEPENDENCE.

SYRIA.		JUDEA.	
	B.C.E.		B.C.E.
Demetrius I, Soter	162	Alliance with Rome	161
		Judas Maccabeus died	160
		Jonathan, High Priest and Tributary Prince	152
Alexander Balas	150		
Demetrius II, Nicator	145		
		Simon—Judea independent	142-
			135

This Temple consecration (forever memorable through the Feast of Hanukkah) was the climax of the Maccabean story, but it was by no means its close. But this event was chosen as the occasion for the institution of the Festival of Hanukkah, not the independence—that was won later. Israel took up arms to defend its Faith, not to win back a separate nation. But its triumph for a spiritual cause awakened the possibility of wresting Judea from the Syrian grasp. For a while swords rested in their scabbards; but it was only an "armed peace." Judas Maccabeus had to build new fortifications against possible invasion. The petty nations around all looked on with ill-concealed jealousy at Judah's victories. Those who in many instances had become Syrian allies had now to be met on the field. The alert and energetic Judas marched out once more and subdued the Idumeans and Ammonites and won peace and security for his people dwelling on their borders. Appeals from brethren whose possessions had been despoiled and their families slain reached him from many sides. With the aid of his brother Simon, whom he despatched to Galilee while he marched to Gilead, these heathen raids were suppressed. Jewish refugees were brought to Judea. So there were new rejoicings at these victories on his return next year (164).

The fight for the restoration of the Jewish faith was now over, but the fight for the restoration of the Jewish nation had only just begun.

Not for very long was Judas allowed to rest. It is far easier to take up the sword than to lay it down. The never-sleeping Syrians were again in the field, defeating two of his generals. But once more victory crowned his arms. In the same year Antiochus, humiliated with defeats in Parthia and Persia as well as in Judea, came to a sad end. The powerful monarch had now to

"Meet face to face a greater potentate,
King Death, Epiphanes, the illustrious."

His death left two rival governors for the regency of the Syrian kingdom.

Death of Eleazar.

The obstinate Hellenist party within Israel had not yet learned their lesson, and appealed to the new monarch, Antiochus Eupator, to take up their cause. So war broke out again in 163. It was the Sabbatic year, when nothing is sown and the land lies fallow. (See Leviticus xxv.) So these circumstances added further embarrassment to the usual evils of war. It meant scarcity of provisions and the terror of long siege. A brave fight in the open field against large odds brought reverse to the Maccabees. One of the brothers, Eleazar, died on the field, a martyr to his bravery. He stabbed an elephant supposed to bear the king, though like Samson, he fell in the overthrow he designed. The army retreated before the second siege was begun. Meanwhile Philip, the rival regent of Syria, raising an army against Lysias, compelled this general's withdrawal from Jerusalem. So Lysias concluded an honorable peace with the Judeans, allowing them the religious liberty for which they had at first taken up arms.

The blessings of peace were now theirs for a space. Judas Maccabeus was made for the time being High Priest. He was not of the priestly line, but the office involved the wielding of temporal as well as spiritual authority. For the former, none more fitted than he. Yet the more strict were not satisfied that it should pass from the traditional priestly family! The Hellenist menace had not yet disappeared, though Jason and Menelaus, its fathers, were now both dead. This party now supported a new Syrian claimant for the throne against the one endorsed by the Maccabees—Demetrius (162), whose agent, Bacchides, appointed one of these very Hellenists, Alcimus, as High Priest. Thus discord was sown anew in Israel.

Death of Judas.

The Syrians with large armies twice repulsed the small army of Judas, but Nicanor, the cruel general of Demetrius, was slain in a brilliant victory by the Jews. This brought such relief to the Jews that "Nicanor Day" was celebrated in Judæa for some years as a day of rejoicing. Judas was certainly at the head of the commonwealth now, even though deprived of the High Priest's office. Hearing of Rome's great power and recognizing that it exercised a kind of sovereignty over Syria, Judas entered into an alliance with it, but too late for its interference to be of aid. For with a meagre force, discouraged by persistent war and overwhelming odds, he had now to meet a large avenging army under Bacchides. With but a few hundred men he went forth to meet the picked thousands of his foes, as brave and as determined as the Greeks of Thermopylæ. When defeat was certain he yet stood fighting and undaunted till wounded unto death. So died a great man who had wrought salvation for Israel. He had made Judah a nation of warrior heroes exalted by religious zeal. His name, his spirit, continued to inspire them to determined resistance against foes without and within. Their religious liberty gained at such fearful cost, even Demetrius, though now holding Judea in subjection, no longer dared defy.

"He put on a breast place as a giant and girt his warlike armor about him. He battled like a lion and the wicked shrunk for fear of him. He cheered Jacob by his mighty acts and his memorial is blessed forever."

Jonathan.

With Judas the Great and his brother John both dead, with Alcimus, the Hellenist, High Priest, and with Syrian garrisons in the capital and all the surrounding places, there was more or less conflict and demoralization. The outlook was not promising. But Jonathan, another of Mattathias' five sons, a worthy brother of Judas, kept the Hasmonean party together. The obnoxious Alcimus died, and there was no religious or political head for seven years. But confidence in Jonathan quietly grew; until eventually he filled both offices. He strengthened his forces sufficiently to withstand a new uprising and even to make it advisable for the Syrians to sue for peace. So when the Syrian throne was seized by a new claimant, Alexander Balas, he realized sufficiently the importance of Jonathan to appoint him High Priest and Tributary Prince in 152; though the deposed Demetrius, who still maintained a partial sway, now sought Jonathan's aid too. The tables were turned and Jonathan held something like a balance of power. Jonathan showed his foresight in remaining loyal also to Alexander Balas, his son, who became Antiochus VI. The Hellenist party quietly died out; it never had the people behind it.

Loaded with honors, Jonathan was now given the golden clasp of independence, and his brother Simon made a Syrian commander. Enemies had become allies. Loyalty to the Syrians meant hard fighting again for the

Jews, but the opportunity was given now to strengthen the defences of Jerusalem and to enable the city and the people to recover from the ravages consequent on a long series of wars. Judea had now an army of forty thousand men. They stood by Alexander Balas when all deserted him. Even then concessions were obtained from the new king, Demetrius II., showing that the Syrian power was broken.

The treachery of Tryphon, a general of the new king, led to Jonathan's death and the massacre of a thousand of his men. Thus passed another of the patriot brothers. It is hard to say to whom Israel owed the greater debt, Judas or Jonathan. Judas saved the nation at a perilous hour; Jonathan reorganized it and gave it an abiding strength.

Independence.

Simon, the last brother, now stepped forward to rally and save Judea. This persistence (characteristic of the resolution of this great family) where only the non-resistance of despair was looked for, completely upset Tryphon's scheme and saved Judea from disaster. Like Jonathan, Simon became at once by popular choice the religious and civil head of his people with the title High Priest included. He felt the time had come to throw off the weak rule of the unreliable, vacillating Syrian power, though this was far beyond the original expectation when the revolt began and far beyond its aims. Yet the march of events made it a logical sequence. He decided to recognize Demetrius II. against Tryphon on condition that Jewish independence be recognized in turn. The terms were accepted—"We release you from the crown which you owe us and we remit the taxes that we laid on Jerusalem." Verily, the yoke of the heathen was taken away from Israel.

The Seleucidan Era (see page 28) was now given up with the Seleucidan sway, and the reckoning of years began anew from 142 with the accession of Simon as High Priest, Commander of the Army and Prince of the Nation. This marked again the independence of Judah, that had been lost since the year 600 B.C.E., when Nebuchadrezzar overthrew Jerusalem and its Temple and took the Jews into Babylonian exile.

NOTES AND REFERENCES.

Calendar:

In the Jewish calendar to-day time is reckoned from the traditional year of the world's creation.

Fighting first against the oppression of an overlord and winning independence as an unexpected outcome—has many historic parallels. In this way the American colonies threw off their allegiance to Great Britain in 1776.

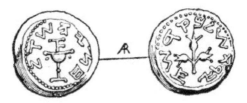

HALF SHEKEL, SIMON MACCABEUS, 141-135 B. C. E.

The issuing of coins marked one of the rights of Judea's independence. See illustrations of these coins, some of which are still in existence.

Theme for Discussion:

Had the Hasmoneans the right to assume the office of High Priest?

A SHEKEL.
SIMON MACCABEUS, 141-135 B. C. E.

CHAPTER V.

THE APOCRYPHA.

In addition to the Book of Daniel there are other writings that throw light on these times; notably the collection known as "The Apocrypha." This is a Greek word meaning hidden or obscure. This title as applied to their *use* was to indicate that the books were used for private circulation, rather than for reading at public worship. This title as applied to their *origin* was to indicate that their authority as sacred scripture was not as certain as that of the Bible books—to be included in the Canon of Scripture. This last application has given a rather sinister meaning to the word "apocryphal." But the collection is full of lofty religious sentiment well worthy to be included in our most sacred treasures.

Like the Bible, this collection was not written all at one time, nor in one land. It spreads over the period between 200 B.C.E. and 150 A.C.E., written therefore under Persian, Greek and Roman rule; some in Judea, others in the Diaspora, lands of Jewish dispersion. While the term covers some writings of non-Jewish scribes, the Apocrypha proper includes the Jewish writings only, and only such will be considered here.

These consist of fourteen books grouped in the following order:

I Esdras,

II Esdras,

Tobit,

Wisdom of Solomon,

Wisdom of Jesus, son of Sirach or Ecclesiasticus,

Baruch (with epistle of Jeremiah),

Song of the Three Holy Children,

Judith,

Additions to the Book of Esther,

History of Susanna,

History of Bel and the Dragon,

Prayer of Manasses, King of Judah,

I Maccabees,

II Maccabees.

Some are narratives, some books of homilies and maxims, here and there an apocalypse, i.e., prophetic vision. While the narratives are not all histories, they are invaluable as revealing the inner life of the people, their brave struggles, their deep convictions, and their yearnings for better things. One idea seems common to all. Each story is presented as an illustration of the temporal trials of good men and women, like Tobit and Susanna, and the ultimate reward of their fidelity; the edifying purpose throughout tending to foster the faith and courage of the people in time of tribulation. In this respect the apocryphal books resemble the book of Daniel, which might be appropriately included in the collection.

While these books as a whole lack the freshness and originality and the exquisite simplicity of the best Bible books, they show in some respects an advance in thought and survey. There is more mysticism in the apocryphal writings. Wisdom is personified, almost merging into a being. Angels and spirits play a larger part. Immortality is brought to the fore, and Asmodeus, a sort of devil, appears upon the scene. Some of these ideas, such as the personification of wisdom and the existence of a devil, were further fostered in Christianity and developed into distinct doctrines, while the inherent rationalism of Judaism gradually threw them off.

Now to consider briefly the books in detail:

I   **Esdras.**

Esdras is a later version in Greek of the events told in the Books of Ezra and Nehemiah, but it begins further back in the reign of Josiah and carries the story through the exile down to the re-dedication of the Second Temple. The author breathes into it some later religious ideas of his own time. The following story quoted from it is known as the "Dispute of the Courtiers":

"Now King Darius made a great feast unto all his subjects and unto all that were born in his house, and unto all the princes of Medea and of Persia.

"Then the three young men of the body-guard that kept the King's person, spake one to another: let every one of us say one thing which shall be strongest; and he whose sentences shall seem wiser than the others, unto him shall Darius the King give great gifts and great honors in token of victory. The first wrote, Wine is the strongest. The second wrote, The King is the strongest. The third wrote, Woman is the strongest: but, above all things, Truth beareth away the victory.

"Then began the first, who had spoken of the strength of wine, and said thus: O sirs, how exceeding strong is wine. It causeth all men to err that drink it: it maketh the mind of the king and of the fatherless child to be all one; of the bondman and of the freeman, of the poor man and of the rich; it turneth also every thought into jollity and mirth, so that a man remembereth neither sorrow nor debt: and it makes every heart rich, so that a man remembereth neither king nor satrap: and when they are in their cups, they forget their love both to friends and brethren, and a little after draw their swords: but when they awake from their wine they remember not what they have done. O sirs, is not wine the strongest, seeing that it enforceth to do thus. And when he had so spoken, he held his peace.

"Then the second, that had spoken of the strength of the King, began to say: O sirs, do not men excel in strength, that bear rule over the sea and land and all things in them? But yet is the King stronger: and he is their lord and hath dominion over them; and in whatsoever he commandeth them they obey him. If he bid them make war one against the other, they do it: and if he send them out against the enemies, they go, and overcome mountains, walls and towers. They slay and are slain, and transgress not the King's commandment. If they get the victory they bring all to the King, as well the spoil as all things else. Likewise for those that are no soldiers and have not to do with wars, but use husbandry, when they have reaped again that which they had sown, they bring it to the King, and compel one another to pay tribute unto the king. And he is but one man. If he command to kill, they kill; if he command to spare they spare; if he command to smite, they smite; if he command to make desolate, they make desolate; if he command to build, they build; if he command to cut down, they cut down; if he command to plant, they plant. So all his people and all his armies obey him: furthermore, he lieth down, he eateth and drinketh, and taketh his rest; and these keep watch round about him, neither may any one depart, and do his own business, neither disobey they him in *anything*. O, sirs, how should not the king be strongest, seeing that in such sort he is obeyed? And he held his peace.

"Then the third, who had spoken of women, and of truth (this was Zorobabel) began to speak: O, sirs, is not the king great, and men are many, and wine is strong; who is it then that ruleth them or hath the lordship over them? Are they not women? Women have borne the king and all the people that bear rule by sea and land. Even of them came they: and they nourished them up that planted the vineyards from whence the wine cometh. These also make garments for men; these bring glory unto men; and without women, cannot men be. Yea, and if men have gathered together gold and silver and every goodly thing, and see a woman which is comely in favor and beauty, they let all those things go, and gape after her, and even with open mouth fix their eyes fast on her; and have all more desire unto her than unto gold or silver or any goodly thing whatsoever. A man leaveth his own father that brought him up, and his own country, and cleaveth unto his wife. And with his wife he endeth his days, and remembereth neither father, nor mother, nor country. By this also ye must know that women have dominion over you. Do ye not labor and toil and bring all to women? Yea, a man taketh his sword, and goeth forth to make outroads, and to rob and to steal, and to sail upon the sea and upon rivers; and looketh upon a lion; and walketh in the darkness.... Yea, many there be that have run out of their wits for women, and become bondmen for their sakes. Many also have perished, have stumbled, and sinned, for women. O sirs, how can it be but women should be strong, seeing they do thus? Then the king and the nobles looked one upon another: so he began to speak concerning truth. O sirs, are not women strong? Great is the earth, high is the heaven, swift is the sun in its course for he compasseth the heavens round about and fetcheth his course again to his own place in one day. Is he not great that maketh these things? Therefore great is truth and stronger than all things. All the earth calleth upon truth, and the heaven blesseth her: all works shake and tremble, but with her is no unrighteous thing; wine is unrighteous, the king is unrighteous, women are unrighteous, all the children of men are unrighteous, and unrighteous are all such their works; and there is no truth in them; in their unrighteousness also shall they perish. But truth abideth, and is strong forever; she liveth and conquereth for evermore. With her there is no accepting of persons or rewards; but she doeth the things that are just and refraineth from all unrighteous and wicked things; and all men do well like of her works. Neither in her judgment is any unrighteousness; and she is the strength, and the kingdom, and the power, and the majesty of all ages. Blessed be the God of truth. And with that he held his tongue. And all the people then shouted and said, Great is truth, and strong above all things."

II   **Esdras.**

II Esdras is an entirely separate work, originally written in Hebrew. It consists of a series of visions of the future of Jerusalem, but it also takes up profound religious questions, as to why man is created to suffer and sin. The answer it offers to these queries is the salvation of the righteous after death. Its view of life is severe and sad. Chapters i and ii and probably xv and xvi are later editions by a Christian hand.

Tobit.

This is the story of the trials of a good man (Tobit—Goodness) in the sad times of the overthrow of Israel by Assyria. He "walked in truth and justice, fed the hungry and clothed the naked" and was a strict observer of every precept of the Jewish Law. A particular duty he took upon himself in those gloomy days of warfare was the giving decent burial to those of his brethren slain in the battle-field—daring the tyrant's edict against it. His property was confiscated, yet he remained undeterred in fulfilling this holy obligation. It was through this very duty, voluntarily undertaken, that he accidentally lost his eyesight. But he never lost his faith in God.

The story now turns from the trials of a good man to those of a good woman—Sara. The spirit of evil, Asmodeus, slew her husband on the very day of her marriage. Again her hand was sought in wedlock and again her husband was snatched from her side. On seven occasions this happened, making her the reproach of her neighbors.

Now kind Providence intervenes to aid its faithful servants. God sends the angel Raphael, who restores the eyesight of Tobit and brings about a marriage between his son Tobias and the much tried Sara. This time the murderous scheme of Asmodeus is happily frustrated. Tobit obtains his lost property and virtue is rewarded.

The following is a part of Tobit's prayer of thanksgiving:

"And Tobit wrote a prayer for rejoicing, and said,
Blessed is God that liveth for ever,
And blessed is His kingdom.
For he scourgeth, and sheweth mercy:
He leadeth down to the grave, and bringeth up again:
And there is none that shall escape his hand.
Give thanks unto Him before the Gentiles, ye children of
    Israel.
For he hath scattered us among them.
There declare His greatness,
And extol Him before all the living:
Because He is our Lord,
And God is our Father for ever.
And he will scourge us for our iniquities, and will again shew
    mercy.
And will gather us out of all the nations among whom we are
    scattered.
If ye turn to him with your whole heart, and with your whole
    soul,
To do truth before him,

Then will He turn unto you,
And will not hide His face from you,
And see what He will do with you.
And give him thanks with your whole mouth
And bless the Lord of righteousness.
And exalt the Everlasting King.
I, in the land of my captivity, give Him thanks
And shew his strength and majesty to a nation of sinners.
Turn, ye sinners, and do righteousness before him:
Who can tell if he will accept you and have mercy on you?
. . . .
Rejoice and be exceeding glad for the sons of the righteous:
For they shall be gathered together and shall bless the Lord of
     the righteous.
O blessed are they that love thee;
They shall rejoice for Thy peace;
Blessed are all they that sorrowed for all thy scourges:
Because they shall rejoice for thee,
When they have seen all Thy glory:
And they shall me made glad forever.
Let my soul bless God the great King.
For Jerusalem shall be builded with sapphires and emeralds
     and precious stones;
Thy walls and towers and battlements with pure gold.
And the streets of Jerusalem shall be paved with beryl and
     carbuncle and stones of Ophir.
And all her streets shall say, Hallelujah, and give praise,
Saying, blessed is God, which hath exalted thee for ever."

Judith.

This is the story of a good and beautiful woman, who, like Esther, saved Israel from a tyrant by stratagem and bravery. Like Tobit, it lays stress on obedience to the Law, of which deeds of kindness form a part. Hence both belong to that period, whence so much emphasis was placed on law enacted. Both Judith and Tobit might be called historical romances.

Additions to the Book of Esther.

These additions introduce the religious note lacking in the biblical Esther, which does not even mention God. A beautiful prayer is ascribed to Esther, in which she, as a devout Jewess, opens her heart to the Lord.

Wisdom Literature.

If Syrian paganism showed the influence of the Greek at his worst on Jewish morals, Ben Sirach and Wisdom of Solomon are indications of the influence of Greek thought at its best on Jewish thinkers. Together with the Bible books of Proverbs, Job and Ecclesiastes, they form a group called "Wisdom Literature." A large part of both books is devoted to the value of wisdom, but it is that wisdom the beginning of which is the fear of the Lord.

Ecclesiasticus.

The Wisdom of Jesus (Greek for Joshua), Ben Sirach or Ecclesiasticus is a commentary on the times. It was written about B.C.E. 180, in Judea, before the persecution began under Antiochus, the Syrian who was so little Greek and so largely pagan. It urges obedience to the Law and Commandments and gives copious rules of conduct in every relation of life.

Ben Sirach was a Jewish scribe. Some of his sayings are edited and some are original. Here are a few quotations:

Woe to the sinner that goeth two ways.

Wine and music rejoice the heart, and the love of wisdom is above both.

The knowledge of wickedness is not wisdom and the prudence of sinners is not counsel.

They (the laboring class) maintain the fabric of the world; and in the handiwork of their craft is their prayer.

He that sacrificeth of a thing wrongfully gotten, his offering is made a mockery.

As one that slayeth his neighbor is he that taketh away his living.

As God's mercy is great, so is His correction also.

Before man is life and death, and whatsoever he liketh shall be given to him.

There is a shame that bringeth sin, and there is a shame that is glory and grace.

A slip on the pavement is better than a slip with the tongue.

Depart from wrong and it shall turn aside from thee.

He that keepeth the law bringeth offerings enough.

He that requiteth a good turn offereth fine flour.

If thou come to serve the Lord prepare for adversity.

Let not reverence of any man cause thee to fall.

Hide not thy wisdom in its beauty.

Rejoice not over the death of thy greatest enemy but remember that we die all.

Forsake not an old friend, for the new is not comparable to him.

Unto the slave that is wise shall they that are free do service.

The bee is little among such as fly; but her fruit is the chief of sweet things.

Judge none blessed before his death.

The rich man hath done wrong yet he threateneth withal. The poor man is wronged and he must entreat also.

Blessed is he whose conscience has not condemned him.

He that despiseth small things by small things shall he fall.

Wisdom that is hid and treasure that is hoarded, what profit is there in both?

He that setteth a trap shall be taken therein.

He that revengeth shall find vengeance from the Lord.

The stroke of the whip maketh marks in the flesh, but the stroke of the tongue breaketh the bones.

Wisdom of Solomon.

The influence of Greek ideas on Ben Sirach is slight, in Wisdom of Solomon it is pronounced. Indeed, this latter book was written in Greek, in Alexandria, the centre of Hellenist government. Its date is about 100 B.C.E. Like most of the books of this collection, it is ascribed to one of the great men of the Bible. Here King Solomon exhorts the rulers of the earth to seek wisdom and to shun idolatry. He expatiates on the influence of divine wisdom on life as exemplified in the noble souls of Israel's great past. Here are some extracts:

Beware of murmuring which is unprofitable: and refrain your tongue from back-biting: for there is no word so secret that shall go for nought.

Honorable age is not that which standeth in length of time, nor that is measured by number of years.

If riches be a possession to be desired in this life, what is richer than wisdom that worketh all things.

Fear is nothing else but a betraying of the succours which reason offereth.

For these men (idolators) there is but small blame, if they peradventure do but go astray while they are seeking God and desiring Him.

Even if we sin, we are Thine. But we shall not sin, knowing that we have been accounted Thine; for to be acquainted with Thee is perfect righteousness.

Court not death in the error of thy life. God made not death, nor delighteth He when the living perish, for He created all things that they might have being.

Wisdom is the effulgence from everlasting light, and the unspotted mirror of the working of God and the image of His goodness.

Surely vain are all men by nature who are ignorant of God,
And could not out of the good things that are seen know Him that is:
But deemed either fire or wind or the swift air,
Or the circle of the stars, or the violent water, or the light of heaven,
To be the gods which govern the world....
For, if astonished at their power let them understand
Through them how much mightier is He that made them....
To know God is perfect righteousness,
Yea, to know thy powers is the root of immortality.

Baruch.

This is a general collection of four different writings.

(a) A Prayer of Israel in Exile (i-iii, 8.)

(b) The fount of Wisdom (iii, 9-iv, 4.)

(c) Consolation to Zion's Children (iv, 5-v, 9.)

(d) The Epistle of Jeremiah.

(e) The folly of idolatry (vi.)

Baruch was the secretary of Jeremiah. See Jer., chaps. xxxii, xxxvi, xliii.

Song of the Three Holy Children:

These "children" are none other than the three young men, who with Daniel dared the fiery furnace in testimony of their faith. The song is presumed to have been sung in the furnace. The book, then, is an amplification of the Bible book of "Daniel." This amplification of Scripture became more and more a favorite custom of the rabbinic age. It is called *Agada*, i.e., story.

To quote:

"At this time there is neither prince, prophet nor leader, burnt offering or place of sacrifice. Nevertheless, in a contrite heart and a humble spirit let us be accepted. Like as burnt offerings of bullocks and thousands of fat lambs may our sacrifice be in thy sight this day, and grant that we may wholly go after thee. For they shall not be confounded who put their trust in thee."

History of Susanna.

This is the story of a chaste woman whom wicked men tried to betray. In the end both her purity and their sin are discovered.

Bel and the Dragon.

Like "The Song of the Three Holy Children" this also is an addition to the story of Daniel. It is an *expose* of the hypocrisy of the priests of the Babylonian idol Bel.

Prayer of Manasses.

This is the Greek spelling of Manasseh, one of the last Kings of Judah. It is a prayer ascribed to him in Babylonian exile. This prayer might be introduced in the confessions of the Day of Atonement.

I and II Maccabees.

The Books of the Maccabees are the classic authority on the Maccabean uprising. The first Book gives a graphic picture of the struggle and the events that led up to it. It is also our source for the subsequent events which will be related in due course, carrying the narrative down to 135 B.C.E. It is written from the strict standpoint of the Chassidim. These, it will be remembered, were the extremely pious party. It is couched in sober historic style. Its value as authentic Jewish history cannot be over-estimated. Written originally in Hebrew (or Aramaic), it has come down to us unfortunately only in a Greek translation.

The second Book of Maccabees was written in Greek and is a condensation of a larger work. It confines itself to the series of events between 175 and 160. Though written in more ornate style, it is less reliable; but it contains some interesting stories, such as the martyrdom of Eleazer, Hannah and her seven sons. Like Daniel, it is written to edify and inspire.

NOTES AND REFERENCES.

Apocrypha:

In most of the Apocryphal Books, the writers have but a vague knowledge of the location of places, or the sequence of historical events. Books are loosely assigned to ancient authors without sufficient consideration of the historic possibility. But then the exact science of history is late.

Ecclesiasticus:

The discovery of fragments of the original Hebrew text of Ecclesiasticus was made by Prof. Schechter and further additions by Messrs. Neubauer and Cowley. See a number of articles in vols. x and xii of the *Jewish Quarterly Review*. (Macmillan, London.)

Wisdom Literature:

Montefiore, *Bible for Home Reading*, Pt. ii, Section i, chaps. i-v.

Read "A Glimpse of the Social Life of the Jews in the Time of Jesus, the son of Sirach." Schechter, *Studies in Judaism*, 2d series, J. P. S. A.

Theme for discussion:

Compare the treatment of wisdom in *Proverbs* (viii) and in *Ecclesiasticus*.

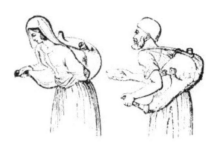

GOAT-SKIN WATER BOTTLES.

CHAPTER VI.

IN THE DIASPORA.

Having brought our story to the close of an epoch, we will pause and glance at the status of the Jew in other lands. The dispersion of Israel in a voluntary way had already begun, though Judea was still the centre of gravity. So the sway of the High Priest reached not only to the Palestinian provinces—Phœnicia, Samaria, Galilee, Gilead, Edom and Philistia—but extended through parts of Asia Minor and to lands on both banks of the Mediterranean Sea. These lands of Jewish settlement outside of Palestine are called the Diaspora.

Egypt.

The land that next to Judea contained the largest number of Jews was Egypt. Our narrative has been moving to and fro between these two lands. In no country outside of Greece itself was the Greek spirit so completely diffused as in Egypt. Alexandria, its new capital, displacing Athens as the intellectual centre of the world, was second in importance only to Rome. While the Greek civilization at its worst was tinctured with an enervated orientalism and had much in it debasing, yet the Greek spirit at its best also found its way to Alexandria, and its influence was intellectually broadening and elevating on the Jews resident there. Look back to Chapter ii.

Under this Greek regime the Jews were given equality at least officially, in Egypt, and also in Cyrene (on the coast of the adjoining country, Lybia). The Greek Egyptian royal house was called the Ptolemaic, from Ptolemy, the family name of its kings. Ptolemy Philometer was a contemporary of Antiochus Epiphanes, and many Jews fled from Palestine to take refuge under his benevolent sway. What a contrast for Israel between Egypt under the Ptolemies and Egypt under the Pharaohs a thousand years earlier!

When settling in lands where they would find themselves a small minority, Jews have usually concentrated in large cities. This has been a source both of strength and of weakness. *Of strength*—for when scattered in twos and threes in country places, the maintenance of their religion and their historic consciousness would become imperilled; while numbers closely grouped offer power of achievement. Cities too, are the intellectual centres of a land. *Of weakness*—for city dwellers lose the simplicity that goes with country life in close contact with nature, which deepens faith; and work on the soil in the open, aids in the building of character. So here, in a land outside of Israel, we find Jews settling in one of the great cities of the world.

The Delta, an Alexandrian district on the sea-coast, was wholly a Jewish colony. The Jews participated in both the commercial and intellectual activities of this famous capital of antiquity. They exported grain, formed artisan guilds, and established schools which were also their synagogues.

The Septuagint.

Interest in Israel was further manifested in its hearty endorsement of the translation of the Jewish Scriptures into Greek given by Ptolemy Philadelphus. But this translation was made first and chiefly for the Jews themselves. Hebrew was growing more and more of a strange tongue to the new generation in Alexandria and its surroundings. Even in Palestine proper they no longer spoke Hebrew, but Aramaic, a sister tongue. A translation of the Bible had already been made in this language; it is called Targum. Indeed, the books of Daniel and Ezra are written in Aramaic; so are some of the prayers in our ritual.

This Greek translation was made, secondly, for the Greeks. It gave the desired opportunity to the Jews to explain their faith and literature to the people with whom they were now brought in friendly contact, and would silence the slanders of ill-wishers such as the Egyptian priest Manetho.

At first only the Pentateuch was translated, each book being assigned to a different scholar. A pretty story that we must not take too seriously says it was entrusted to seventy-two persons, six from each tribe. The tradition survives partly in name—Septuagint—(seventy), written lxx. The anniversary of this really great event was commemorated by the Jews as a holiday. We may say that this translation of our Scripture into this widely spoken tongue was the beginning of the mission of the Jew to carry God's Law to the Gentiles. The Greeks were among the great educators of the world. Now that the Bible was revealed in their tongue, it became the property of the world and its lessons reached the hearts of many, scattered far and wide.

Onias and His Temple.

Onias, son of the Jewish High Priest of the same name, was the most renowned of the Judean settlers in Alexandria. He was entrusted with an army in one of Philometer's campaigns. He was likewise chosen by the Judeans of Egypt as their Ethnarch (governor), to direct the affairs of the Jewish community. Around him the people coalesced into a strong body.

He conceived the idea of building a Temple for the benefit of the Alexandrian Jews whom distance practically debarred from the benefits of the Temple in Jerusalem. If justified at all, the right to establish it was most naturally his as heir of the High Priest at Jerusalem. Yet it was a bold step, a daring precedent, since only one sanctuary, that at Jerusalem, had been recognized since the days of Josiah. Such was the law. (See Deut. xii, verses 13-15.) The new Temple was, not unnaturally, condemned by the Jews of Jerusalem.

We might say, if it was a daring innovation, it was abundantly justified by the changed conditions. The Deuteronomy law was of great value at the time instituted, in preventing the spread of idolatrous notions through the ministrations of ignorant village priests; but "new occasions bring new duties;" that was no longer to be feared. Again, the two-and-a-half tribes in the days of Joshua (see Josh. xxii) offered a precedent in building a second altar, when nothing but the Jordan separated them from the rest of Israel. Lastly, it was almost a realization of the exquisite Messianic picture in Isaiah xix, 19-25, where an altar would be built in Egypt, and Israel, Assyria and Egypt would be united under God's blessing.

So built it was, at Leontopolis, in old Goshen, land of early Israel's sojourn, and near the famous Memphis. It received royal sanction and aid; but it never acquired for Egyptian Jews the validity and sanction of the Temple at Jerusalem.

Philometer's confidence was further shown in appointing Onias Arab-arch, i.e., commander of the Arabian province Heliopolis, and also custodian of the Nile ports.

In the following pages we shall see Egypt gradually losing power and independence through the growth of Rome; but we will notice also that through all these changes the status of the Jews remains almost undisturbed— that unfriendly attacks are confined almost wholly to literary slanders. But then, grave persecutions often began with the pen throughout all Israel's history.

NOTES AND REFERENCES.

The Septuagint:

So many Hebrew terms and constructions were used in this Greek translation that it became a modification of the language, a sort of Jewish-Greek.

Schürer, *Jewish Life in the Times of Christ*, 2d Division iii, (Scribner). This is a very valuable work on this era, but should be accepted with reservation.

Temple of Onias:

A "mound of the Jews" recently unearthed near Leontopolis, doubtless marks the ruins of the Temple of Onias.

Read articles "Alexandria" and "Diaspora," *Jewish Encyclopedia*, Vols. i and iv respectively.

Christianity.:

The fairest presentation of the Judaism of these times by a non-Jewish author is Toy's *Judaism and Christianity*.

Theme for Discussion:

"Are there traces of Greek philosophy in the Septuagint?" Freudenthal, *Jewish Quarterly Review*. Vol. ii.

BOOK II.

JUDEA INDEPENDENT

Judea's Rulers and Teachers.		ROME.	
	B.C.E.		B.C.E.
Jose b. Joezer and Jose		Final subjection of Carthage	
b. Jochanan	170	and Greece	146
Judea independent	142		
Simon, Prince	142	Pompey takes Syria and	
Joshua b. Perachia and		closes the Seleucidan	
Mattai the Arbelite	140-110	dynasty	65
John Hyrcanus I	135		
Aristobulus I	105	**Pompey takes Jerusalem**	63
Alexander Janneus	104		
Judah b. Tabbai and Simon		1st triumvirate Caesar,	
b. Shetach	100-90	Pompey and Crassus	60
Salome Alexandra	78	Caesar	48
Aristobulus II	69		
Shemaiah and Abtalion	65-35		
Hyrcanus II (tributary to Rome)	63	2nd triumvirate, Antony,	
		Octavius and Lepidus	44
Antigonus	46-37	1st Emperor, Augustus	30
Hillel and Shammai	30	B.C.E.—14 A.C.E.	
	Herod 37—4 B.C.E.		

THE TEMPLE OF JERUSALEM.—AS RESTORED BY CHIPIEZ.

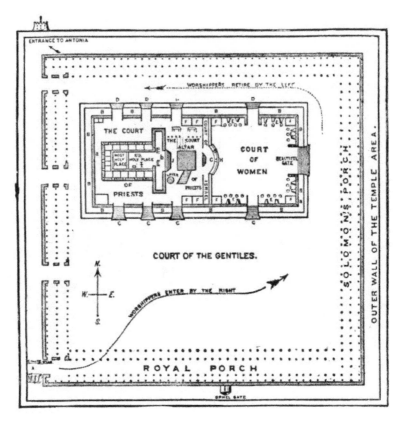

GROUND PLAN OF THE TEMPLE AREA, REPRESENTING ONE THOUSAND SQUARE FEET.

A.: The colossal Royal Bridge, on arches, that spanned the Tyropoeon valley from Mount Zion to Mount Moriah, and led eastward into the Court of the Gentiles.

COURT OF THE GENTILES: The outer portions of the Temple area within the walls. The dots in the dotted lines show the number and position of the Corinthian columns forming colonnades that enclosed the Court. Within these colonnades was the Royal porch on the south, and Solomon's Porch on the east. In these porches the oxen, sheep, and doves selected for sacrifices were sold, as in a market.

BEAUTIFUL GATE: The broad gate leading from Solomon's Porch into the Court of Women.

B. B. B.: A terrace ten and a half feet high and fifteen feet broad, which bounded the inner wall of the Sanctuary.

A. A.: The inner wall of the Sanctuary.

THE SANCTUARY consisted of the three courts: The Court of Women, the Court of Israel, and the Court of Priests, beyond which were the Holy and Most Holy Places, forming lower apartments of the Temple proper.

C. C. C. C.: Four south-side flights of steps that led up to the gates in the terrace that opened into the Courts above.

D. D. D. D.: Four north-side flights of steps that led up to the gates on the north side.

E. E.: The thirteen money chests, forming the Treasury of the Temple.

F. F.: Courts and chambers within the Sanctuary.

G.: Nicanor Gate, leading from the Court of Women into the Court of Israel.

H.: The fifteen terrace steps on which the Levites stood when they sung the fifteen "Psalms of Degrees" at the Feast of Tabernacle: and in the door-way of the gate, all took place that was ordered to be done "before the Lord."

J.: Twelve steps leading up to the Porch of the Temple.

B.: The two Tables, the one of marble, the other of gold, within the porch.

THE HOLY PLACE contained the Tables of Shewbread, the Golden Candlestick, and the Altar of Incense. In the "Holy of Holies" a solitary stone marked the place where should have stood the ark, which Nebuchedrezzar had taken away.—From *The Wonderful Story of Old.*]

———————————

CHAPTER VII.

PHARISEES AND SADDUCEES.

Simon.

The new kingdom acquired *de jure* (by treaty), must yet be fought for to be maintained *de facto*. The citadel of Jerusalem, as well as that key to the mountain passes, Gazara, had still to be mastered. Successful in both enterprises, Israel could enjoy some years of long needed peace. Simon furthered the religious as well as the political welfare of his country. The people could till their ground in peace and for a time at least "sit under their own vine and their own fig-tree"; though it could not yet be said "there was none to fray them away." Simon, moreover, "strengthened those who had been brought low, the Law he searched out, and he beautified the sanctuary." He used the time of quiet for building a haven at Joppa, for enlarging the boundaries and for encouraging agriculture.

The office of High Priest, maintained hitherto in a hereditary priestly family, had been gradually transferred to the Hasmonean House, and hence now devolved on Simon. By this time the people had become reconciled to the transfer. He renewed the treaty with Rome, which had taken the place of Greece in becoming the greatest power in the world and in deciding the fate of nations.

When Tryphon was slain, Antiochus turned against the Jews, but was defeated by Simon's sons. Alas, Simon's fate was not to be an exception to that of the rest of his warrior brothers. None died a peaceful death. Simon, together with two of his sons, was treacherously slain by his own son-in-law, Ptolemy, an unscrupulous man, cruelly ambitious for the throne.

Hyrcanus I

John Hyrcanus, the oldest surviving son of Simon, became the next Jewish ruler. So, imperceptibly a royal house had been created, and the princely honor came to Hyrcanus by *hereditary succession*. In just that way have all royal lines been created—starting with a great deliverer, like Judas Maccabee. But the *title*, King, came later. Hyrcanus had not only to rout the usurper Ptolemy before the rulership could become his, but had also to resist the siege of Antiochus VII., the next Syrian king, who would not yet renounce Judea without another struggle. Peace was at last reached by Hyrcanus agreeing to the payment of an indemnity and tribute for a few outlying towns.

This first repulse showed that the new kingdom was not very strong and that it owed its independence to Syrian weakness (due to the continued conflicts of rivals and pretenders), rather than to its own material power. But Syria's embarrassment was Judah's opportunity. After Antiochus had been slain in a Parthian conflict, John Hyrcanus, once secure, began a vigorous campaign to enlarge his boundaries. Very soon he had incorporated the old land of the Ten Tribes, now called Samaria. The complete conquest of the Samaritans was undertaken toward the end of his life. Their famous temple on Mount Gerizim was destroyed. Idumea (Edom) was also conquered and Judaism imposed on it by force. But that kind of conversion was always against the free and tolerant spirit of Judaism and against its very genius. We shall later see that it brought its own retribution and weakened the cause of Israel.

Pharisees and Sadducees.

Let us not forget that the rise of the Hasmoneans had come about in a measure through a conflict for religious integrity between the extreme pietists on the one hand, the Chassidim, and the worldly Hellenists on the other, with varied shades of opinion in between. These religious divergences had now crystallized into two schools that acquired the names Pharisees and Sadducees. It is hard to say just when these distinctions began. Perhaps they were always there; for we meet the two groups—conservative and progressive —under different names in all creeds and in nearly all eras. The division is naturally inherent in the human temperament. It marks broadly the two grand divisions into which all men become grouped in organized society.

Now let us consider in particular the distinctions that differentiated these two parties in the Jewish State. The Sadducees were largely composed of the priestly families; but the priestly caste was not necessarily the religious class. It corresponded rather to what we would call the aristocracy—we have seen that the High Priest was also a prince. In this party, too, were largely the military. They were faithful to the Mosaic Law, the Pentateuch, which they rigorously enforced, but gave slight allegiance to the later religious injunctions that came to be developed from the Law by the Scribes; in so far they were religiously unprogressive. Still in their attitude toward life in general, they did not approve of holding aloof from the world, but encouraged a mingling with it and entering into intimate commercial and political relations with other nations. They regarded it their patriotic duty to aggrandize the nation in every way and to make it a splendid power.

The name Sadducee is derived from Zadok, of the family of Aaron, the chief priest of the time of Solomon's Temple, who thus gave his name to the priestly house, "Sons of Zadok."

The Pharisees, while interpreting Biblical law more leniently in certain respects than the Sadducees, were determined supporters of all the mass of legal minutiæ that had been evolved from the Law proper and which had become a "Second Law." These rites and ceremonies that were added to the original Mosaic code (occasionally by a rather forced deduction) they considered equally binding with it. They called it the *Oral Law* to distinguish it from the *Written Law*, and the tradition was that it, too, was revealed to Moses.

In their political policy they equally diverged from the Sadducees, believing in standing somewhat apart from the peoples about them. They looked askance upon too intimate relations with the world at large; for they believed it their duty to subordinate all interests, national and commercial, to the religious, trusting the outcome rather to divine providence than to the judgment of their statesmen or the enterprise of energetic leaders.

Further, as against the priestly aristocracy, that wished to confine all ecclesiastical functions to the priestly order, the Pharisees were more democratic in that they desired to extend the privileges of priestly sanctification and holiness to all. Purifying ablutions, they claimed, were obligatory on the whole people. *Their* meals should also be consecrated, even as the repasts of the priests—so that all Israel should be a "Kingdom of priests and a holy nation." Hence, "Second Maccabees," the work of a Pharisee, declares, "Unto *all* are given the heritage, the kingdom, the priesthood and the sanctuary."

The chief characteristics of the Pharisees are expressed in their name: *Pharash*, the Law expounders; *Pharash*, the separatists—though the former is probably its true derivation.

The Pharisees, it will be seen, were the more pious, the Sadducees the more worldly, though the Pharisees as a whole were not as pious as the Chassidim had been, nor the Sadducees as worldly as the Hellenists had been. The Sadducees further denied belief in bodily resurrection or in judgment after death (though not necessarily renouncing immortality), on the strength of the famous teaching of Antigonus of Socho, "Be not as servants who serve the Master for the sake of reward, but rather as those who serve the Master without thought of reward." As distinct from the Pharisees they were strong believers in free-will, that the destiny of men is in their own hands. We might call the Sadducees the rationalists and the Pharisees traditionalists.

Some Pharisees again did carry the fulfilment of rites and ceremonies too far; a few, perhaps, were even ostentatious in their piety. By strange mischance these few have transferred their dubious reputation to all Pharisees as such. Most unjustly however, for the Pharisees earned the confidence of the great bulk of the people and were on the whole identified with them. So strangely has that sinister repute persisted that "Pharisee" is to-day defined in some dictionaries as self-righteous or hypocritical (see note). How undeserved as describing those whose trust in God was absolute, without reservation or misgiving. This is but one of many instances where the world's verdict has been unjust to the Jew.

Essenes.

We meet also a third party nearer in sympathy to the Pharisees. The old Chassidim, the extremists, had developed into an ascetic party under the name of *Essenes*, with a similar meaning—pious. They lived the life of a celibate brotherhood, holding the little they allowed themselves, in common. They hardly affected the national life of Israel, because they were too few and because they slighted patriotic obligations. They practiced all the self-denial of the Nazirites of old and sought to reach from cleanliness to godliness. Another derivation of the name Essene is "bather," baptist, from their frequent ablutions. Yet another is "healer."

The Hasmonean royalty—to what party did they belong? Well, we might say that they began their career with all the religious enthusiasm of the Pharisees, they closed it with the political outlook of the Sadducees. This was something like an anti-climax.

John Hyrcanus perhaps represents the dividing line. He started on a career of conquest simply to satisfy national ambition; though he had forced Judaism on the Idumeans. In his later years, he rejected many traditional observances of the Oral Law that completed his estrangement from the Pharisees. Taking a material and external survey, Hyrcanus left the Jews at the end of his life with an independent State, that in power and extent was as great as Northern Israel in its palmy days, as great perhaps as the realm of Solomon. He could mint his own coins, on some of which, still in existence, we find inscribed, "Jochanan, High Priest of the Commonwealth of the Judeans." Yes, it was all very splendid! But surely the Jews had learned by now the insufficiency of national glory that was material and external, that that kind of splendor was apart from the Jewish ideal, "not by might, not by power, but by my spirit, saith the Lord." The age needed a Jeremiah again. Alas, the era of the Prophets was over!

NOTES AND REFERENCES.

Hasmonean:

This was the family name of Mattathias, afterwards assumed by his descendants.

Pharisees and Sadducees:

Geiger, *"History of the Jews,"* vol. i, chapter viii, translation.

The fact that Jesus of Nazareth condemned the false Pharisees—as Micah condemned false prophets (see Matthew xxiii and Luke xi) has much to do with their general condemnation in literature.

The Talmud is also bitter against the false Pharisees, the *Zebuim*, the tainted ones, who do evil like Zimri and claim the goody reward like Phineas. In its severe denunciation of the false Pharisees, it divides them into six classes:

1. Those who do the will of God for earthly motives. 2. The ostentatious who go with slow steps and say "Wait for me, I have a good deed to perform." 3. Those who knock their heads against a wall because in their looking up they fear they may see a woman. 4. Those who pose as saints. 5. Those who say, "Tell me of another duty." 6. Those who are pious because of the fear of God.

"Who are the genuine Pharisees?" asks the Talmud. "Those who do the will of their Father in Heaven because they love Him."

King:

Carlyle reminds us of the derivation of "King" from *Können*—the man who "can"!

Samaritans:

See *People of the Book*, vol. iii, p. 244.

Theme for Discussion:

Compare modern with ancient parties in Israel.

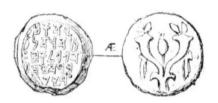

COIN OF JOHANAN THE HIGH PRIEST.

CHAPTER VIII.

A ROYAL HOUSE AGAIN.

Aristobulus.

In Aristobulus, eldest son and successor of John Hyrcanus, we see the Hasmonean further and further estranged from the generous spirit that called them to the fore. Judas Maccabeus wished to be the *Saviour* of Judaism and the Jews, Aristobulus wanted only to be their *king*. The story of Abimelech in the days of the Judges and Jotham's parable come forcibly to mind (Judges ix). Aristobulus began his reign by inprisoning his mother, to prevent her succession to the throne, according to his father's wish, and likewise all his brothers but one, on suspicion of their treason. Antigonus was his favorite brother, and he shared the royal power with him. The king was certainly unpopular with the people, who accused him of being more Greek than Jew. Slander made him even worse than he was, ascribing to him the death of his beloved brother Antigonus, who was assassinated toward the close of his reign. He continued his father's policy of conquest, and subdued portions of northern Palestine, including Galilee, and, like his father again imposed Judaism upon them. While in both instances the motive for the forced conversion was probably ancestral pride, still it showed religious zeal too— though not of the highest kind.

Alexander Janneus.

The widow of Aristobulus, Salome Alexandra, released her husband's brother from prison at his death and by marrying Alexander Janneus, the eldest, and appointing him to the office of High Priest she allowed the kingly power to devolve upon him. Like his brother, he was not a man of peace, but of war. He further increased Judea's territory by conquest on the western Philistine side bordering on the Mediterranean.

He was not the man to quiet the growing dissensions between Pharisees and Sadducees, but rather to foment them. For the royal Sadducean party was getting more and more estranged in policy and aim from the national and religious aspirations of the people. There was a not always silent protest against the warrior king officiating as High Priest. At the Feast of Tabernacles, the people pelted him with their citrons, which they were carrying together with palms (*lulab and esrog*), symbols of the harvest, for this is also called the Feast of Ingathering. This could not end without a tragedy, and a large number were slain by his foreign mercenaries. (Royal body guards were usually composed of foreigners.) This conflict grew into a civil war, both sides in turn hiring foreign troops, and resulted in a terrible decimating of Judah's numbers, the Pharisees losing more largely. Such is one of the evils of uniting religious authority with temporal power. The rebellion was finally put down, but only with an iron hand.

This king, who could not be at peace, spent his last days in fighting the Arabians, who were just beginning to be Judea's most dangerous neighbor. But he inherited from his Maccabean ancestors love of arms without inheriting their military genius. This meant much wanton waste of life and some reverses. How vain this purpose of spending blood and substance in extending his territorial sway and making it nominally Jewish by force of arms, while fomenting religious antagonism at home—always destructive of religion itself. He left an even bigger State than his father, John Hyrcanus. Judea now meant the whole seacoast (with the exception of Ascalon) from Mount Carmel to Egypt and reached far east of the Jordan.

Queen Salome Alexandra.

The throne went by will to Alexander Janneus' widow, who, it will be remembered, was also the widow of his elder brother, Aristobulus. Upon her eldest son, Hyrcanus, Queen Salome bestowed the high priesthood. Her sympathies, however, were entirely with the Pharisees. The exiles came back and political prisoners were released. The land enjoyed a pleasing contrast under her pious and gentle sway. All the Pharisaic ordinances, abolished by the late king, were reinstituted. Indeed, all religious interests were placed in their hands. It was a prosperous, peaceful reign, and was later looked back upon as a blessed day. In the stormy days that were to follow, it might well seem in retrospect, a golden age.

COIN OF THE TIME OF ALEXANDRA.

The "Pairs."

We have seen that the priesthood and Temple were no longer the religious centres around which the people rallied. The Jews had outgrown the age of priestism, although the splendid ritual of the sacrificial altar still continued. The religious guides and teachers were the scribes, learned in the Law, who for sometime had been presiding in couples. Hence they are called the "Pairs." The first of each pair held the office of *Nasi*, Prince or President of the Sanhedrin, and the second that of *Ab Beth Din*, Father of the Court or Vice-President.

Here are their names with some of the most famous sayings attributed to them:

Jose ben Joezer—Let thy house be a meeting place for the wise. Cover thyself with the dust of their feet and quench thy thirst with their words.

Jose ben Jochanan—Let thy house be opened wide and let the needy be thy household.

Joshua ben Perachia—Procure for thyself an instructor, possess thyself of a worthy associate, and judge every man in the scale of merit.

Mattai the Arbelite—Associate not with the wicked and flatter not thyself that thou canst evade punishment.

Jehudah ben Tabbai—Constitute not thyself dictator to the Judges.

Simon ben Shetach—Be guarded in thy words; perchance from them men may learn to lie.

Shemaiah—Love labor and hate pomp and suffer thyself to remain unknown to the head of the State.

Abtalion—Ye wise be guarded in your words; or you may be exiled to a place of evil waters (false doctrine) and your disciples may drink and die.

Hillel and *Shammai*, the last "Pair," will be treated in a separate chapter.

Simon ben Shetach flourished in this reign. He was brother-in-law of the king, by whom he had been nevertheless imprisoned. But when the queen came to the throne he was practically placed as the religious head of affairs. Simon ben Shetach and his associate, Judah ben Tabbai, reorganized the Council and hence were called "restorers of the Law." From this time on the Pharisaic became the official interpretation of Judaism.

In all large towns Simon ben Shetach established schools for young men for the study of the Pentateuch and the laws interpreted from it. As President of the Council, he was very severe on those who infringed on the law. He has even been called the Judean Brutus, as he did not spare his own son. He reinstituted many customs that had been neglected during the Sadducean regime. Among these was the joyous "Water Celebration" during Tabernacles, a trace of which still survives in the ritual of *Shemini Atzereth* (the eighth day that follows and concludes the festival of Succoth). The celebrations were accompanied by illuminations and torchlight processions, religious music and dancing. The water drawing at the Spring of Siloah was heralded by blasts of the priests' trumpets. Another national custom revived was the summer "Wood Festival," on Ab 15. It had relation to the use of wood at the altar fires, and was a further opportunity for joyous unbending among the youths and maidens.

The Pharisees on the whole were the more democratic party, and decided that the maintenance of the Temple should be borne by all and not merely by voluntary offerings of the rich few. This new law brought enormous revenues to the Temple which later became its menace, attracting the covetous rather than the worshipful.

Notes and References.

Sayings of the Fathers:

Sayings of the Jewish Fathers, chapter i. Taylor. Cambridge Press. Translations and notes.

These sayings, which form one book of the Mishna, will be found in the Sabbath Afternoon Service of the Jewish Prayer Book.

Water Festival:

For a vivid description see *Poetry of the Talmud*, Seckles.

Theme for Discussion:

Contrast the Wood Festival of ancient Judea with Arbor Day in modern America. Mark the difference of purpose.

THE POOL OF SILOAM.

CHAPTER IX.

RIVAL CLAIMANTS FOR THE THRONE.

Aristobulus II.

Even before the good Queen Salome died storm clouds began to darken the horizon of Judah. Her second son, Aristobulus, inherited all his father's fierceness and tyranny. The throne had been naturally left to the elder brother, Hyrcanus, but the headstrong Aristobulus seized the reins of power on the dangerous theory that he was more fit to rule. Civil war began before the good queen had quite breathed her last. Hyrcanus, the weak, yielded, and all might have been well were it not for the interference of a new enemy who was eventually to bring about the ruin of the Jewish State.

Antipater the Idumean.

It will be recalled that John Hyrcanus had conquered the Idumeans and made them, seemingly, Jews. We shall now see the kind of Jews they were. One of them, Antipater, was the local governor of this Idumean province. He was a man who lusted for power and had absolutely no scruples as to the means of gaining his ends. He saw that if only he could place the weak Hyrcanus on the throne, he might become a power behind it.

He began by insinuating himself into the favor of the Jewish nobility, and, ostensibly, as a pleader for justice, emphasized the evils of Aristobulus' usurpation. Letting that poison work, he came to the innocent Hyrcanus and played upon his fears with a made-up story of conspiracy against his life. Most reluctantly was Hyrcanus persuaded to flee with him from Jerusalem to an Arabian prince, Aretas. Aretas was induced to lend his aid in the expectation that Hyrcanus, once in power, would restore the cities Alexander Janneus had taken from the Arabians.

So unhappy Judah was plunged in war again to gratify the unworthy ambitions of unworthy men and men not of their own people. Aristobulus was defeated in battle by Aretas and was besieged in the TempleCitadel.

Prayer of Onias.

An interesting incident is told at this juncture that recalls the Bible story of

Balaam. (Numbers xxii-xxiv.) In the party of Hyrcanus there was a man, Onias, who, so said credulous rumor, had brought rain in times of drought through his fervent prayer. He was now brought into the camp and asked to invoke God's curse on Aristobulus and his allies. But such prayer he considered blasphemous, therefore he voiced his petition to heaven in these words: "O God, King of the whole world, since those that stand now with me are Thy people and those that are besieged are also Thy priests, I beseech Thee that Thou wilt neither hearken to the prayer of those against these, nor bring about what these pray against those." Alas, the temper of warfare had not patience or appreciation with this sublime attitude. The man was stoned. But in a sense his prayer was answered.

Pompey Takes Jerusalem.

For the Aesop fable of the two bears quarrelling over a find, thus affording opportunity for a third to step in and seize it, was here to be exemplified. Rome was ever on the watch to bring all outlying provinces into her net. Pompey, her victorious general, whose head Julius Caesar was later to demand, was just now making his triumphant march through Asia. The warring brothers, Hyrcanus and Aristobolus, appealed to his lieutenant. To leave the decision with Rome was a dangerous precedent, for the power that could grant a throne by its decision might also take it away. So, while the decision was rendered in favor of Aristobulus, it was as vassal rather than as independent king that he held his throne for some two years. The real gainer was Rome. It had now the right to revoke its decision; and it did. The people, disgusted with their unworthy leaders who cared nothing for the nation, but only for its honors—appealed to Rome to abolish the monarchy that had been gradually introduced and restore the old regime of the High Priesthood.

But the headstrong Aristobulus dared resist even Rome and entrenched himself against invasion. This was fatal both for him and Judea. The temple mount was besieged. It was taken with frightful massacre by lustful Romans. This was in 63. Pompey sacrilegiously entered the Holy of Holies, in which to his surprise he found no idol; a spiritual God was an unfamiliar concept to the pagan mind. He curtailed the Jewish state and made it tributary. Aristobulus must grace Pompey's triumph at Rome.

So much for the vain conquests of John Hyrcanus and Alexander Janneus. They evaporated with a word from Pompey. Thus ended the Judean independence for which the early Maccabees had fought so nobly. It had endured but seventy-nine years. Over this tributary State Hyrcanus II. was made High Priest. The kingship created by the first Aristobulus was short-lived indeed. The scheming Antipater had won, but graver issues were to be the outcome.

CHAPTER X.

JUDEA UNDER ROMAN SUZERAINTY.

Growth of Rome.

Rome, from the city on the Tiber, had spread over all Italy. Then gradually it mastered the lands on both sides of the Mediterranean. Greece and Carthage were absorbed in the same year, 146 B.C.E. Soon its tide of conquest reached Asia, and nearly all the lands in the East conquered by Alexander—excepting Persia—were under its sway. When Greco Syria—which had included Judea until the Maccabean independence—fell before its arms, it was to be expected that the never-satisfied Rome would not rest until the land of our fathers had been added to its possessions. We have seen how an unhappy series of events played into its hands and hastened this end. In a sense Rome was becoming the "mistress of the world." Nor was her sway as transitory as that of earlier world powers—Assyria, Babylonia, Persia or Macedonia. It was to endure for many centuries and it has left a lasting impress upon the world's civilization.

Already the Jewish captives that Pompey took to Rome, later freed and called Libertini, formed together with earlier emigrants the beginnings of an important Jewish community. Here later still we find this Jewish colony on the Tiber quietly influencing Roman affairs.

Judea, with the rest of Palestine, was now placed under the general supervision of Rome's Syrian governor. Internally its life was not interfered with, but all temporal—that is political—power was taken from the High Priest. His authority was confined to the Temple. Both Aristobulus, who had escaped from Rome, and his son, Alexander, made foolhardy attempts for the throne, which only resulted in further curtailing of Judah's power. Yet another desperate attempt was made for the throne. Alas, it only resulted in thirty thousand of the defeated malcontents being sold into slavery. This chafing against Rome's rule only brought its mailed hand more fiercely against ill-fated Israel.

From First Triumvirate to Empire.

But Rome now entered upon its own period of civil war at home and men lustful of power drenched this country in blood. In 60 B. C. E. Julius Caesar, Pompey and Crassus divided the Roman possessions between them and formed the First Triumvirate (Crassus given Syria, plundered the Temple treasures). On the death of Crassus, Caesar, ambitious for supreme power—the fatal weakness of this really great man—crossed the river Rubicon that was the boundary of his province of Gaul, made war on Pompey, who was soon slain, and held for a brief time sole sway. In 44 Caesar was killed by Brutus and Cassius. These in turn were overthrown by Cæsar's avenger, Marc Antony, and a new Triumvirate was formed, consisting of Antony, Octavian (Augustus) and Lepidus. These were as disloyal to each other as the first group. Antony, seduced from his duty by the witchery of that fatally beautiful woman, Cleopatra of Egypt, was finally defeated and overthrown in the battle of Actium, 30. Octavian Augustus now held the reins alone and the *Roman Empire* was launched. Augustus, the first emperor, reigned from 60 B.C.E. to 14 A.C.E.

JULIUS CAESAR

These few outlines of Roman history will have to be kept in mind to follow events in Judea, for much was to happen to storm-tossed Israel between the first Triumvirate and the empire of Augustus. Every change in government at Rome affected the land of Israel and its people.

Indeed, in all their subsequent history no great event occurred in the world without affecting the Jews in some way, and many of these world events were in turn influenced by them.

When Pompey was killed in 48, that arch-conspirator, Antipater, who had sided with him while in power, now with Hyrcanus, his puppet, professed friendship for Caesar and helped him with Jewish troops for his Egyptian campaign. Caesar extended favors to both. Hyrcanus, as High Priest, was once more given political authority, and Antipater was made Procurator of Judea. We have witnessed the thin entering of the wedge; behold the Idumean now head of Jewish affairs. Caesar now granted permission to rebuild the walls of Jerusalem, and concessions and privileges were also conferred on the Jews of Alexandria and Asia Minor, for Rome's sway reached far. Caesar's good will made the rulership of Antipater tolerable for a while and when the news of Caesar's death reached the Jews they mourned him as a lost friend.

The political power granted to Hyrcanus as High Priest carried with it the title of Ethnarch, which means governor of a province. But all power was really exercised by Antipater who, as Procurator of Judea, made his son Phasael governor of Jerusalem, and his son Herod governor of Galilee. How this intruding stranger had tightened his grip on the land of our fathers!

Herod Enters on the Scene.

Herod was to play an important role in Judah's fortunes. Already as governor of Galilee, a youth of twenty-five, he showed his masterfulness in the summary execution of a marauder. Summoned to the Sanhedrin to answer for this action, he dared defy it. Why? Because Cassius, now master of Syria (including Judea) at Caesar's death, was put under obligation by the crafty Antipater and his equally cunning son Herod. Together they succeeded in squeezing money from Judæa for the maintenance of an army against Antony. Thus the Jews were embroiled in Rome's conflicts to further the ambitions of these Idumeans. As a result Herod was now made governor of Celo-Syria (Palestine) and could snap his fingers at the Sanhedrin. Judea, in fact, was a prey to anarchy brought about by conspiracies and usurpations.

In 42 Brutus and Cassius were defeated at Philippi by Antony and Octavian, and it seemed that an end had come to the fortunes of Herod. Antipater had been slain, caught in a final act of heartless duplicity against Hyrcanus. But Herod had the adroit cunning of his father and knew how to desert a sinking ship and change his allegiance to the man of rising fortunes. With plausible words Herod made his peace with Antony. Nor did the complaints against him and his brother by the Jewish nobility avail. On the contrary Antony made them both *tetrarchs*—subordinate governors—of Judea at the expense of the weak and aging Hyrcanus.

The Last Hasmonean Ruler.

Antigonus, a son of Aristobulus, taking advantage of a Parthian uprising, made one more effort to seize the Jewish throne. He succeeded. Herod was put to flight and Hyrcanus deposed altogether. This last scion of the Hasmonean house held a brief royal sway from 40 to 37. He lacked the greatness of the earlier Maccabeans to hold the nation; and, antagonized the Sanhedrin instead of attaching it to him. Herod, after varied shifts, sailed to Rome, making an appeal at headquarters. Deceiving all by his plausibility, he obtained an appointment as "King of Judea" from Antony's senate. But for that throne he must now fight "the man in possession." There followed a series of engagements in which Jewish blood flowed freely. With the aid of Rome, Herod was of course successful, ultimately taking Jerusalem itself. Antigonus was put to death. Thus ended the Hasmonean rule in Judea so gloriously begun a little over a century before.

Theme for Discussion.

Single out great events in history influenced by and influencing the Jews.

COIN OF ANTIGONUS, 40 B. C. E.

CHAPTER XI.

HEROD.

What had been the result of the attempt of Alexander Janneus to force Judaism upon Idumea? It had begun by giving the Idumean Antipater, from the intimate relations created, the opportunity to make Hyrcanus his puppet, and ended by placing the Jewish crown upon the head of Herod, who was absolutely un-Jewish in ancestry and sympathies, and really a pagan at heart. Herod, in fact, delivered Judea to Rome that he might be made its vassal king.

He had married Mariamne, the beautiful grand daughter of the weak Hyrcanus—a stroke of policy, to be allied in marriage to Judah's royal family.

Herod as Man.

Undoubtedly he was a man of power of a sort, born to command; but there was no soft spot in his nature. He had all the instincts of a tyrant, and neither scruple nor pity deterred him from carrying out his passionate will and his insatiable ambition. He inherited all his father's cunning, allied with fine judgment and untiring energy. Though of undoubted bravery, he knew how to fawn before those in power.

The first dozen years of his reign were marked by storm and conflict with enemies both without and within. The feelings of the Jews can be imagined in having this alien thrust upon them by all-powerful Rome and whose first act was to slay their patriots and confiscate their property. Rebellion was put down with a merciless hand. Step by step he carried out his relentless purpose and put to death all the survivors of the royal line, the flower of the Jewish nobility, and likewise every member (except Shemaiah and Abtalion) of the Sanhedrin that had some years before censured one of his misdeeds.

Very unwillingly he appointed his wife's brother as High Priest. It was a fatal distinction for the young man, for the people too openly expressed their regard for this scion of the Hasmonean line. What was the consequence? One day when refreshing himself in the bath, he was held under the water till life was extinct. It was called an accident! Alexandra, his mother, a hard woman, appealed to Rome through Cleopatra to punish this murder. Herod was summoned to answer for his conduct before Antony, but his plausible manner aided by bribery won his acquittal. The tyrant marked his return by the execution of another brother-in-law, to whom he had entrusted Mariamne in his absence, and whom he jealously imagined disloyal.

That Antony at this time gave part of Palestine proper to Cleopatra, including even a bit of Judea, and that Herod must bear it without protest, showed on what slender tenure he held his throne. So completely was he under Rome's control that Antony, to satisfy the whim of Cleopatra who disliked Herod, commanded him to undertake a campaign against the Arabians, while she secretly assisted them.

When Antony fell at Actium in 31 in that contest between continents, Herod managed adroitly at the right moment to go over to the side of the victorious Octavian Augustus. Before departing for Rome to curry favor with the Emperor, he took a precaution, which only his cruelty deemed necessary. He put to death his own kinsman, the aged Hyrcanus, to whose weakness he in a measure owed his throne.

He returned in the good graces of Augustus, and received back all the lands taken from him by Antony for Cleopatra. But before his departure, he had repeated the order given prior to his previous visit, that Mariamne should be put to death in case his cause should take a fatal turn in Rome. Learning of this revolting plan in his absence, she upbraided him on his return. This gave his envious relatives opportunity to slander her and defame her honor. The jealous Herod believed the calumny against his innocent wife—and think of it —ordered her to be put to death, though, in his savage, sensual way, he loved her. Remorse came too late, which wild excesses could not drown. Soon her mother followed her to the block on the better founded charge of conspiracy. More deeds of needless bloodshed were perpetrated by his wanton command until every remnant of the Hasmonean house was destroyed.

Herod as Builder.

Herod was a renowned builder. He wanted to have a splendid capital with which he might dazzle Roman grandees and foreign plenipotentiaries. Notice the bent of his mind—his conception of a monarch—not a father of his people living up to such a maxim, for example, as *ich dïen* (I serve) but the possessor of glory and with the power to play with the life and death of his subjects. He must needs have grandeur without, though there was misery enough within. He erected temples, amphitheatres and hippodromes. He built for himself a palace that was a fortress too, with parks and gardens around it. New cities were laid out, not for the honor of Israel but for the honor of Augustus Caesar and named after him. Samaria was rebuilt and renamed Sebaste. He rebuilt a city on the coast and called it Caesarea, with a fine haven. One he named Antipatris after his father, another after his brother, Phasaelis; Agrippaeum, after Agrippa, and Herodium, a stronghold, after himself. Existing fortresses were restored and strengthened. Nor did he neglect to mark the outlying provinces with examples of his building passion.

EMPEROR AUGUSTUS.

The old Temple, built in the days of Ezra and Nehemiah, now looked shabby among these fine edifices, and he determined to rebuild it. This was one of his great achievements. There was no religious motive whatever in the project, for he had built outside of Jerusalem many heathen shrines. The purpose was wholly worldly. If there is to be a Temple, let it be gorgeous to gratify my vanity! It took many years to build and was not finished till long after Herod's death. The whole circumference of the Temple, including the fortress of Antonia connected with it, covered almost a mile. It must have been magnificent, for a proverb arose, "He who has not seen Herod's Temple has never seen anything beautiful." Yet, with all his grandeur, he was but a subject king under the sway of the Roman emperor. He could not make treaties or war without the consent of the emperor, to whom he had to supply on demand troops and money.

The introduction of heathen games in theatres and race-courses, in which the lives of gladiators and runners were lightly sacrificed to gratify the brutal instincts of the spectators, deeply grieved the Jews, imbued with the sanctity of human life. It was in such violent antagonism to the ethics of Judaism. But what could they do? They were in the power of this pagan tyrant.

He gathered in his capital, too, Greek litterateurs and artists. To these scholars were given state positions of trust. But this was no more an indication of love of culture than Temple building was love of religion. Ostentation was at the root of both.

Yet the Pharisaic party (the great mass of the people) was too strong for him to carry his paganizing influence as far as he wished. He ungraciously yielded, out of prudence, now and then to the religious sensibilities of the people. The building of the sanctuary proper he entrusted to priests, nor were images placed on the Jerusalem buildings. But the Roman eagle was later erected over the Temple gate. For an attempt to remove it, forty-two young men, zealous for the law, were burnt alive. The Jewish Sanhedrin was shorn of all power.

He appointed unfit men as High Priests and removed them when they did not do his bidding. That such appointments should be left in his unsympathetic hands. Finally, the people were heavily taxed to support heathen splendor of which they did not approve. So his reign, so hateful to them, was maintained only by despotism and force. An attempt was even made to assassinate him. The populace had to be watched by spies. Yet in the year 25 he brought all his energies to the fore to save the people from the consequences of famine. Let us remember this in his favor; also that he used his power to secure protection for Jews in the Diaspora.

Herod as Father.

By paying lavish court to the emperor and his son-in-law, Agrippa, his territory was gradually doubled. A splendid kingdom viewed superficially, but it brought no happiness to this unscrupulous man. Peace in the home, domestic joy, these are the things that prowess and power cannot buy. The story of how this barbarian had put to death his favorite wife, Mariamne, has already been told. Her two sons were now grown to man's estate. But Herod's sister, the wicked Salome, who had plotted against their mother, now tried to fill the king's mind with suspicions against her sons. In this purpose she was aided by Antipater, son of Herod by another of his wives. Learning that their mother had been put to death by their father's mandate, they openly expressed their anger, which so increased the king's suspicions, that he accused his sons before the emperor. The mildness of Augustus could only postpone the eventual tragedy—the execution of the young men by order of their own father. Antipater—the real conspirator against Herod, though his favorite son, —was at last detected, and of course executed also. Surely the latter days of this king were bitter.

These domestic troubles were aggravated by bodily disease and the knowledge that he was hated by his people. Determined to be mourned at all costs, he imprisoned some of the most distinguished men of the nation with orders that they were to be killed at the moment of his death. Thus would he obtain a mourning at his funeral! Was not this the climax of savagery! This fiendish purpose was, however, never carried out; so he died unwept and unmourned.

He is called "Great" to distinguish him from some puny Herods that followed in the fast dying Jewish State. We can call him "Great" only in a bad sense—an awful example of the abuse of power in the hands of an unscrupulous and blood-thirsty man.

NOTES AND REFERENCES.

Mariamne.

Zirndorf, *Some Jewish Women.* (Jewish Pub. Soc.) Grace Aguilar, *Women of Israel.*

Rome.

In Talmudic literature "Edom" is often a disguised term for Rome, because in the Bible story Esau is the rival of Jacob. When we remember that Antipater and Herod were Idumeans (Edom) and that they practically delivered Judea to Rome for the price of a crown, the rabbinic usage is peculiarly appropriate.

Herod.

In Stephen Phillip's dramatic poem of this name, the character is idealized.

Theme for discussion:

Did Herod succeed or did he fail?

CHAPTER XII.

HILLEL

Let us now take a glance at the religious life of Judah in this reign. The picture is brighter. Hillel was made president of the Sanhedrin in the year 30. A new direction was given to the development of rabbinic Judaism under his guidance. He was the greatest Jewish teacher since Ezra. Like Ezra he came from Babylon, which had remained a Jewish centre since the exile, 600 B. C. E., and was to continue to be a Jewish centre for many centuries later. Pleasing stories are told of the sacrifices made by this poor boy to gratify his thirst for knowledge. Once he was almost frozen to death while lying on the skylight to hear the discussion, since he was not allowed to hear it from within. Ultimately he was placed at the head of the Sanhedrin where at first he was a beggar at its doors. Great as he was as an expounder of the Law, he is perhaps best known by the sweetness of his character. None could put him out of temper, it is said. This story is given as illustration. A man who ventured a wager that he would rouse Hillel's wrath called thrice at the most inopportune time asking the absurdest questions, and each time more rudely than before. The attempt failed. On hearing the explanation of this strange behavior, Hillel, unruffled to the last, said, "Better that you should lose your wager than I my temper." He united in himself gentleness and firmness.

Hillel as Moralist.

Many interesting instances are given of his evenness of disposition that disarmed the violent and won many a convert to the fold, where the brusqueness of his colleague—Shammai—often drove them away. "Be patient like Hillel, not passionate like Shammai," ran the saying. Thus Hillel became the peacemaker in those troublous Herodian days. In this connection he taught, "Be of the disciples of Aaron—loving and pursuing peace, loving mankind and bringing them nigh to the Law." His consideration for others went so far that, a man of standing, becoming suddenly poor, he provided him with a horse and servant that he might still enjoy some of the comforts of his earlier life.

He is the author of the famous Golden Rule in its earlier form, uttered in reply to a heathen who would have him teach the whole Law while he stood on one foot: "That which is hateful to thee do not unto thy neighbor; this is the principle, all the rest is commentary." Another heathen must needs be made a priest if converted: Hillel gently showed him the prohibition of the Law. But the instances show that proselytism was encouraged.

In the following maxims many phases of his character are revealed:

"He who craves to raise his name, lowers it."

"A name inflated is a name destroyed."

"My humility is my pride, my pride my humility."

"He who will not learn or teach deserves death."

"He who does not progress, retrogrades."

"Say not, 'when I have leisure I will study,' for you may never have leisure."

"Study God's word; then both this world and the next will be thine."

"Trust not thyself till the day of thy death."

"In a place where there is no man, strive to show thyself a man."

"Judge not thy neighbor till thou art in his place."

"If I am not for myself, who will be for me? But if I am for myself alone, what am I? And if not now, when?"

Do you realize how much is contained in that last maxim? Unravel it and you will see revealed his philosophy of life.

Hillel as Legislator.

So gentle, he was yet daring. When an old law was abused, he ventured to modify it. The Law, for example, for release of debts every seventh year, made particularly for the benefit of the poor (Deut. xv), hampered the growth of trade in more complex times and changed a generous purpose into an occasional embarrassment. There is a gulf of difference between a loan to buy bread and a loan for business enterprise. In the latter case Hillel allowed the stipulation to be stated in the contract, called *prosbul*, that the law of release was to be suspended.

To Hillel is due the important service of devising a logical system of seven rules of deduction by which new laws to meet new needs could be developed out of the fewer and more general principles in the Bible code. It must be confessed that these deductions were occasionally far-fetched. None the less the custom prevailed among the rabbis to make laws for all exigencies in that way for many centuries to come. The practice arose from the reverence paid the five books of Moses that induced them to seek authority for every regulation they found needful, in their pages. We might say it was a virtue carried to the extreme of a fault. Hillel's method earned him the title "Regenerator of the Law."

Last Days.

"Where goest thou, Master," said Hillel's disciples one day when he hastened from the house of learning. "I go to meet a guest," Hillel replied. "Who is this guest of whom thou so often speakest?" The sweetness of the master's face deepened into earnestness. "My guest is my soul. Too often in intercourse with the world must its claims be pushed aside."

But the day came, as indeed it must, when the soul was summoned to a greater tribunal than his own. The day of Hillel's death was a day of mourning in Israel. "O, pious, gentle, worthy follower of Ezra," cried the sorrowing people. Contrast his death with Herod's.

Such was the love and esteem in which he was held by the scholars of his own and later ages, that the presidency of the Sanhedrin was kept in his family for four centuries (like a royal succession), and in this way his memory reverenced for many generations.

Shammai.

In Hillel and Shammai, the "Pairs" referred to in chapter viii reached their culmination. A teaching of Shammai ran, "Say little but do much." These two men were the founders of two distinct schools of interpretation of Jewish Law. They were as distinct in their character as in their exposition of Scripture. Hillel was broad, tolerant and original; Shammai—narrow, strict, and conservative. (Hillel's opinions were usually accepted by later generations.) Shammai was a pessimist saying "It were better not to have been born." Hillel was an optimist, and said, "Being born, make the most of life."

To the Shammai school we owe the many stringent prohibitions with regard to the Sabbath and to ecclesiastical purity. They objected even to teaching the young, visiting the sick, or comforting mourners on the Sabbath day. We are glad to state that Jewish practice has taken the opposite view. The rabbis of the Shammai school were not only severe in their religious decisions, but also in the interpretation of patriotism and in their views of life generally. Their gloomy philosophy is shown in Second Esdras: see chap. v., on the Apocrypha. We might compare them with the first Puritan settlers in America.

———

This school, also unlike Hillel's, opposed the admission of proselytes from the heathen. Yet in those stormy times, these severe views against the heathen found the larger following. From these doubtless came the band of Zealots whose fanatic hatred of Rome and its institutions became almost a religion, and whose deeds, to be told later, form a lurid chapter in Judah's closing days.

NOTES AND REFERENCES.

Law and Equity:

According to ancient Jewish law a city home sold could be redeemed within a year. "But suppose the owner lock it up and depart." "Break the lock and lodge the money with the court," said Hillel. He touched a modern need in showing here that craft must not defeat the benevolent purpose of the Law.

See Geiger's *History of Judaism*, vol. i, chap. viii.

Golden rule. See Tobit iv, 15.

Sayings of the Jewish Fathers, Taylor, pp. 34 to 37.

Theme for Discussion:

Is it possible as Hillel said, to evolve the whole law from the Golden Rule?

———

CHAPTER XIII.

HEROD'S SUCCESSORS.

The selfish Herod had split up his kingdom among his three sons—Archelaus, Antipas and Philip. Before Rome had yet confirmed the succession, and while a procurator was placed in temporary charge, already the sons were intriguing against each other. Rome carried out Herod's wishes, only that his sons were made tetrarchs instead of kings. How steadily Rome moved toward its purposed end!

Archelaus was made tetrarch of Judea, Samaria, and Idumea. The realm of Antipas was Galilee and Perea, the Jordan dividing the two districts. To Philip was given the remaining provinces of Batanæa and Trachonitis in northern Palestine. Look at the map in front of this book.

A word on each of these principalities in the inverse order of importance. Philip held a mild sway for thirty-seven years. There is nothing to record in these outlying provinces, partly because they were far removed from the Jewish centre of gravity.

Antipas and John the Baptist.

The realm of Antipas, often mentioned in the New Testament, was a little nearer. His recognition of Judaism was only formal. He inherited all his father's vices and like his father, too, he was a great builder. He built Sepphoris in Galilee, and Tiberias on the Lake of Gennesaret. In his reign and realm flourished John the Baptist of Perea, and also Jesus of Nazareth in Galilee. As this term, *Baptist*, was applied to the Essenes, because of their frequent ablutions (see p. 82), John may have been a leader of that party.

We know that John preached in the wilderness in the neighborhood of the Jordan, the centre of the Essenes. His bold words, in which he denounced the king, led to his imprisonment, on political grounds, as an agitator. His influence on the people was feared by Rome, for it was hard then to separate religion and politics. It is sometimes hard now. It is said he was finally put to death at the wish of a dancer, Salome, but really to please her mother, Herodias, a wanton woman, to marry whom Antipas had divorced his wife, the daughter of an Arabian king. This not only involved him in a disastrous war, but Herodias caused him eventually the loss of his government and his freedom. For, aiming at a kingship at her instigation, he was banished, and his tetrarchy given to Agrippa, of whom we shall hear later on.

The Last Herodian.

To come now to Judea proper; together with Samaria and Idumea, it was entrusted to the unfit Archelaus; like his father he, too, had to secure his throne through bloodshed. Plots and counterplots with the appearance of pretenders for the thrones of Judea and Galilee, characterized this unhappy time. The Jews were disgusted with the rule of Rome and its creatures, and some began open rebellion. The Syrian governor finally quelled the revolt, but thousands were slain. Had the Jewish malcontents been organized under trustworthy leadership, something might have been achieved. As it was, it ended in their more complete subjection.

There is little else to tell of the reign of Archelaus. Serious charges were brought against this tyrant; so serious that the emperor recalled him to Rome and deposed him. He had reigned ten years, 4 B.C.E. to 6 A. C. E., thus crossing the dividing line of what is called the Christian Era, from the tradition that it marked the birth of Jesus of Nazareth; he was actually born four years earlier than this date.

Herod had brought Judea so completely under Roman control, that bit by bit all the old vested rights, privileges and local powers had been taken from its Sanhedrin, its High Priest and its royal family. Herod had practically sold Judea to Rome for the privilege of subserving as its king. Its fate was now wholly in Rome's hands.

Judea Part of a Roman Province.

Leaving the outlying provinces under the rule of tetrarchs, Rome now decided to govern Judea absolutely as a part of the province of Syria. It sent out governors or, as they were called, *Procurators*, to administer its affairs under the more immediate direction of Syria. The Jews were now to be ruled by strangers who had no understanding of their religion and no sympathy with their traditions or social needs; by men possessed in fact, for the most part, of an ill-concealed antagonism to the rites and obligations that entered into the lives of conscientious Jews.

At its best Judea had been a Theocracy, i.e., a kingdom in which religion, represented by the priesthood and the Sanhedrin, directed the affairs of the nation. Roman rule, therefore, would be revolutionary, even had the procurators been good men and had sought to administer the province in kindness and equity. As a matter of fact, they were nearly all tyrants, lustful for gain at any price and absolutely indifferent to the welfare of the people under their charge; even as we shall see, in many instances wantonly wounding Judea's sensibilities to gratify their cruel pleasure. No wonder the Jews were eventually goaded into a war of desperation.

As to the Jews in other lands under Roman sway, we find Augustus Caesar well disposed to them. He placed the harbors of the Nile under Judean Alabarchs (same as Arabarch). His kindness to the Alexandrian Jews was in marked contrast with his severity toward the Alexandrian Greeks. In the city of Rome he allowed the Jewish settlers—Libertini—to observe their religion undisturbed, and to build synagogues.

So in the deepening shadows there was a glimmer of light too.

NOTES AND REFERENCES.

For the relation of Baptism to the Essenes, read articles on those topics in vols. ii and v, respectively, of the *Jewish Encyclopedia.*

Tetrarch:

Literally, governor of a fourth part of a province.

BOOK III.

JUDEA UNDER ROME.

ROMAN EMPERORS AND PROCURATORS.		JEWRY.	
	C.E.		C.E.
Augustus.			
Coponius	6	Archelaus, tetrarch of Judea,	
Marcus Ambibulus	9	deposed	*
Annius Rufus	12		
Tiberius.		Philo, philosopher, born	16
Valerius Gratus 5	15		
Pontius Pilatus	26		
Caligula.			
Marcellus	36	Death of Jesus of Nazareth	28
Claudius.			
Marullus	37-41	Josephus, historian born	38
	Agrippa, King 41-44		

CHAPTER XIV.

PILATE THE PROCURATOR.

Procurators in general.

The Procurators fall into two groups, with a Jewish king intervening. The table above is the first group of these administrators of Judea. Their seat of government was Caesarea, a city that had become Jerusalem's rival. The Jews had a certain freedom under this regime. "The oath of allegiance to the Roman emperor was more an oath of confederates than of subjects." The Sanhedrin was still supposed to be the governing body for home affairs with the High Priest as its president. But the arbitrary appointment and removal of High Priests by the procurator, placed these powers at the mercy of his caprice, and ultimately the Jews were robbed of these prerogatives altogether. The procurator then could always interfere with the carrying out of Jewish law. It is important that these facts should be borne in mind in the events of the next chapter. Even in religious offenses where the High Priest with the Sanhedrin could pronounce the death sentence, the confirmation of the procurator was required for the execution. So heavily were the people taxed that the tax-gatherers (called *publicans*) were looked upon with opprobrium. Doubtless many of them dishonestly abused their power.

Still Judea was the only province in which the worship of the emperor was not compulsory. The reason is obvious. To pagan communities it was a command which they could obey complacently; to the monotheistic Jews recognizing one sole spirit God, it was simply impossible. It was attempted by the Emperor Caligula, but failed. Even the local coinage bore no figure, nor were the standards bearing the likenesses of the emperor tolerated, as such was regarded as an offense by the strict interpreters of the second commandment. One tyrant tried and failed to force these banners on Judea. They violently opposed a census in the year 7 both on religious and on political grounds, as they regarded it as an infringement of their sacred rights and the precursor of slavery. But Joezer, the High Priest, quieted them and induced them to submit.

Still, from such incidents the stern determination of the Jews may be inferred. Judas of Gamala, a Galilean, and a religious enthusiast, went about preaching the duty of rebellion and the sin of submission. Gradually these malcontents formed themselves into a new party of extremists—the *Zealots*, who believed in using the sword against the heathen to hasten the Messianic realization. They already began nursing the smouldering embers of rebellion.

Pilate in Particular.

Such was the status under the procurators in general. We will treat in detail the regime of only one—Pontius Pilate. It is characteristic of all, but especially eventful in many ways.

The Jewish historian, Josephus, and the Jewish philosopher, Philo, have much to tell of his doings. From the trustworthy Philo we are told that he was of "an unbending and recklessly hard character." "He has been charged with corruptibility, violence, robberies, ill-treatment of the people, continued executions without even the form of trial, endless and intolerable cruelties."

On his first entry into Jerusalem he determined to outrage the religious sensibilities of the people he was sent to protect, by bidding his Roman soldiers hoist a flag with the Emperor's likeness. They petitioned for its removal. He refused. For five days they stood outside the palace urging their request. When the soldiers with drawn swords stood ready to slay at his signal, the people bared their necks, preferring death to toleration of this idolatrous emblem. Such was the intensity of the Jews of these last years of their national life, such was the stuff of which they were made. Even tyrants reach limits beyond which they dare not pass. The emblem was sullenly withdrawn.

At another time he appropriated the Temple treasures, sacredly set aside for religious purposes, for the building of an aqueduct to Jerusalem. This time he resorted to violence to quell the opposition, many lives being sacrificed.

With the purpose only of annoying the people, he put up votive shields inscribed with the emperor's name. But they appealed to Tiberius who not only ordered them removed, but rebuked Pilate for raising them.

On another occasion the Samaritans, to whom Gerizim had all the sanctity that Sinai had for Israel, because the Mosaic Blessings were announced from its heights (see Deut, xi, 29, Joshua, viii, 33), gathered there on a rumor that sacred vessels were hidden in its soil. Pilate sent soldiers wantonly to slaughter them. This led to his recall by Tiberius.

Proselytes.

The Emperor Tiberius decided that it was kinder to the Jews to appoint procurators for long terms than to make frequent changes. It meant the greed of a smaller number to be satisfied. But, on the whole, his attitude was less friendly than that of his predecessor, Augustus. This may have been due to the fact that many Romans of high birth had, unsolicited, accepted the Jewish faith, and had sent gifts to the Temple at Jerusalem. Among these converts was Fulvia, wife of a Roman senator. This led to the banishment from Rome of many thousands of Jews to a dangerous climate. Here was the beginning of a religious persecution.

The incident, however, shows that the worthier Romans were becoming more and more distrustful of pagan cults and were looking for something better. We shall see later how zealous Jews from Judea, and more particularly from Alexandria, began making converts to Judaism all through Asia Minor. The influence of these converts on future events was farther reaching than their sponsors ever dreamed.

NOTES AND REFERENCES.

Read "A Procurator of Judea" in *Mother of Pearl*, by Anatole France. Trans., N. Y., John Lane, 1908.

Theme for discussion:

(a) Does official Judaism discourage conversion?

(b) Why did the Jews oppose a census on religions grounds? See II. Sam. xxiv, and article Census in *Jewish Encyclopedia*, vol. iii.

CHAPTER XV.

JESUS OF NAZARETH.

So far the rule of Pontius Pilate as it concerned Judea. But his rule has become of wide import because of his relation to Jesus of Nazareth, who was put to death during his administration, though born in the province of Galilee governed by Herod Antipas. To explain how a great religion sprang up around this Galilean Jew, which came afterwards to regard him as its father, can be explained only by a complete grasp of the political and religious aspirations of the time.

The Messianic Hope.

The ominous mood in which the Jews realized their gradual deprivation of country and independence indicated the stirring of deep forces in their nature. Judea was to them a Holy Land, for "from Zion had gone forth the Law." Love of country had become part of their religion. Every political function had its religious aspect. The Sanhedrin was at once a civil and a religious body, and this dual characteristic pervaded all the civil institutions. So the longing for the restoration of the royal line of Judah, i.e., the coming of the Messiah, expressed the religious as well as the political hopes of the nation. Not that the word Messiah had any peculiarly religious significance. It is the Hebrew word *M'sheach*, meaning "Anointed (king)," and was applied in the Bible to Saul, David, and even to Cyrus, the Persian, Isaiah xlv—1. In post-exilic times the coming of the Messiah implied the re-establishment of the throne in the Davidic line.

Many of the pious felt further that with a king once more on an independent throne, the glorious pictures of the coming day foretold by the Prophets and not attained in the first monarchy, would be realized in the second. Such as "The Lord's house will be established on the top of the mountains; all nations will flock to it, saying, Come let us go up to the house of the Lord, to the house of the God of Jacob. He will teach us His ways, we will walk in His paths." (Isaiah and Micah.) Again, "The earth will be full of knowledge of God as the waters cover the sea." The conviction expressed by Jeremiah (chap. xxxi, 33-34) would then be fulfilled, that all would "know the Lord from the least of them to the greatest." One of the latest of the Prophets —Zechariah—had foretold a day when "ten men would take hold of the garments of him who was a Jew and would say, We will go with you, for we believe that God is with you." So we might quote nearly every prophet from Amos to Malachi, the last prophet, who said that the day of Judgment would be heralded by the undying Elijah. A Jewish poet in Alexandria voiced the same hope; heathendom would disappear and the kingdom of God would be established.

Alas, the outlook for either the spiritual or the temporal realization seemed farther removed than ever. Every now and then, more particularly under the disturbing rule of the procurators, a deluded enthusiast would appear upon the scene and claim that he was a Messiah. Theudas was one who made this claim in the year 45. So desperate were the times that these agitators always found followers. They were always ruthlessly put to death by Rome for the claim of Messiahship, i.e., "King of the Jews," was treason against Rome. Was not Judea a Roman province now?

Jesus the Man.

In chapter vii the Essenes have been mentioned. This sect, that lived as a brotherhood in the vicinity of the Dead Sea, shared all goods in common, condemned wealth and passed simple lives away from the great world. They, too, looked for the coming of the Messiah. But it was the religious climax of the prophets just quoted that would follow the Messiah's advent—the ushering in triumph of an independent nationality, that most appealed to them. This lofty view was also shared by the more saintly among the Israelites in general; nor was it ever entirely absent even from the popular view.

We have already heard of John the Baptist (Essene), who so stirred the people by preaching that "the kingdom of God" was at hand; this was the Messianic hope. He evidently inspired one youth, who was in close sympathy with the Essene brotherhood, Joshua (Greek Jesus) from Nazareth, in Galilee. Galilee, like the other provinces in northern Palestine, was away from the learning and culture of Jerusalem. It was the home of simple folk who spoke a corrupt dialect, and who credulously accepted popular superstitions; such as, every disease comes from an indwelling spirit or demon.

Of the life of the man Jesus who came from these surroundings *little is really known*, but from a few bare facts very much has been deduced and still more imagined. Apart from the fact that he was the son of a carpenter, Joseph, we only hear of him about two years before his death, and that occurred at the early age of thirty-two. We find him preaching and expounding the Law and sympathizing with the unfortunate classes.

Though by no means a profound scholar in the Law, he exhibited fine moral perception and lived up to the pure ideals of the strict, peace-loving

Essene brotherhood. In his teachings or rather preachings, he followed the models of the great prophets, laying stress upon the spirit of religion and minimizing the value of ceremonial. For there were formalists in those days as there were in the days before the Exile. Indeed, every age reveals the experience that the multitude is often more impressed by the ceremony than the idea it is intended to convey—and gives more attention to the outward, tangible form than to its inward, spiritual purpose, the exaltation of life. Nor is that tendency confined to the ignorant either. Religion so easily sinks into a mechanical routine unless we keep vigilant watch. This lesson is preached by the moralists of every age. It was preached by Jesus of Nazareth with rare power. He had soon a large following, perhaps, too, for the reason that he was now regarded as John the Baptist's successor.

Jesus the Messiah.

But it was not so much his ethical teaching, lofty though it was, that brought him into prominence and caused the crowds to gather about him, though a modern school of Christian apologetics lays stress upon that now. It was partly because he was regarded as a "healer," a power claimed by the Essenes; but chiefly because he was regarded as the long-looked for *Messiah* who would deliver Israel from the thraldom of Rome and gratify their wildest expectations. Whether he first of his own accord laid claim to this mysterious title, or whether he was persuaded into it by his admirers, we cannot gather from the few records that tell the events of his life. For even the earliest of these records, the so-called Gospel of Mark, was not written till nearly fifty years after his death, at a time when startling opinions had already been formed about him; and they do not agree even as to his parentage and birthplace. In fact, once regarded as the Messiah, his biography was *recast* to fit the Messianic prophecies in the Scriptures! This made the Jesus of the Gospels largely a mythical character.

Jesus could quite honestly have believed himself to be a Messiah in some religious sense, though he was rather evasive when bluntly questioned. For many sincere enthusiasts both before and since his time have believed themselves specially chosen messengers of God to bring redemption to their people. It will be seen at the end of this volume that Mohammed, who flourished several centuries later, believed himself to be sent by God to bring salvation to the Arabians. In a sense he was; to call him an impostor, an earlier practise of the Church, is uncharitable and untrue. In Israel's history, since the days of the procurators not a century has passed but some one has come forward claiming to be the Messiah. Some were honest, though mistaken; some were mere adventurers.

Jesus probably accepted the Essene idea of the Messiah, that is, he was less concerned with ushering in an earthly than a heavenly kingdom.

This distinction was not clearly realized by the simple masses of the people, groaning under a hated yoke; certainly it was not realized by the Romans, who saw in every Messianic claim treason against Rome, a plot to win independence for Judea again. On the other hand, Jesus applying to himself on one occasion the term "son of God"—that may mean so little or so much—awakened the alarm and antagonism of the priesthood and lost for him many supporters. So Jesus, who was probably innocent of any blasphemous assumptions against Judaism and guiltless of any conspiracy against Rome to seize the throne and be made "King of the Jews," was nevertheless condemned to death like the Messiahs before him and was executed by the Roman method of capital punishment, crucifixion. But unlike the Messiahs before him—all mediocre men—his name has been treasured ever since as one of the great religious teachers of the world.

Christianity.

For although he died without bringing the redemption which would have proven his Messiahship, his followers did not lose faith in him. His turning kindly to the poor and despised folk, even to the sinful and degraded with his message of comfort, had won all hearts. As they believed he had performed miracles in his life-time, so now they tried to persuade themselves that a greater miracle had been fulfilled in his death—that he had not really died, but had been translated to heaven like Elijah or Enoch and that he would return some day and complete his unfinished work. In those unlettered days belief in the supernatural was very common. Among certain folk it is not so uncommon to-day.

So these believers that Jesus was the Messiah became a new sect called *Christians*. What does "Christian" mean? Christ (Christos) is the Greek for Messiah. So the name Christians meant Messians, and the name Jesus Christ means Jesus the Messiah. Though Jesus himself did not speak Greek, but Aramaic, the Christian Scriptures were written in Greek.

The Jewish Christians continued to live much as the Essenes before them, like them assuming voluntary poverty and faithful as of old to the Jewish Law. But in later years when many pagans joined this sect, they introduced into it many idolatrous notions, borrowed from the cults of Greece, Rome and Egypt. The man Jesus was exalted into a divinity and worshipped as such. The shedding of his blood at his execution was regarded as a sacrifice intended by God to atone for the sins of mankind, based on the ancient idea that the priest shed the blood of an animal in atoning for the sins of the people; but the Hebrew prophets and some of the psalmists had all condemned animal sacrifice as a means of atonement. This belief was a stage of religion beyond which the Jews were advancing. It died out altogether before the century was over—just when it was being revived in this way by Christians.

The next step which separated the Jews from the Christians was the depreciation and ultimately the abrogation of the Jewish Law. This was brought about by a later teacher, Paul, at first opposed to Christians, but later their most eloquent advocate. This abandonment of the Law, ultimately conceded by the early Messians, who had so far still clung to it, severed their relationship with the parent faith. Thus Paul made Christianity a new religion for the heathen world.

The process by which this Jewish sect became a new religion, most of whose adherents came from the heathen world, was slow and gradual. We shall refer to the different steps in the development of this Faith as they occur, and we shall see how this sect, born in Judaism, became its antagonist and persecutor in later days.

NOTES AND REFERENCES.

Biography of Jesus:

In recasting his life from the meagre data at hand his biographers ascribed to him all of the miracles told of Elijah and Elisha—feeding the multitude with a few loaves, curing the sick, reviving the dead and being transported to heaven.

Teachings of Jesus:

He taught nothing heretical or startlingly new; he preferred to emphasize the old. The phrases of "the Lord's Prayer" are biblical; the Beatitudes (a group of Blessings in the New Testament) are rabbinic; his communistic views, those of the Essene school.

The chief source of his teachings was the *Didache*, i.e., a summary of the Faith used by the Synagogue for proselytes. It contained the *Shema* followed by "Thou shalt love the Lord God, etc.;" love thy neighbor as thyself—

Hillel's Golden Rule; the Ten Commandments; a disquisition on "the two ways"—right and wrong.

He followed the rabbis in teaching largely by *Mashal*—parable. Even the form "Ye have heard, etc., but I will go further yet, etc.," is rabbinic.

The Crucifixion:

The reasons why the death of Jesus should not be attributed to the Jews, may be summarized as follows. (See *Jewish Encyclopedia*, vol. iv.)

Crucifixion was not a Jewish, but a Roman method of capital punishment. Prior to the open rebellion against Rome, 30-66 C. E., many Jews were crucified as rebels, and on very meagre evidence. A Messiah in its eyes was a rebel; the inscription placed on the cross was "King of the Jews."

"The mode and manner of Jesus' death undoubtedly point to Roman custom and law as the directive power," though Jews may have administered a soothing cup to lessen the suffering.

None of the well established measures of precaution were taken that always preceded a Jewish execution. It is very doubtful whether Jewish law would tolerate a three-fold execution at one time.

A Jewish execution on Friday is almost impossible. If Jesus died on Nissan 14, the execution on the eve of a festival would be irregular. If on Nissan 15 (Passover), the execution could not be held. There is no corroboration of the custom to liberate a condemned person on account of a holiday.

Read *As Others Saw Him*, Joseph Jacobs; Macmillan.

Jesus of Nazareth, Schlesinger. Albany.

Cradle of the Christ, Frothingham.

The Religious Teaching of Jesus, C. G. Montefiore, Macmillan, 1910.

Matthew, Mark and Luke are called Synoptic Gospels as distinct from the Gospel of John, a later and more doctrinal work.

Theme for discussion:

Why cannot Jesus be accepted by the Synagogue to-day?

CHAPTER XVI.

THE ALEXANDRIAN SCHOOL.

Jew and Greek.

Before resuming the story of Judea under the procurators, let us take another survey of Jews and Judaism in lands outside of Palestine. The voluntary dispersion still went on. The Jews were now scattered over all the Roman Empire, which included Asiatic and European lands from Syria to Spain. We also find our ancestors, at the beginning of the Christian era, in Arabia and in Parthia, an Asiatic kingdom south of the Caspian Sea. But, however widely scattered, religion was the bond of union and Jerusalem the spiritual centre. From distant lands many would from time to time make pilgrimages to the Temple.

The attitude of the heathen world was on the whole not unfriendly to the Jews. They were disliked for their rejection of the heathen gods, for their aloofness, their stern morality, their sobriety, and their material success; while their exclusiveness—partly but not wholly justifiable—led to the erroneous supposition that they were hostile to mankind. But the Jews of the Diaspora were less exclusive and more tolerant than those of Judea. This was particularly true of Alexandria, capital of Egypt, now part of the Roman Empire. There had existed here—apart from occasional outbursts of racial antagonism among the populace, a cordial interchange of ideas in which the Jews met the Greeks more than half way. (chaps. ii and vi.)

The Jews admired the culture of the educated Greeks and felt drawn toward the lofty philosophy of Plato, the nearest Greek approach to the monotheism and morality of the Hebrews. The broadening effect of this infusion of Greek thought, gave to Judaism in Alexandria a distinct character, and it came to be known as Hellenistic Judaism, and its espousers, Hellenistic Jews. We have used the term Hellenist in an earlier chapter, in a bad sense as descriptive of Jews who yielded to those Greek influences that were pagan, to the detriment of Judaism. Here we apply the term in a good sense to those who were open to Greek influences that were intellectual, to the advantage of Judaism. We have already marked the effect of Greek thought in some of the Apocryphal writings, particularly in the "Wisdom of Solomon." Appreciating the metaphysics of the Greek philosophers, the Jewish Hellenists were anxious to bring home to the Greeks and to others the spiritual and moral truths of Judaism.

Jewish Missionaries.

But how to present the revelation of the Law and of the Prophets in a manner that would most appeal to the Greeks? In their fervor to make proselytes to the Law of Moses, they resorted to a strange expedient. There existed among the Greeks women-seers called Sibyls, who were supposed to foretell in mysterious oracles the destinies of nations. So some Jewish writers cast the Bible teachings of God and morality in the literary form of Sibylline oracles. Like the Bible prophets, these Jewish Sibylline writers, warned those who followed false views and bad lives, and promised salvation to those who accepted the law of the God of Israel. They popularized the teachings of the Mosaic law and so generalized it as to present it as a religion for mankind. These writings exerted a salutary influence on many followers of Greek thought.

The Hellenists went so far as to try to prove from Jewish Scriptures many of the loftier ideas of Greek philosophy. In this way Judaism was represented as anticipating the highest knowledge of the time. In their enthusiasm, this reconciliation of Judaism and Greek philosophy was occasionally carried further than conditions quite warranted. The attempt was also made to explain every biblical law allegorically, as though it was intended to convey ideas other than those that appeared on the surface. Thus they read Greek philosophy into the Bible. The habit of reading the science of the day into the old Bible books still prevails. This poetic explaining away of many injunctions of Scripture led in some instances to their actual neglect. This was the dangerous extreme.

The assumption that Jews discourage proselytes has been refuted in chaps. xii and xiv. It is certainly not true of the Alexandrian Jews who were most zealous in their missionary efforts. They not only felt that it was the mission of the Jew to carry his message to the world; they did it. The translation of their Scriptures into Greek, the presentation of the message of their faith in the form of Sibylline oracles, and the allegorizing away of many of their ceremonials were all employed for the bringing of Judaism to the Gentile. So successful were their efforts, that just when the Jewish state was dying, many heathens were seeking this Faith of their own accord, attracted by its ethics and repelled by heathen uncleanliness. Philo says that the adoption of Judaism by many heathens immediately resulted in a marked moral improvement in their lives. The number of female proselytes in Damascus, Asia Minor, Egypt and Rome steadily grew. Pagan writers remark it. Josephus writes:—"There is not any city of the Greeks or of the barbarians … to which our custom of resting on the seventh day has not been introduced and where our fasts and dietary laws are not observed." He adds further how enthusiastically these converts fulfilled all Jewish rites. A zealous Jewish missionary converted Helen, the queen of Adiabene, a province on the Tigris, and all her family. She made a pilgrimage to Jerusalem, sent valuable gifts to the Temple, and helped the people in the time of famine.

So, although Judaism was a religion that imposed on its followers severe restraints and, although the Jews were a very small people, whom some heathens despised, still, many knocked at its doors to be admitted into the fold, even for fifty years after its Temple was destroyed and its nationality overthrown—tragedies which we shall presently have to tell. Yes, many of the very people that overthrew it—the Romans—accepted the Jewish faith. The Emperor Domitian made severe laws against proselytes to Judaism, in order to discourage the practice. Indeed, a cousin of the emperor, who was also a senator and consul, together with his wife, accepted Judaism.

But ultimately the stream of converts was diverted to the new creed, born of Judaism, Christianity—more particularly as in its second stage it sent its missionaries to the heathen world proclaiming that acceptance of Jesus as savior and divinity would bring them salvation without conforming to the burdensome Jewish Law. Furthermore it became a doctrine of the new religion that the death of Jesus abrogated the Law. Thus, salvation made easy, brought thousands to the fold. The Jewish missionaries had really simplified the task for the Christian missionaries who followed later. They prepared the soil.

This is looking a little further ahead to events yet to be related. By that time the followers of the two religions had become people of two different races: Judaism followed almost exclusively by Jews who were Semites; Christianity by Aryans, Greeks, Romans and other Europeans. This racial distinction became the final barrier which completely separated them.

NOTE.

Aryans and Semites:

Not all Semites are Jews, for example the Arabians; nor are all Aryans Christians p. e. the Persians. Religious and racial lines are no longer identical.

Theme for discussion:

Why did most heathen converts to Judaism ultimately become Christian?

CHAPTER XVII.

PHILO-JUDEUS.

We are now ready to consider one to whom frequent reference has been made—the greatest of the Alexandrian Jewish missionary philosophers, styled the "noblest Judean of his age"—Philo-Judeus. He was born in Alexandria of good family, about 15 C. E., just when Herod was ruling and Hillel was teaching in Jerusalem. His brother, Alexander, was given the influential post of farmer of taxes. Both received the best education the times afforded in literature, music, mathematics and natural science. Philo early showed a taste for literature in general, and philosophy in particular. His circumstances enabled him to devote himself to a literary life, for which he was peculiarly gifted. He showed his warm interest in the cause of his people in his journey to Rome as one of the ambassadors to plead before the mad Emperor Caligula (to be told in the next chapter). Of this whole incident he himself gives a graphic account in his chronicles of the Jewish events of his time.

His Bible Commentary.

A many-sided genius, he was the best exponent of that Hellenistic school that sought to harmonize the revealed religion of the Torah with the conclusions of Greek philosophy. He was thoroughly versed in both. His works, as those of all this school, were written in Greek. While the form may be that of Plato, the spirit is that of the prophets. In his commentary on Scripture, following the allegorical method already referred to, he treats all the incidents in Genesis, for example, as symbolic of human development and moral truths underlying the historic facts on the surface. He did not, however, go to the extreme of neglecting Jewish observance on the strength of metaphoric interpretation. Indeed, he even rebuked those who did. He writes "just as we must be careful of the body as the house of the soul, so must we give heed to the letter of the written laws. For only when these are faithfully observed, will the inner meaning of which they are the symbols become more clearly realized."

But he warningly adds "If a man practice ablutions and purifications, but defiles his mind while he cleanses his body ... let him none the more be called religious."

In his interpretation of the Mosaic Law in the Pentateuch, he has the education of the heathen chiefly in mind. He reveals the harmony of its precepts with the laws of nature. He groups all duties under the Ten Commandments. He points out with enthusiasm the humanity of the Law, and completely refutes slanders against Judaism by citing examples of its purity, breadth and philanthropy, such as the Sabbatic year and the jubilee to eliminate poverty, the freeing of slaves, the boon of the Sabbath for the servant, the social equality in the festival rules, the restraints of the dietary laws, the tenderness and consideration for all human needs in the code of Deuteronomy. His contrasts are the severest condemnation of Greek and Roman morals.

His Philosophy.

In his philosophy he again applies the allegorical method to the Pentateuch. In this field of *Midrash* (homiletic exposition) he may have influenced the later rabbis of the Talmud, even though rejected by them. He attempts to show that the lofty ideas found in the Platonic, Stoic and Neo-pythagorean philosophies were already taught in the Jewish Scripture. From Moses, the greatest teacher of mankind, the Greek philosophers derived their wisdom. From Mosaic Law comes the highest and truest religious revelation. Thus he endeavored to win Jews to an appreciation of Greek literature, and Greeks to an appreciation of Jewish Scripture.

Philo is the first Jew to present a complete system of philosophy, yet he weaves it out of the Bible. Just a word about it. It is hard to treat the philosophy of any one writer separately, for it is usually linked with a whole chain of theories of earlier schools. A deep believer in the spiritual God of his fathers, it was one of the aims of his life to attain fuller knowledge of Him. While in his treatment of the divine idea he shows the influence of the Greek philosopher Plato, yet as Jew he brings to the philosophic abstraction the religious warmth of a believer in the living God.

God alone is perfect, unchangeable, devoid of all qualities and indefinable. Absolutely perfect, He cannot come in contact with matter, which is defiling. How does Philo bridge the gap from the spiritual God to the material world? God acts on the world indirectly through intermediary causes or powers, which He first created.

The Logos.

These intervening powers he at times calls angels and at times ideas. He uses a Greek word *logos* meaning Reason. Whence comes this *logos* which we are to think of partly as a spirit and again as a thought? It is a product; or as he expresses it in a Greek idiom, a *child* of divine intelligence. By means of this *logos*, the perfect spiritual divinity creates the world.

This sounds unfamiliar, but the eighth chapter of Proverbs and some of the books of the Apocrypha speak of Wisdom as though it were a kind of being and that with it God laid the world's foundation. Of course, this is only figurative. But later the fathers of the Church put a new and startling construction upon Philo's Logos and read into it a literalness he never intended. They changed the *logos* into an actual human being. Unlike Philo they did not call it a child of divine intelligence in the Greek idiomatic sense, but a "son of God" in an actual and physical sense. It was then but a step for the Church to declare that Jesus, its Messiah, was the *Logos*! He was therefore a species of divinity too. It was not till Christianity's second stage that Jesus of Nazareth was in this way raised from a real man into an imaginary divinity. Thus the link with Judaism was broken in the rejection of its fundamental principle of monotheism—the belief in one indivisible God.

Philo is, of course, only unconsciously the cause of this doctrinal change, for he did not come in contact with the new sect of Christians and never mentions it, and this idea developed after his day. In fact, the divinity of Jesus had already been adopted, and Philo's writings were later construed to fit it.

His Ethics.

A word on his ethics. Evil is a necessary consequence of our free will. Without it there could not be the contrast of good. Evil is associated with the body which he depicts as the opponent of the soul. The soul emanates from God like the *logos*, but attracted by sensuous matter it descends into mortal bodies. This earthly body then is the cause of evil. But Philo was too wise to infer from that the duty of asceticism. He did not teach that man must suppress his desires and passions and earthly longings, but that he should suppress them. For this, man needs the help of God. The wise and virtuous are uplifted out of themselves to a closer knowledge of God, and God's spirit dwells in them. This is highest happiness. While we cannot quite accept his theories, his conclusions ring true with all the inspiring elements of lofty religion.

NOTES AND REFERENCES.

The Logos:

The Greek *logos* also means Word. Just as Proverbs personifies wisdom, so

100

the Targum (Aramaic translation of the Bible) identifies the "word of God" with the divine presence. Here again the Christian mystic goes a step further and changes a metaphor into a fact. "The Word of God became flesh; Jesus is that Word!" (Gospel of St John.)

In his popular but exhaustive work on *Philo-Judaeus*, (J. P. S. A. 1910) Norman Bentwich writes:

"It is idle to try and formulate a single definite notion of Philo's Logos. For it is the expression of God in His multiple and manifold activity, the instrument of creation, the seat of ideas, the world of thought, which God first established as the model of the visible universe, the guiding providence, the sower of virtue, the fount of wisdom, described sometimes in religious ecstacy, sometimes in philosophical metaphysics sometimes in the spirit of the mystical poet."

Philo:

Philo represents an important type, then new—a Jew loyal to his faith when living in a non-Jewish atmosphere. Not all so nobly withstood these surrounding allurements. His own brother drifted from the fold. Philo wrote for indifferent Jews as well as for pagan Greeks.

According to Montefiore, the Greek, according to Bentwich, the Hebrew note in Philo, is the more pronounced.

Greek Law and Jewish:

Philo brings out the following contrast. The Greeks were bidden not to refuse fire and water to those who needed it, but Judaism bids its followers to give to the poor and weak all that life requires.

For examples of Philo's teaching read "Florilegium Philonis," by Montefiore, *Jewish Quarterly Review*, Vol. vii; in the same volume, "Philo Concerning the Contemplative Life," Conybeare; and in Vol. v, "Latest Researches on Philo," Cohn.

Theme for discussion:

Why did rabbinic Judaism neglect Philo?

CHAPTER XVIII.

A JEWISH KING ONCE MORE.

In taking up again the thread of Judea's story, let its relation to the Roman State be clearly understood. It was under the immediate supervision of the procurator. He in turn was subject to the higher power of the governor of Syria. Both were answerable to the supreme authority—the emperor at Rome. Though the Syrian governors came little in contract with Judea, at times their intervention was important. We may instance Vitellius, who deserves passing mention in Jewish history. In contrast with the behavior of Pilate the procurator, was his consideration shown for Jewish sensibilities by this Syrian governor. "He was the noblest Roman of them all." He exhibited an uncommon forbearance by remitting some burdensome taxes; he sympathetically inquired into the needs of the people and removed from the High Priesthood the unworthy Caiaphas in whose time Jesus of Nazareth was executed. He also ordered Pilate to Rome to answer for his misgovernment.

The Mad Emperor Caligula.

As to the emperors: Some of these gave no thought to the Jews apart from appointing their procurators. With others the Jews came in clashing contact. Such was the case with Caligula who donned the purple in 37. This demented man believed himself to be a divinity, so that obeisance to his image was not merely an act of allegiance, but of worship. The consequences of this sacrilegious command to worship him was the first felt by the Jews of Alexandria; for the Ptolemaic and the Seleucid empires were both Roman now. An actual persecution here took place in which the Jews were besieged in their own quarter, the Delta. Their refusal to obey the emperor's childish demand gave excuse to their tormentors to attack them under the guise of patriotism. Patriotism may be the mantle for so many sins. Synagogues were defiled and many persons were slain. Philo, now advanced in years, led a deputation to Rome, to intercede for his brethren. He made an eloquent plea, assuring the emperor of Jewish loyalty. "They sacrifice for you daily an offering in the Temple." "*For* me," sneered Caligula, "not *to* me." The deputation suffered many indignities and returned dispirited.

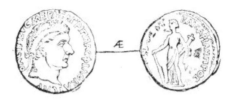

To Judea likewise came the same blasphemous demand with the threat of similar punishment. At last the mad monarch ordered his image to be set up in the Temple and entrusted the task to the Syrian governor, Petronius, a man of the stamp of Vitellius. He did his best to delay the wanton edict at the risk of the emperor's displeasure. At last yielding to the agonized entreaty of the people he imperilled his life by asking the emperor to revoke the order. Agrippa, a Jewish favorite of Caligula, succeeded in persuading the emperor to renounce the abortive project. Soon, however, he repented and determined on its execution. But relief came to Alexandria and Judea at one stroke—the emperor was murdered in 41.

The next emperor, Claudius, restored to the Alexandrian Jews all the privileges that had been taken from them during the rule of his predecessor, and their rights were more firmly established than before. Religious freedom was now granted to the Jews throughout the whole Roman empire. But best of all, he stopped the regime of the procurators by appointing as king of Judea, one of their own brethren—Agrippa.

Agrippa's Youth.

Agrippa was the grandson of Herod the Great and Mariamne, thus having both Idumean and Hasmonean blood in his veins. As a child he was sent for his education to Rome. The influences of Rome were not healthy. They made the lad luxurious and extravagant. Loaded with debts he returned to Judea and was assisted by his uncle and brother-in-law, Antipas, tetrarch of Galilee. After varied fortunes he came again to Rome, befriended by Philo's brother Alexander. Tiberius, emperor at that time, received him favorably and gave him charge of his grandson. But still his extravagant habits continued, and an incautious word sent him to prison, where he remained till the emperor died in 37.

The next emperor, Caligula, who was mad enough to think himself a divinity, was also sane enough to make Agrippa his friend and even to be dissuaded by him from putting his statue in the Temple. Agrippa's fortunes began now to rise. On the death of tetrarch Philip and on the deposition of tetrarch Antipas, their Palestinian provinces were bestowed on him (see p. 117). He was honored with the titles of King and Praetor, and his iron chain was exchanged for one of gold. So, like Joseph, he was transferred from a prison to a throne. At Caligula's death he assisted Claudius in obtaining the imperial crown. In grateful recognition, Judea, Samaria and Idumea were added to Agrippa's dominions. And thus it happened that Judea had a king again.

Agrippa the King.

His kingdom, uniting the various tetrarchies of Herod's three sons, was now even vaster in area than that of his grandfather, Herod. But he was a very different type of man. In spite of his Roman associations, he possessed strong Jewish sentiment and decided to become the father instead of the tyrant of his people.

The wild habits of his youth he laid aside and he hung up in the Temple the golden chain that replaced his prison fetters, as a mark of thankfulness and humility. His rule was a golden age for Judea—all too brief. Though partly of alien blood, the Pharisees said on one occasion, "Thou art our brother, Agrippa." He was amiable, benevolent, grateful and showed a forgiving disposition. His magnanimity changed opponents into friends.

He entered with hearty enthusiasm into all the ceremonial of Judaism. The Mishna, explained in chap. xxxi, speaks of him in high praise, and tells how he carried the first fruit offering to the Temple with his own hand. He looked after the interests of Jews and Judaism at home and abroad. Through his representation, some statues that had been wantonly put in a Phoenician synagogue were removed. Still, outside of Judea he permitted the amphitheatre with gladiatorial combats, and bestowed gifts upon many Grecian cities and upon some heathen towns of Palestine.

Rabbi Gamaliel.

The Sanhedrin was invested by him with new power and dignity, and under the wise presidency of Rabbi Gamaliel, *hazaken* (the elder), a descendant of Hillel many liberal laws were made. Gamaliel showed the same consideration to heathen as to Jewish poor. He was so esteemed that the saying arose, "When Rabbi Gamaliel died, the glory of the Torah passed away." One of his teachings ran: "Procure thyself an instructor; avoid the possibility of doubt; and do not tithe by conjecture."

Agrippa Slain.

Agrippa would fain have furthered the hopes of Israel in making them more independent of Rome, but he was watched by envious eyes. A conference of local vassal kings, called by him, was broken up by the suspicious Syrian governor. He wished to strengthen Judea's fortifications, but again the Syrian governor induced the emperor to stop the work. In fact, many jealous Romans feared that a longer continuance of his kingdom might develop into a menace against Rome. So the assassin's knife was called into play! Suddenly at a moment of triumphal glory, he was stricken down at the early age of forty-five. The kindly disposed emperor would have given the kingdom to his son, but he was dissuaded by his counselors. The old regime of the hated procurators was restored once more.

Agrippa II.

It is true this son, called Agrippa II. was given a small dominion, but with little independent power. He was also entrusted with the superintendence of the Temple which he did not always exercise wisely. He was well-disposed to the Jews, and even used his influence at court to intercede in their favor; but he felt akin with them far less than had his father. He imported wood for the Temple use and employed the discharged workmen of the finished Herodian Temple to pave the city with marble. At first, he did all he could in his impotent way to prevent hostilities between Rome and Judea, but his training had been Roman and his spirit was pagan. He moved on the line of least resistance—that meant his ultimate drifting toward victorious Rome. His was a weak nature entirely under the control of his sister Berenice. She became later a favorite of the Roman emperor Titus, who played so large a part in Judea's last days.

Note.

Agrippa II. continued to hold his petty kingdom for some time after Judea had fallen, and lived to read Josephus' history about it. He was the Agrippa before whom Paul appeared, and to whom he indolently said, "With little wouldst thou win me over to be a Christian."

Paul also appeared before a later procurator, Felix.

Theme for discussion:

If Agrippa had lived and reigned as long as Herod—?

COIN OF AGRIPPA **II**, **60** C. E.

CHAPTER XIX.

THE LAST PROCURATORS.

Roman Emperors and Procurators.		Jewry.	
	YEAR.		YEAR.
Claudius	41		
Fadus	4		
Tiberius Alexander	45	Theudas the Messiah	45
Ventidius Cumanus	48		
Felix	52		
Nero	54	Death of Philo	55
Festus	60		
Albinus	62		
Gessius Florus	66	Josephus Gov. of Galilee	66

Agrippa's death was a signal for general indignities by Greeks and Romans throughout Palestine against the people who had lost their defender. Burdensome taxation alone would have been borne; but each in turn of the second group of procurators placed over them seemed actuated by the wanton purpose of trampling upon everything the Jews held sacred, holding their religion up to scorn, and forcing them into rebellion through the madness of despair.

Fadus, the first of the second group, was the most harmless. A deluded enthusiast named Theudas claiming to be the Messiah and to be gifted with supernatural powers, was apprehended and put to death together with many of his followers.

The Zealots.

Tiberius Alexander, the next procurator, was a nephew of Philo, but unlike his uncle, had abandoned Judaism, and therefore was a very unfit appointee. He found it necessary to put to death two sons of the Zealot Judas, the Galilean. These Zealots already briefly referred to were a group of irreconcilables that at times resorted to desperate remedies. They were the advance guard of a revolution. Rebellions continued to grow in gravity with each successive rule. During the administration of Ventidius Cumanus a rebellion broke out through the wanton indecency of a Roman soldier during the Passover celebration. In putting down the insurrection Cumanus ordered many thousands slain. On another occasion the Zealots started to lead an attack against Samaria to punish the murder of some of their brethren, for the base Cumanus allowed marauders to rove unmolested on the payment of sufficient bribe. Against the Zealots, however, he led an army, for their offenses were political, not moral. Through the intervention of young Agrippa, Cumanus was banished.

But the worst Procurator was to follow—*Felix*. He goaded the Jews beyond endurance. All the appointees to the procuratorship had been bad, but the appointment of this man as Judea's ruler was an outrage. He was a freedman, i. e., one from the low classes. His tyranny in public and his lust in private life revealed his base origin. How natural that Judah should come to hate Rome when she was represented by such hateful creatures! How natural that the rebellious element—the Zealots—should grow in number and determination. These Felix punished with cruel recklessness, resorting often to treachery to entrap them. By such doing he fomented the evil. Rebellion was now rife and could no longer be quelled.

The Sicarii.

For a still more fanatical group now made their appearance—outcome of these unhappy times. They were called *Sicarii*, from the short dagger, *sica*, with which they secretly slew their opponents. These political assassinations made Jerusalem unsafe. Felix was even unscrupulous enough to make use of these desperate men to slay the High Priest Jonathan, whose influence had brought about his own appointment. His only crime against Felix was begging him to administer his office more worthily, and his only crime against the Sicarii was not sanctioning their outrages. These wild, misguided men were religious enthusiasts of a frenzied sort, for wanton injustice breeds such types. They would gather with crowds of deluded followers in the wilderness, claiming a divine call to overthrow Rome; Felix always had his cohorts ready to hew them down. He knew no remedies other than bloodshed. In one instance an Egyptian Jew appeared as a would-be deliverer. At once Felix ordered a massacre. The leader escaped; some of his surviving followers awaited his return as a Messiah, who would re-establish the throne of David once more.

Gradually a large part of the nation was imbued with the spirit of rebellion. The mismanagement of Felix also brought quarrels among the priests. Conflict arose in Caesarea between Syrians and Jews as to civic rights and privileges. Felix partially decided in favor of the Syrians and again increased the disturbance by resorting to slaughter. In return for large bribes he deprived the Jews of Caesarea of their civic rights, which they had possessed from the days when the city was founded. At last, having done all the mischief he could, this creature was recalled in 60 by Emperor Nero.

His successor *Festus*, meant well, but could do little in this demoralized state. Things had gone too far to be smoothed over. The upheaval had to come. The Sicarii continued their assassinations, regarding all the moderates as their enemies.

At the death of Festus and after an interval of anarchy, Albinus—a second Felix—was appointed—a public plunderer, a bribe-taker from all parties. Well-to-do criminals could buy their freedom from him; only the poor remained in prison. The high-priesthood at this time was held by a most unscrupulous man, Ananias, who took by violence the tithes of the priests. At last Albinus secretly joined the robber bands of Sicarii. When recalled in 62, he maliciously opened all the prisons and set the malefactors free to fill the country with lawless men. How the lives and fates and fortunes of these hapless Judeans were bandied about to gratify the wanton lust of these tyrants and scoundrels!

The last procurator, *Gessius Florus*, held the post till 66 and then the storm burst. For the climax of outrageous rule was reached in him. Josephus says that, compared with him, Albinus whom he describes as "an arch-robber and tyrant," was a law-abiding citizen and to be praised as a benefactor! Need we add more? He did not, as Albinus, even hide his crimes. His plunderings were conducted by wholesale. He was verily a partner of robbers. Surely the time for Judah to strike a blow for freedom had come.

Theme for discussion:

Compare zealots of antiquity with to-day's Russian revolutionists, the Sicarii with the Anarchists, the local governors with the procurators.

CHAPTER XX.

JUDEA'S WAR WITH ROME.

Revolution.

When Florus, after robbing the people, began openly to rob the Temple, the last thread of endurance snapped. Called in bitter irony a beggar, for whom forsooth alms must be collected, Florus took a bloody revenge. A second wanton attack upon the long suffering people by his arriving cohorts, compelled them to rise against the Roman soldiers in self defense. They gained possession of the Temple Mount and Florus at last, seeing the mischief he had effected, fled to Caesarea. Agrippa tried hard to dissuade the people from a hopeless struggle against Rome, but he was a man without influence. The Temple offerings for the Roman emperor were stopped—that was, so to speak, the official renunciation of their allegiance. The more temperate could not restrain the masses from this determination.

A Peace Party.

These moderates, who represented the judicious, formed a "Peace Party." Conflict arose between them and the advocates of war, in which Agrippa who aided the former with his troops, had his palace burned and his soldiers put to flight. Soon the fortress towers held by the Roman soldiers had to yield and the garrison was slain. The revolution extended to all the outlying towns in which Jews and Gentiles fought against each other, and spread even as far as Alexandria.

The governor of Syria, Cestius Gallus, thoroughly alarmed, came to Jerusalem with a picked army, but after a partial success he was forced to retreat. So vigorously was he pursued by these dauntless men, that only by leaving most of his baggage behind him—of great value to the revolutionists —could he escape at all, and then with but a remnant of his army. This unlooked for success left the Peace Party in a hopeless minority. Roman allies could do naught but leave the capital. The Jews now began to organize their forces and some of the highest men in the city led in the defense.

Josephus.

At an assembly of the people Joseph ben Gorion and the High Priest Ananus were given charge of Jerusalem itself. Two men of the high-priestly family were sent as generals to Idumea. In Jerusalem the walls were strengthened and the youths trained for soldiers. Josephus, a man of but thirty years, later historian of this war and known so far only as a scholar, was sent to Galilee. Here he was to gather an army from among the people and to meet the first brunt of Rome's experienced hosts as they would arrive via Syria. For the time being he was the governor of Galilee and appointed greater and lesser councils to strengthen the fortifications of all the cities. He had further to meet the opposition to his appointment in the province itself, chiefly by one John of Gischala, a leader bold and violent. For Josephus was not entirely trusted. His attitude was altogether too moderate to satisfy these determined rebels. In his heart of hearts he realized the impossibility of success. That very conviction at once unfitted him for leadership.

The Emperor Nero, hearing of the defeat of the governor of Syria, entrusted the task of quelling the rebellion to the experienced general, Vespasian. He at once sent a garrison of six thousand to the important Galilean city, Sepphoris, which took possession before the Jewish army arrived. As the Roman host approached Galilee, Josephus' untrained soldiers retreated to the highlands, leaving the whole Galilean plain in possession of Vespasian without his striking a blow.

Josephus sent word to Jerusalem that if he was to meet the Romans, he must have an army. The request came too late. His troops, such as they were, retired to the fortress of Jotapata, north of Sepphoris. Vespasian appeared before it and a desperate struggle followed. Josephus was a skilful commander and his men showed dauntless courage, but Rome on its side had all the experience of war together with overwhelming numbers. The first attack failed and a siege began. Josephus showed wonderful craft in obtaining food for his garrison and in breaking the force of the Roman battering rams. But these means could only delay the end; they could not change it. The besieged were worn out by sleeplessness and starvation after holding out for forty-seven days. The wall was scaled when the exhausted watchmen were asleep. All were either slain or sold into slavery. The city and its fortifications were levelled to the ground.

Josephus with forty companions escaped to a cave. Against his advice to surrender, they all decided that they would die by their own hands. Josephus by strategem alone managed to escape this fate. He appeared before Vespasian and by adroit flattery was favorably received into his camp.

Theme for discussion:

Make clear the difference in principle between Judea's "Peace Party" and the "Royalist Party" among the American revolutionists in 1776.

A BATTLEMENT ON THE HOUSE-TOP.

CHAPTER XXI.

THE SIEGE.

The North Succumbs.

When Vespasian reached Tiberias, on the Sea of Galilee, the people opened their gates and at the request of Agrippa—who had now wholly thrown in his fortunes with the Romans—they were well treated. In the meantime the army of Titus, son of Vespasian, took the city of Tarichea.

Glance for a moment at the map of Palestine, (front of book) so that a mental picture may be formed of the territory involved in the great struggle: Phoenicia, the Lebanon Mountains and Syria ran across the north. Immediately south was the province of Galilee, partly bordering on the Mediterranean and bounded on the east by the province of Gaulonitis and Decapolis, the Jordan and the Sea of Galilee being the dividing line. Batanaea lay to the east again of Gaulanitis. Still farther south was Judea, with the Jordan dividing it from Perea. Idumea lay in the extreme south.

Vespasian was still in the north and next attacked the strong fortress of Gamala in Gaulonitis. But after an entrance was gained into the city, the Jews fought so desperately that the Romans was repulsed with severe loss and for a time were afraid to renew the attack. But in a second determined sally it was taken. At the same time Mount Tabor was taken by a Roman force. There was now left in Galilee only one unconquered fortress to be taken—Gischala. Its conquest was entrusted to Titus. Its gates were soon opened, but its controlling spirit, John of Gischala, with his band of Zealots escaped to Jerusalem. By the end of the year 67 all northern Palestine was in the hands of the Romans.

Rival Parties in Jerusalem.

These defeats brought consternation to Jerusalem. The leaders, who had been taken from the aristocracy, were blamed and deposed. Some were imprisoned and leaders from among the people were put in their place. But the change was not made without bloodshed. Alas, here was the beginning of a civil conflict as well—war within war. Judea's cup of misery was full. John of Gischala, the escaped Zealot, was soon at the head of the extreme fanatic party. Fighting contingents of malcontents came to Jerusalem from all over the country and joined the Zealots, which thus became the ruling power. They threw discretion to the winds. An ignorant man of the common people was also chosen as High Priest though this office had always been in the hands of the aristocracy.

The Idumeans were now invited to enter Jerusalem and join forces with the Zealots. They began at once a bloody attack on the party of law and order. The old leaders, men of high birth, were put to death. Verily it was Judea's "reign of terror." After assisting in all this mischief, the Idumeans departed. The new Christian community also left Jerusalem, deserting their brethren in the sore hour of need, and took refuge in a heathen city. The shrewd Vespasian made no haste to attack the capital, hoping that the opposing parties left to themselves would weaken each other and make his task more easy. He contented himself with placing fortified garrisons in the chief surrounding places.

EMPEROR TITUS.

In the meantime Nero died, in the year 68. Galba was made emperor only to be murdered a few months after. These events were watched by Vespasian with keen eyes. The man who had the army with him might win the purple. He therefore made a pause in the war.

Another wild Zealot, Simon Ben Giora, began a plundering expedition, carrying devastation wherever he went. In 69, after a year's pause, Vespasian vigorously renewed the struggle by subduing the remaining outlying districts. There was now left for subjugation a few fortresses and the capital.

Stopped from his robber raids by Vespasian's vigor, Simon ben Giora was now hailed in Jerusalem. Here all was confusion and demoralization. The reckless tyrant of Gischala had indulged in terrible excesses. The people hoped that the admission of Simon would rid them of John's bloodthirsty rule; but there was little choice between them.

Although Vitellius was now made emperor of Rome, the armies in Egypt and Palestine decided to nominate Vespasian. He hastened to Rome, found Vitellius murdered, and his own candidature unopposed. So in the year 70 he was acknowledged emperor by both east and west, and the prosecution of the Judean war was left in the hands of his son, Titus.

In Jerusalem the reign of terror continued. There was now a third war party under one Eliezar. Each regarded the two others as enemies, and each held a certain portion of the city as jealously against the others as against the Romans. Simon ben Giora held the upper part of the lower city situated on one hill, and the whole of the upper city situated on another hill called Acra. John of Gischala was entrenched in the Temple Mount. Eleazar held the court of the Temple, but soon overpowered by John was forced to join forces with him. In the madness of their folly they played into the hands of the Romans by destroying grain rather than let it fall into the hands of their rivals.

Titus with an immense army appeared before the walls of Jerusalem in the spring of the fatal year 70. Still he by no means carried all before him. When we read of the brave and stubborn resistance of the Jews in spite of the unfortunate conflicts within, we can better realize how successful their resistance might have been had they presented a united front to the enemy.

The situation of the city had its natural advantages. It was built on two hills with a ravine between, while the Temple standing in spacious grounds, surrounded on all sides by strong walls, was a citadel in itself. Attached to it was the castle of Antonia. The upper and lower divisions of the city had their own separate walls, a town's main protection before the days of gunpowder. There was a common wall around both divisions and a third around the suburb, Bezetha.

COIN OF THE REIGN OF TITUS, ABOUT 73 C. E.

When the battering rams of Titus began attacking the outer walls in three places, John and Simon stopped their feud and banded together at last to meet the common enemy. It was only after desperate fighting for many days that the Romans got possession of the first wall. Five days later the second wall was taken, though the enemy was held back for four days longer. Earth defenses were now built by the legions of Titus against the different fortifications, but no sooner were these built than they fell, undermined by the vigilant Simon and John.

Titus now applied new measures of severity. A stricter siege was maintained. The city was reduced to famine and poor creatures stealing out to gather food were crucified in sight of the defenders. Then he built a wall to shut off all possible escape and so tried to starve them out. The sufferings of the besieged, vividly portrayed by Josephus, were desperate indeed and led to still more desperate remedies.

NOTE.

How history repeats itself! The antagonism of the masses to the aristocracy, characteristic of the French Revolution, found its precedent in Judea's war against Rome. But the motives were far from identical.

CHAPTER XXII.

THE FALL OF JERUSALEM.

Titus built new fortifications and this time the attempt to destroy them was not successful. But no sooner had the last city wall fallen under the catapults shot from the Roman battering rams than a second wall appeared behind it, built by the foresight of John of Gischala. After many attempts this wall was scaled. The Romans now reached the Temple walls and took the Antonia tower, which they immediately destroyed.

During all this time the daily sacrifices were continued in the Temple. In the presence of the grim monsters, war and starvation, this religious obligation was not forgotten. A proposition of surrender was made at this dire hour, but the besieged would not yield. For Titus chose an unfortunate ambassador—Josephus. He was received with a storm of arrows, for he was regarded by the warriors in Jerusalem as a traitor.

Now, within the narrower compass of the Temple site, the siege was maintained, though it was but the beginning of the end. First, ramparts were erected by Titus against its outer walls; but these walls were so strong that he could only gain admittance by burning down the gates. Terrifically did the Jewish soldiers, wasted by famine, contest every inch of the ground, giving to the Romans many a repulse. But overwhelming numbers told. Titus had decided to save the Temple, but his vandal soldiers set it on fire. The attempts of Titus to quench it were in vain. The beautiful structure of marble and gold —monument of Herod's pride—was reduced to ashes. While it was burning the Romans began an indiscriminate slaughter of men, women and children.

John of Gischala and Simon ben Giora with a small band, now fell back to the last refuge, the upper city. Their request for liberty on condition of surrender was refused. The lower city was now burnt and new ramparts built against the last stronghold. Yet it took some weeks before entrance was finally forced, and the Romans continued their savage work of burning and massacre.

THE GOLDEN CANDLESTICK.

(*From the Arch of Titus.*)

DEPICTING CARRYING THE SPOIL OF JUDEA.

The city was razed to the ground—a few gates of Herod's palace and a piece of wall were alone left standing. The survivors were sent to labor in unwholesome mines to gather wealth for their despoilers. Some were reserved for Roman sport in the amphitheatre. John, discovered in a subterranean vault and begging like a craven for mercy, was imprisoned for life. Simon ben Giora graced the Roman triumph.

Thus fell the city of Jerusalem—the religious capital of the world—in the year 70 C. E., on the same date it is said—the 9th of Ab—on which it had fallen nearly seven hundred years earlier under the attacks of the Babylonians. So the Fast of Ab commemorates the double tragedy.

Masada, the Last Fortress.

The final work of conquest and the barbaric rejoicings, consisting of forced gladiatorial combats between Jewish prisoners, together with games and triumphs, continued some two years longer. There were still three outlying strongholds to be conquered—Herodium, Macharus, on the other side of the Dead Sea, and Masada, far to the south. The first two soon fell, but Masada offered a stubborn resistance which its natural position favored. Under Eleazar ben Jair and some Sicarii the dauntless bravery of Jerusalem and

Jotapata was repeated. They determined not to die by the swords of the Romans, so when the soldiers entered they found the little band all slain by their own hands.

On the site of the old Temple there was subsequently built another, dedicated to Jupiter Capitolinus, and, with a refinement of cruelty, the Jews throughout the Roman dominions had to pay toward its maintenance the taxes they had hitherto paid to the support of their own beloved sanctuary. So ended the Israelitish nation that under varied fortunes had continued unbroken, except during the Babylonian captivity, since the days of Saul, i.e., for over a thousand years.

Judea remained a separate Roman province, but was no longer a home for the people whose possession it once was. So completely was it levelled to the ground that there was nothing left to make those who came there believe it had once been inhabited. Rebuilt at a latter day, even the name was changed to Aelia Capitolina. But great names cannot so easily be erased by the ruthless hand of man.

The Remnant Again.

What was now to become of the remaining Jews? What was their status in the world? Nation, temple, independence were gone. Gone too were their arms, their means, their nobility, and all political power. Would it not seem that this must be the end, that their name and identity must be ultimately merged with their surroundings? Such had been the fate of other nations as completely conquered—Ammon, Moab, Assyria, Phoenicia. But Israel was made of different stuff. Its epitaph was not yet to be written.

NOTE.

In the history of Rome, the conquest of Judea occupies a small place. It was only a little province in the East! But Greece, which it had also conquered, was insignificant in size. Still Hellas and Israel were the greatest intellectual and spiritual powers in the world. Rome itself received its education from the one and its religion from the other.

CHAPTER XXIII.

JOSEPHUS AND HIS WORKS.

What literature did this sad period produce? There was neither heart nor leisure to turn to poetry or philosophy, or even to write a second "Lamentations." But in the prosaic field of history some important works were produced by one individual, who hardly deserves to be included in the fold of Israel—Josephus.

His Early Life.

He was born in Jerusalem in the year 38 C. E. under the regime of the procurators; so he never knew an independent Judea. Of studious bent, he was consulted (so he tells us) on points of law at the early age of fourteen. At the age of 26 he went to Rome like Philo, to intercede with the Emperor Nero for some of his brethren, falsely charged by the procurator, Felix. His persuasive address and political shrewdness won the day. He returned dazzled with the splendor and magnitude of the city on the Tiber. He realized now the impossibility of Israel undertaking a successful war against it. Therefore he never should have been chosen to command one of Judea's campaigns.

Josephus vs. Jeremiah.

After the war he sought and obtained the liberty of some of the captives. But he was satisfied to receive Roman citizenship from the hand of the emperor who had overthrown the Jewish State—Vespasian, and even appended the emperor's first name, Flavius, to his own. When we see him living at ease on a pension and a tax-free estate given by Rome while his brethren were working in the lead mines of Egypt or glutting the slave markets of Europe we cannot but contrast his character with that of Jeremiah who had been placed in similar circumstances some centuries earlier.

FLAVIUS JOSEPHUS.

In the last days of the first nationality, when Babylonia was thundering against the gates of Jerusalem, Jeremiah had belonged to the Peace Party of his day, not for reasons of expediency, such as actuated Josephus, but from intense religious conviction. (See vol. iii, *People of the Book*, chap. xxviii.) Nebuchadrezzar, regarding this attitude as friendly toward Babylon, had offered to Jeremiah ease and liberty after Judah was laid in the dust. But he scorned to receive gifts from the enemies of his country or to enjoy benefits through their misfortune. Though Judah had rejected his advice and even persecuted him for it, he made their lot his own, miserable though it was. Like Moses, he died in the wilderness with the generation who had brought that fate upon themselves, because they lacked his faith.

History of the Jews.

Let us forget Josephus the soldier; let us remember Josephus the scholar. Though in his last years he may possibly have lived as pagan, he certainly wrote as Jew. He loved his people, but lacked the magnanimity to share their misfortunes. This was his fatal weakness. Posterity is grateful to Josephus for his History of the Jews, called "Antiquities of the Jews" in twenty volumes, the writing of which may have formed the chief occupation of his later years. Perhaps he felt that he might yet serve Israel's cause in this way. He begins his chronicle with the Bible records, which he embellishes with many a Midrashic story such as that of Moses being given choice of a plate of gold and of fire. He carries the narrative right down to the procuratorship of Florus. Writing for Greek and Roman readers, he sought to give them a better and truer estimate of his people. Indeed, in all his works, he never loses an opportunity to defend the honor of Israel. In his next work, "Wars of the Jews," in seven books, he begins with Antiochus Epiphanes, thus duplicating part of his history. But the first two books are but introductory to his real theme, the war with Rome. This history is not only his greatest work, but one of the greatest of antiquity. He presents a vivid picture of the last scenes of Judea's death struggle, of which he was an eye witness and in part an actual participator. It is carefully and skilfully compiled and as a contemporary record it is invaluable.

It was first written in his mother tongue, Aramaic, (p. 69), and later rewritten in Greek. The work was endorsed by Vespasian, Titus and Agrippa. It may be said that such a man was not of fine enough character to be an impartial historian; but impartial historians are quite a modern institution. All ancient historians took great liberties both with events and numbers, and put speeches of their own composition in the mouths of the leading characters.

In connection with this work we may mention his autobiography, covering chiefly his questionable achievements as commander-in-chief in Galilee in 66. It is his *apologia pro vita sua*.

Contra Apion.

To his merit, be it further said, he gladly became the advocate of his people in the land of the Gentile, and jealously guarded their reputation. Against the traducer, Apion, an Egyptian grammarian, he launched a work in Israel's defense, "Josephus Against Apion," or "The Great Age of the Jews," in the form of a letter to a friend. It is in two books. In the first he replies to other traducers of the Jewish people. For the bad fashion had come into vogue of inventing absurd slanders against the Jews—a fashion, by the way, that has not yet passed away.

He easily refutes the charges of Manetho that the Jews were expelled from Egypt as lepers. "If lepers why should they have been kept so long as slaves."

Of Apion, the offender, who gives title to the book, he says: His writings show palpable ignorance and malevolent calumny; but as the frivolous part of mankind exceeds the discerning, I find myself under some kind of necessity to expose the 'errors of this man.' He shows how Apion ridicules the Sabbath by misrepresenting its origin.

To the slander that Jews worship a golden ass placed in their holy of holies, he replies that such charge could only have been brought by an Egyptian, for they *do* worship animals.

He dismisses the preposterous charge that Jews annually sacrifice a Greek, with the information that at the time of Moses, "the Jews knew not the Greeks." How old "the blood accusation" is!

But Josephus finds that the best and most dignified reply to all aspersions on Israel lies in giving an outline of their law and belief. This gives him an opportunity to testify to the faith that is in him still. He writes:

"There never was such a code of laws framed for the common good of mankind as those of Moses—for the advancement of piety, justice, charity, industry, regulation of society, patience, perseverence in well doing, even to the contempt of death itself."

"God is the source of joy and to Him they turn in all woe. This worship of the one God is combined with morals."

"They weekly gather even their servants and children (on the Sabbath), having suspended work to read the Law, that they might know what to do."

He points out the sobriety of the Law, its strict chastity, reverence for parents and elders, duties to the stranger, moderation towards enemies, easement of prisoners, especially women, kindness to animals and vigorous punishment of sin. It regards death, he says, as a blessed means of being transported from this life to a better. Hence Israel's record of martyrdom:

"Such is our reputation that there is hardly a nation in the world that does not conform in some respect to our example."

"How many there are of our captive countrymen at this day, struggling under exquisite torments because they will not renounce their laws nor blaspheme the God of their forefathers."

Like Philo, he regards Judaism as a universal religion that should be accepted by all mankind.

His works are couched in simple and attractive style. Written in Greek, they have been translated into all tongues. They were read much by Christians of the Middle Ages, who regarded Josephus as a second Livy; but till recent years he has been neglected by his own people. But then so was Philo.

NOTES AND REFERENCES.

Historians:

Justus of Tiberias also wrote a history of the Jewish War; it is now lost.

Defenders:

Among writers in defense and appreciation of the Jews just a little prior to Josephus, were Alexander Polyhistor, Strabo, the geographer, and chiefly Nicolaus of Damascus.

Josephus and Christianity:

Josephus relates fully the story of John the Baptist, but does not mention Jesus of Nazareth! This would seem to indicate that, prior to the coming of Paul, Jesus left but a slight impression on his age. This omission seems to have so disconcerted some members of the Church that one actually inserted a paragraph about Jesus in the History of Josephus. But the clumsy forgery was later discovered.

Theme for discussion:

Should Josephus be regarded as a traitor?

THE ARCH OF TITUS.

RAISED TO COMMEMORATE THE OVERTHROW OF JUDEA.

BOOK IV.

THE TALMUDIC ERA.

CHAPTER XXIV.

JOCHANAN BEN ZAKKAI.

The Jews now belonged to no land, yet for that very reason, they, in a sense, belonged to all lands. They were cosmopolitans, citizens of the world. To follow their history after their dispersion by Rome, we shall have to turn to all the settled parts of the globe. What henceforth became the link to hold together their widely scattered members and preserve them from being absorbed by their surroundings? Their religion. Religions outlive states and spiritual bonds are stronger than temporal. But now that Judaism's centre, the Temple, was no more, now that the sacred capital, Jerusalem, the only sanctioned place for sacrificial worship, was lost—how could they maintain their continuity and what would become of their priesthood? Just here will we witness the wonderful adaptability of Judaism in the hands of this deathless race. It only awaited a genius to revive the Faith, apparently in the throes of death, and to endow it with new strength and vitality. The hero who undertook this sacred task was named Jochanan ben Zakkai.

The Academy at Jamnia.

Jochanan ben Zakkai had been a leader in the Sanhedrin, in the last days of Judea. When many were urging war he had stood for peace and he became the exponent of the Peace Party. For he saw that the madness of the Zealots in blindly plunging the country into conflict could end only in ruin. He may have felt, too, that the fulfilment of Israel's mission did not rely on national independence and that it could preach its message in a way other than in bloody conflict. So when the war was at its height, he managed to escape from Jerusalem in a coffin, since the Zealots treated all peace advocates as traitors. Welcomed by Vespasian, who saw the value of so influential a pleader for surrender, he was allowed to ask a favor. His reply showed that he was not of the Josephus, but of the Jeremiah type. He asked naught for himself, but pleaded for the privilege of establishing an *Academy*, where the principles of Judaism might be taught. This small request was granted, perhaps contemptuously at its apparent insignificance. Yet by that grant Judaism was enabled to continue its development—aye, to outlive the great Roman Empire at whose mercy it now stood.

Jamnia, a place near the Mediterranean and not far from Joppa, was chosen as the seat of the new academy. Here came many who, being of the conciliatory party, were left free and untouched by Rome at the close of the War. Here Jochanan ben Zakkai summoned a Sanhedrin, and by a bold stroke decided to continue the authoritative powers of that body in spite of the tradition that to be effective, it must sit in the "hewn stone hall" of the Jerusalem Temple.

Prayer replaces Sacrifice.

But he took a more daring step still. According to the Law, now that the Holy City was taken, sacrifice was no longer possible; therefore Jochanan ben Zakkai declared that it was no longer indispensable; saying, charity is a substitute for sacrifice. Prayer, which had been an accompaniment to sacrifice was now treated as an independent mode of worship. The synagogue, which had in later years existed side by side with the sacrificial Temple, now altogether replaced it. Thus does genius adapt itself to altered conditions.

The change was revolutionary and marked a new era in Judaism's development. The epoch of the Priest was over, the Altar was outlived—one of the ideals of the Prophets was attained. Again necessity was the teacher and adversity was found to "wear a precious jewel in its head." Furthermore, the creation of a centre of Jewish authority outside of Jerusalem freed Judaism from bondage to a particular locality. Its complete fulfilment was now confined neither to a city nor a nation. The whole earth could become its legitimate home. This also had its moral value. To the simple-minded it made clearer the idea that God was manifest everywhere; that verily "the heaven was His throne and the earth His footstool." It gave tangible application to the text, "In every place where I cause my name to be remembered, I will come unto thee and bless thee."

So the survival of Judaism after the destruction of the sacrificial Temple, after the loss of the sacred capital and the Holy Land, and after the dispersion of the Jews throughout the world, made it more manifest that it was indeed a perennial and a universal Faith. Perhaps then even in this sad tragedy we may discern the hand of Providence.

It is true that some pious souls took a disconsolate view of the outlook and, renouncing the world's joys, gave themselves up to ascetic lives of penitence. A few drifted toward the new Christian sect that was now severing all relations with Judaism, thinking it doomed. But under the guidance of Jochanan ben Zakkai, the great majority faced the future more hopefully and more bravely. The land was gone, but the religion was saved. Henceforth its rallying centre was to be—not a *Temple*, but a *Book*.

The Tannaim.

We have already seen that the Scribes interpreted the Bible in a way to derive from it new laws to meet new needs, (pp. 19-20; 80-81.) These deduced rules grew into a Second Law, more voluminous than the first. The patient continuance of this process to meet all religious, social and economic requirements of Israel's altered life became now the chief work of the Jamnia Academy and of other schools that sprang from it. To this work of laying bare "the whole duty of man" the scholars now devoted themselves and regarded it as sacred as divine worship. "The study of the Law," said they, "outweighs all virtues." The first order of these great expounders were called *Tannäim* (*tanna* means teacher). Very preciously did the students who sat at the feet of the sages treasure their decisions (for they were contained in no book) and handed them down from generation to generation.

The people at large now learned to look to the Jamnia Sanhedrin, for such it became, as their authority in all religious duties and also for guidance in varied perplexities. In those days there was no fixed calendar; the new month was ascertained by watching the heavens for the new moon and from the date of its appearance the Sanhedrin decided the festivals of each month for the community. The new moon was announced from place to place by messengers and fire signals on the hills. These could not reach distant places of Jewish settlement far beyond Judea, and, in some cases the signals were tampered with. So, as there was a doubt of one day as to the new moon's appearance, they introduced the custom of observing an additional day of each festival.

Halacha and Agada.

Jochanan ben Zakkai, then, revealed his greatness in boldly abrogating institutions that had lost their application with the Temple's fall, bridging the transition between epochs, just as Samuel had done in his day. His great personality strengthened the union between the dispersed Jews. Further, like his master Hillel, he combined in his character gentleness and firmness (*suaviter in modo, fortiter in re*) and like him, too, he also exercised an elevating influence on his pupils by his ethical teachings. He showed them how to search the Scriptures to discover its noblest lessons. This was distinct from that branch of the Bible study already referred to, enabling the student to evolve new rules and new observances. The latter was judicial, the former homiletic. These gradually came to form the two great divisions of the scholarly activities of the Rabbis, the judicial division called *Halacha* (legal decision), the ethical styled *Agada*. This latter word means narrative—for many a story, anecdote, moral maxim or bit of history would be brought in to illustrate a legal point or to relieve the tension of argument by a pleasing diversion. So Agada implied much miscellaneous material and included everything not strictly judicial.

Here are some of the maxims of Jochanan ben Zakkai:

"No iron tool was to be used on the altar, suggesting that religion's mission is peace."

"If thou hast learnt much, do not boast of it, for that wast thou created."

"Fear God as much as you fear man."

"Not more?" asked his pupils in surprise? "If you would but fear him as much!" said the dying sage.

NOTES AND REFERENCES.

Sacrificial Worship:

The pupil has already been made familiar with the prophetic views on sacrifice (see *People of the Book*, vol. iii). Here follow some opinions of the Rabbis as to its relative place in Judaism:

"The humble-minded is considered by God to have offered all the sacrifices, for it is said that the sacrifices of God are a broken spirit."

"Acts of justice are more meritorious than all the sacrifices. Unless the mind is purified, the sacrifice is useless; it may be thrown to the dogs."

"He who engages in the study of the Law, requires neither burnt offering nor meal offering."

"A day in thy courts is better than a thousand," Psalm lxxiv. is thus explained: God said to David, "I prefer thy sitting and studying before me to the thousands of burnt offerings which thy son Solomon will offer on the alter."

"He who prays is considered as pious as if he had built an altar and offered sacrifices upon it."

"As the Altar wrought atonement during the time of the Temple, so after its destruction, the Table of the home."

With the abolition of sacrifice, the Paschal Lamb was indicated only in a symbolic way by a lamb bone on the Passover table.

R. Jochanan b. Zakkai asked his disciples: "Find out what is the best thing to cultivate." The first replied a generous eye; the second, a loyal friend; the third, a good neighbor; the fourth, prudence and foresight; the fifth, Eliezar, a good heart. "I consider R. Eliezar's judgment best, for in his answer all of yours are included."

Theme for discussion:

Whether the Temple's fall suspended or abolished animal sacrifice is a point of difference between Judaism's two schools today.

BRASS COIN STRUCK IN ROME, **74** C. E., DURING REIGN OF VESPASIAN.

INDICATING JUDEA'S OVERTHROW.

CHAPTER XXV.

THE PALESTINIAN ACADEMIES.

Jamnia was the first of many Palestinian schools; one was located at Sepphoris, another at Tiberias, both in Galilee; another at Lydda in the south not far from the Mediterranean. So the good work grew, and under sadder auspices the thread of life was taken up again. A new royalty, so to speak, was created in Israel. The first literal royalty of the House of Judah had been overthrown by Babylon seven hundred years earlier. After the restoration, the priests became the monarchs of the state, exercising almost regal powers. Now in the dispersion the teacher was king. Rabbi Simeon taught: "There are three crowns: the crown of the Law, the crown of the priesthood, and the crown of royalty; but the crown of a good name excelleth them all."

The head of the Academy was called Nasi (prince), also Patriarch. His sway was voluntarily yet gladly accepted in matters both religious and civil (as far as the management of internal affairs was granted) by the congregations in Rome, Babylonia, Greece, Egypt and the Parthian lands.

Rabban Gamaliel II.

The first Nasi at Jamnia was Rabban Gamaliel II. of the family of Hillel, for Jochanan ben Zakkai had held a unique position, *sui generis*, demanded by the exigencies of the time. But it was the wish of all that the official position should remain in the House of Hillel.

Gamaliel was noted both as scholar and man. He was so conscientious that in farming his estate he would take no interest. He was so expert as easily to master the astronomical and mathematical knowledge needed for the regulation of the Jewish calendar. He was a stern man, but these troublous times needed a firm hand, religiously as well as civilly, for it was a period of unrest; the air was full of schemes and fantastic notions. Even so, he was perhaps too severe, and for a brief period during his thirty years of Patriarchate, he was actually deposed; the incident will be related presently. One indication of his severity was his frequent imposition of *Niddui*— excommunication. The person so condemned had to remain aloof from the community and live as one in mourning. He was thus ostracised until the ban was removed.

As in the days when the Temple stood, there were still two parties—

Hillelites and Shammaites. Rabban Gamaliel, however, endeavored to place himself above party, as the leader should.

The following incidents will show the temper of these Jewish scholars: One Akabiah ben Mahallel was asked to recede from a particular decision. It was even intimated by some that if he would yield, he would be made *Ab Beth Din* (Vice-President, next in order to the Nasi). To this suggestion he answered, "I would rather be a fool all my life than a rogue for one hour." Is not that magnificent? Living aloof and asked by his son for a letter of recommendation to his colleagues, the stern father refused. "Thine own works must recommend thee."

Another famous teacher was Eliezer ben Hyrcanus, who opened the school at Lydda. His weakness lay in the fact that he would never trust his own judgment to deduce a rule. He accepted and taught only what he had learned on the authority of his teachers. That type of man has its value in the world and is like the priest, who treasures past traditions. But we need originators too, who boldly open up new highways; for if we mistrusted our own powers altogether and walked only in the old paths, knowledge would not grow and the world would not advance. Rabbi Eliezer taught: "Thy fellowman's honor must be as dear to thee as thine own. Do not allow thyself to be easily angered. Repent one day before thy death."

R. Joshua.

In contrast, let us single out a more interesting figure, a man who left his impress on his age—Rabbi Joshua ben Hananiah. Broad, versatile and gifted, he as a youth had been a chorister in the Temple, now laid waste. His mother, like Samuel's, destined him for a religious life from his birth. Like a true genius, he broke through many of the disadvantages that handicapped him and became one of the Tannäim and the founder of a new academy at Bekiim. He was miserably poor and eked out a scanty existence as a needle-maker. For these great teachers received no emolument for their labors in the religious Academy. It was a service of love. They followed the principle laid down by Rabbi Zadok, "Do not use the Law as a crown to shine therewith or a spade to dig therewith." Rabbi Joshua was, however, so severely plain that a Roman emperor's daughter, combining at once a compliment and an insult, asked why so much wisdom should be deposited in so homely a vessel. Tradition says he advised her to put her father's wine in golden jars with a lamentable result, to prove that, good wisdom, like good wine, may be best preserved in plain receptacles.

Many of the scholarly leaders belonged to the Jewish aristocracy, that was still prized even in their fallen state. Joshua was a man of the "common people." Yet that became for him a source of power, as, being closer to the masses, he was the better able to influence them, and he helped to bring the upper and lower classes closer together. By his gentleness and moderation he prevented many a split in Judaism that often threatened when divergence of view reached the danger point.

Although, like Gamaliel, a great mathematician and astronomer, he was modest and obedient and submitted to a humiliating ordeal imposed by this stern Nasi because of a mistaken calculation as to the date of a holy day. He must travel with purse and staff on the very day, according to his error, Yom Kippur would have fallen. He came. Gamaliel embraced him and said, "Welcome, my master and my pupil; my master in wisdom and my pupil in obedience." Such examples by great teachers were most beneficial to the people at large.

Very valuable to the cause, too, was his shrewd and common sense that exposed the folly of extreme and fantastic views. "The Law," said he, "was not revealed to angels but to human beings." Some misguided pietists would not partake of wine or meat because, now that the Temple had fallen they could not be offered at its altar. "Why not," said he, "abstain also from bread and water since they too were used in the sacrificial service?" Nothing like ridicule at times to explode fallacies.

Most important perhaps of all his service was his endeavor to close the breach between Israel and the Romans, which the unforgiving Shammaites would have widened. He advised a graceful submission to the inevitable. In consequence he enjoyed the confidence of the Roman rulers. Like Jochanan ben Zakkai, he turned out to be the man of the hour; and when a little later Israel again sailed into stormy seas, he was called to the helm.

Rabbi Ishmael ben Elisha deserves a brief mention as one of the great Tannäim of this age who, avoiding strained interpretation, explained the Law with logical common sense. He gladly devoted his wealth to the maintenance of girls orphaned by the war. He too founded a School and was destined, alas, to die a martyr's death.

Ordination of Rabbis.

These men and others like them assured the continuity of their holy work by training students in the exploration of the Law and transmitting to them the *Halachoth* that they thus far deduced. When proficient, they were ordained as teachers by the ceremony of *Semicha* (laying on of hands). This gave them right of membership in the Sanhedrin and certain judicial functions, and also the title of *rabbi*, introduced after the Temple's fall by Jochanan ben Zakkai.

Outside of Judea, schools were also being established in Babylon, Parthia, Asia Minor and Egypt. In Alexandria a modest academy replaced the pretentious Temple of happier days. But all turned to Jamnia, where the Sanhedrin met as the centre of religious authority. It was for the time being their spiritual capital. To the presiding Nasi, Rome granted some civil jurisdiction in the administration of internal Jewish affairs. So the Sanhedrin was still quite a House of Legislature in its way.

The Prayer Book.

Here were regulated the institutions of Judaism and here was now more completely formulated the ritual of prayer already inaugurated in the synagogues while the Temple stood. Here is its outline:

(a) *The Shema* the prayer beginning "Hear, O Israel," (Deut. vi. 4-9), was the centre of the first division of the service. It was *preceded* by two benedictions, the first expressing God's providence seen in Nature, in the morning for the glory of light, in the evening for the soft restfulness of night; the second God's love for Israel manifested in the bestowal of the Law. The Shema was *followed* by another benediction voicing gratitude for divine redemption. (b) The second division of the service was called *Tefillah*, the "eighteen benedictions" prayer, containing a set form of praises at the opening and close, with the central part variable to fit the different occasions of week-days, Sabbath and Holy Days. (c) The third section of the service was the reading from the Pentateuch and the Prophets.

The Reader was no special official; any Israelite could "stand before the Ark" where the scrolls were placed, and read the service. Here again prevailed the idea that religious service was not to be paid for. Prayer for the restoration of the Land and Temple was now a fixed feature of every service. Perpetually to commemorate the Temple's loss by outward signs, such as shattering a glass at a wedding, became a duty in which patriotism and religion were blended. Two of the fasts instituted in Babylon for the fall of the first Temple were given a second sad sanction now, to commemorate the downfall of the second.

As may be well understood, a long and disastrous war had demoralized the masses, especially the country folk. The educated classes rather held aloof from the *Am Haaretz*, "people of the soil," i.e., the ignorant masses. This is rather surprising on the part of the scholars, otherwise so conscientious and so benevolent. But the times were rude and ignorance usually went hand in hand with many evil practises.

The Prayer Book:

The ritual scheme given in this chapter was gradually amplified by passages from Scripture especially Psalms, by additional introductory and closing prayers and by poems for the Festivals.

See Singer translation of the old *Prayer Book*; also the *Union Prayer Book*, closer to the ancient, shorter ritual.

In addition to complete services, the rabbis drew up a series of Benedictions for daily occurrences. Darmesteter thus puts it:

"Each day, each hour is unalterably arranged by regulations from on high ... benedictions before the meal, after the meal benedictions. At sight of the imposing phenomena of nature, of a storm, the sea, the first spring blossoms, thanksgivings. Thanksgiving for new enjoyment, for unexpected good fortune, on eating new fruits, at the announcement of a happy event. Prayers of resignation at the news of misfortune. At the tomb of a beloved being, set prayers; words all prepared to console the sorrow-stricken. Every emotion and every feeling, the most fugitive as well as the most profound, are foreseen, noted and embodied in a formula of prayer ... sanctifying the present hour and keeping one in perpetual communication with the divine."

The Temple Fasts:

Gedalyah's Fast (Tishri 3d); Tenth of Tebeth, 17th of Tammuz, 9th of Ab. Only the last two apply to loss of Second Temple.

See *People of Book*, Vol. iii, p. 200.

Theme for discussion:

In what respect did the "Academy" differ from a school?

CHAPTER XXVI.

JUDAISM AND THE CHURCH.

The Development of Christianity.

In the meantime the new religion that had sprung from Judaism was entering its second stage of development. We have seen (p. 133) how its adoption of pagan ideas tended to separate Jews from Christians theologically. We will now see how the trend of events tended to separate them socially. There were still two Christian sects—the pagan Christians, many of them Greeks, to whom Jesus was the Son of God, whose blood shed on the cross was an atonement for the sins of mankind and whose coming abrogated the Law. These had small sympathy with the Jews in spite of the fact that it was the lofty morality of the Hebrew Scriptures that formed the backbone of the new Faith.

On the other hand there were the Jewish Christians, the original group, but now the small minority, who remained Jews in all respects, but clung to the belief that Jesus of Nazareth was the Messiah, that he had risen from the grave and would come a second time to gratify the hopes not fulfilled in his first advent. They also fostered the belief that they could cure by miracles and drive out demons by declaration of a formula of their faith; for Jesus had also believed in this power of exorcism. They still maintained to a degree the customs of the Essenes (from which body, perhaps they may have been an outgrowth),—particularly the duty of voluntary poverty. Indeed, the Sanhedrin seriously considered whether they might not be regarded as Jews.

But when Judaism and Jews became discredited through loss of land and Temple and Jews were taxed for the privilege of remaining loyal to the former, these Jewish Christians began to drift away from a people who had lost power and status in the world, and threw in their lot with the controlling majority. Such is the way of the world. Furthermore, some of the Jewish country folk, losing faith in the validity of Judaism through the loss of its Temple, were attracted to Christianity with its new scheme of salvation, in which Jesus took the place which had been filled by the altar of sacrifice. In this way many of the Gentile proselytes to Judaism in Alexandria and Asia Minor went over to the new creed. So the loss of the Temple with its priestly service had much to do with the spread of Christianity.

Although great bitterness at first existed between the two Christian sects, the pagan branch soon absorbed the small Jewish branch and all too soon the Christians "knew not Joseph." For the antagonism of Gentile against Jew was now transmitted to the new church and, sad to say, it became a more bitter persecutor of the people from which Jesus and Paul had sprung than most of the heathen nations had been.

Old and New Testaments.

New ceremonials grew up in the new faith. Passover was turned into the Easter sacrificial service. The unleavened bread and wine were supposed to be transformed in some mystic way into the flesh and blood of the Savior (as Jesus was styled). Many Roman rites and symbols were consciously or unconsciously taken up by the new creed in the first few centuries of its foundation; for it grew less and less Jewish as the years went on. Depreciation of Judaism became now the accustomed tactics of the Church Fathers, for Christianity's justification depended in some respects on the theory of Judaism's insufficiency. Jews were said to be blind and obstinate in still clinging to the Law, now that Jesus had come. This unfortunate spirit of antagonism to the parent faith pervades the Christian Scriptures and mars its ethical teachings. These Scriptures were known as the *New Testament*, to distinguish them from the Jewish Scriptures which were called the *Old Testament*; the theory being that the testament or *covenant* between God and Israel, there recorded, was now obsolete and superseded by a "new" covenant in which, as already explained, belief in Jesus, the Messiah, took the place of obedience to the Law. Many passages from the Psalms and Prophets were retranslated to fit the impression that they had really foretold the coming of Jesus and the events of his life. The whole Hebrew Bible in fact was treated as but a preparation for Christianity's grand climax! Even the history of Israel was regarded as but an allegorical picture of the life of the man of Nazareth.

Gnostics.

We cannot pass this period of religious upheaval, without a word about certain strange sects, neither wholly Jewish, Christian nor pagan, but something of all, that arose at this time. They were for the most part called Gnostics, from the Greek "know," claiming to obtain through weird processes a clearer knowledge of God. Very fantastic were the views of some on the problems of life and sin. Some of the sects were led into all sorts of absurdities and excesses. A few Jews were seduced by these fascinating heresies, notably one Elisha ben Abuyah, learned in the Law though he was. Having left the fold, he is said to have became a persecutor of his people. The

Rabbis only accounted for the sad change by a complete revolution in his nature—so they called him *Acher*, "another man."

The Sanhedrin found it wise to prohibit the reading of such mystic literature that would tend to lead youth astray from the sound and healthy teachings of Judaism.

NOTES AND REFERENCES.

For an elucidating picture of the compromise of paganism with Christianity by a Christian writer, read "Is Catholicism a Baptized Paganism?" by Rev. Heber Newton, in the *Forum Magazine*, New York, 1890.

Jewish Scripture and Church Doctrine:

Isaiah (particularly ch. ix, 6-7 and ch. liii), was a favorite book among Christian theologians from which to deduce the doctrines of the church. Notice the quotations used in Handel's Oratorio "The Messiah." Also Daniel, hence the prominent place among the prophets, given it by the Church. Modern critics altogether abandon this forced method of Biblical exegesis. (See Skinner's *Isaiah* and Driver's *Daniel* (Cambridge Bible).

Theme for discussion:

Contrast the ancient gnostic with the modern agnostic.

CHAPTER XXVII.

ROME'S REGIME AFTER JUDEA'S OVERTHROW.

Roman Emperors	Jewry	
Titus	79 Jamnian Academy	70
Domitian	81 Clemens, Roman proselyte,	
	put to death,	95
Nerva,	96 Revolt of the Diaspora,	115
Trajan,	98 Aquila's Bible translation	
	about	128
Hadrian,	117 Akiba, president of Sanhedrin	130
Antoninus Pius,	138 Bar Cochba insurrection,	132-135

Proselytes Again.

The Emperor Vespasian, who had permitted the institution of the Jamnian Academy, was succeeded by his son Titus. Titus lived too briefly after he became emperor to exert a decided influence on Israel, but it could never forget that to his hand had been entrusted the final overthrow of Judea. His brother Domitian, however, the next emperor, was a tyrant and a degenerate. It is said that at one time he contemplated the extermination of the Jews. The Jewish tax (*Fiscus Judaicus*) was collected with needless cruelty and indignity. He bitterly persecuted those Romans who in spite of Israel's fallen fortunes, were still drawn to its Faith and made severe laws against those who encouraged conversion. Proselytes came in sufficient numbers to make the subject an important theme of discussion in the Jewish Academy. It was probably in Rome itself where the spread of Judaism most alarmed the emperor. Perhaps its teachings reached the Romans through the Jewish prisoners of war. Certainly many high born Romans were enthusiastically prepared to make sacrifices for its cause. It is said that even Flavius Clemens and his wife Flavia Domitilla, relatives of Domitian and possible heirs to the throne, were pledged to Judaism. Clemens was put to death and his wife was exiled. But a step, and Judaism might have mounted the imperial throne of Rome and have exchanged destinies with Christianity. Perhaps not even then, for its unbending monotheism and strict Law brooked no easy compromise. However, it is one of the might-have-beens of history.

One of the most famous proselytes was Aquila, a Greek of scholarship and wealth. Dissatisfied with the later Greek translations of the Bible, distorted to fit Christian doctrine, Aquila made a literal translation from the Hebrew that so commended itself to the Rabbis that it became the "authorized version," so to speak, for the Synagogue. An Aramaic (p. 60) translation of the Bible, following his model, was called after him *Targum Onkelos*—which means "a translation like that of Aquila." It is often printed with the Hebrew texts of Scripture to-day.

Revolt against Trajan.

It was the unhappy fate of Israel that the mischievous Domitian should have reigned so long and that the good Emperor Nerva, his successor, should have reigned so briefly. So although the injunctions against proselytes were removed during the sixteen months of Nerva's rule as soon as Trajan came to the throne many anti-Jewish laws were restored. Like Alexander the Greek, Trajan the Roman cherished the wild desire of conquering Asia. When he attacked Parthia, the Jews living in semi-independence there became his most vigorous opponents. In Babylon they stubbornly held the city of Nisibis against his legions. No sooner had he subdued the lands on the Euphrates and the Tigris than the Persian provinces revolted.

All the Jews of the Diaspora now seized the occasion to throw off the hated Roman yoke. For they had never become reconciled to it; and, their children, now grown to manhood, had been brought up in the assurance that soon Judea would be won back again and the Temple rebuilt. "Carthage must be destroyed" had been the Roman cry; "Jerusalem must be rebuilt" was now the Jewish. In Egypt, in Cyprus, a Mediterranean island, and in Cyrene, further west on the African coast—they rose against their opponents. At first success came to their arms, though much blood flowed on both sides; but there could be no doubt of the ultimate outcome with Rome's overwhelming numbers. Yet so vigorous was their resistance that the historian Graetz ventures to think that, in spite of lacking cavalry and being indifferently armed, had these three separate Jewish uprisings been organized under one directing control it would have gone hard with the Roman legions. As it was, their beautiful synagogue in Alexandria was destroyed, all the Jewish inhabitants of Cyprus were slain and the island forbidden them in the future. Many lives were lost in other places of Jewish insurrection, including Judea itself. The revolt certainly nipped in the bud Trajan's foolish ambition to conquer all Asia, and he died in mortification at his failure.

Gamaliel was now dead and Rabbi Joshua had become Patriarch. The reins of power could not have been entrusted to wiser hands, for he seized the moment of the accession of the new emperor, Hadrian, to counsel conciliation. Like Jochanan ben Zakkai, he saw the futility of Israel wasting its strength in fighting with colossal Rome. The Sanhedrin was removed from Jamnia to Oosha in upper Galilee. Joshua's sway was less rigorous than that of Gamaliel. At a time when many of his brethren felt nothing but hatred toward the heathen, he uttered the famous dictum: "The virtuous of all peoples have a share in the heavenly bliss of the life to come." This has since been accepted by the House of Israel as the classic expression of its attitude towards other religions.

The new emperor Hadrian also seemed at first inclined to a policy of concession; but there was little choice, for revolt burst out in all parts of the empire, from Asia Minor in the East to Britain in the far West. The discouraged emperor gladly met many of his enemies half way. Parthia was restored to the control of its own princes. In Judea proper a cruel general, Quietus, was checked in his terrible purpose of exterminating the Jews and was ultimately executed.

Hadrian's "Promise."

To win peace and adherents, Hadrian was willing to make many fair promises at the opening of his reign that he had no serious intention of fulfiling. One of these was an offer to the Jews to rebuild their Temple, which they had exacted as the condition of laying down their arms. Imagine the boundless joy with which this news was received—a Cyrus come to power once more! Hebrew poets sang of the glories that were to come. Christians and Samaritans were much disconcerted at the news.

But as soon as Hadrian had obtained the mastery of the situation and quiet was restored, he resorted to subterfuge. They might rebuild their Temple, but not in the same place! He knew it was that place or none. The Jews saw through the pretense; their hopes were blasted. There was talk of war again, but the wise Rabbi Joshua still counselled submission. So for many years the embers of revolt slumbered in the breasts of the Jews, but did not die out, though as long as Rabbi Joshua lived they did not break into flame.

Notes and References.

Proselytes:

Read the article on this subject in the *Jewish Encyclopedia* for fuller list of Roman proselytes. Notice here first, the different degrees of proselytism;

secondly, the attitude of the synagogue toward the convert, favorable or unfavorable in different periods of its history, varying with its changing relations with the outside world. Based on the laws given to Noah (Genesis ix) the Tannäim deduced seven Noachian rules, which they regarded as obligations binding on all mankind. To these humane laws strangers living in their midst must conform. For they felt this sense of responsibility to those not of their religion.

BRASS COIN OF NERVA, 96 C. E.

MARKING THE WITHDRAWAL OF CERTAIN ABUSES IN CONNECTION WITH THE JEWISH TAX.

CHAPTER XXVIII.

AKIBA.

Love and Law.

The man who now came to the fore was of a different mould—the famous Rabbi Akiba. He was born in Palestine in the year 50 C. E. that is, some 20 years before the Temple fell. Many a pretty legend is woven around his life. Have you ever realized that it is only around great men that legends most luxuriantly grow? Imagination does not seek to picture incidents in the lives of the commonplace. Not only poor, but ignorant, Akiba despised scholars and scholarship. One day, so runs the story, this humble shepherd met Rachel, the beautiful daughter of his master, Kalba Sabua, and fell in love with her. Angry at his daughter's attachment for this boor, the rich Kalba disinherited her. Her sweet self-sacrifice in sharing poverty with him rather than wealth without him, roused the noblest qualities dormant in Akiba's nature. She was determined to bear yet further privation that he might become a scholar in the Law. For it was to his ignorance, rather than to his poverty, that the father had objected. Among no people was illiteracy so great a disgrace as among the Jews, and among none did learning simply, confer so much honor. So at her urgency, he reluctantly left his home to sit at the feet of the Rabbis of the Schools. The chronicles of chivalry furnish pretty stories of knights-errant hieing forth at the bidding of fair ladies to make conquests in distant fields of battle. Akiba went forth at Rachel's bidding; and is not the mastery of knowledge a victory as renowned as that of war? A wonderful pupil he became, for he had the gift of enthusiasm. But while he was winning renown at the Academy, she, alone and at a distance, was battling with poverty, at one time having to sell her hair to buy food for her child. But still the self-sacrificing woman would not permit his return.

One day it was announced in the village in which she lived that the great scholar, Rabbi Akiba, was about to visit it. He came, surrounded by many disciples, and as the crowd of admirers gathered about him, they pushed aside a poorly clad woman who tried to reach his side. But espying her, he parted the crowd and caught her in his arms. To the astonished spectators he declared, "All that I know I owe to her, for she was my inspiration."

So far the romantic side of his life. On its literary side he was a great *Tanna*, and famous scholars came from his School. His method of interpreting new Law from old was based on the theory that no word or particle in the

Pentateuch was redundant; if any appeared in the text that it seemed could be dispensed with, then it must have some hidden significance. This changed the law of Moses from a limited group of unvarying precepts to a living fount of continuous tradition, and made the laws of the days of the Jewish monarchy capable of modification and enlargement to fit Israel's life under the Roman Empire. Interpretation that would produce new precepts to meet the changing conditions of later times was undertaken by Hillel (p. 113) but never before reduced to so complete a system as was done by Rabbi Akiba. On such a principle there was no end of the possible deductions from Scripture. Yet the Rabbis were too earnest and too conscientious knowingly to abuse it. The theory worked in the interest of progress. The institution of this method has earned for Akiba the title of "father of rabbinic Judaism."

He further gave an impetus to the classification of the *Halachoth* already begun before his day. This classification of the Oral Law was called *Mishna*, or Second Law, of which we shall hear more later on.

He, too, had a voice in fixing the canon of Scripture.

Akiba's Ethics.

Here follow some of his sayings:

"How favored is man for he was created in the Image" (of God).

"—Who slays a man sins against the devine image."

"Take thy seat below thy rank until bidden to take a higher place."

"God is merciful but He does not permit this mercy to impair His justice."

"Everything is foreseen, yet freedom of will is given to man."

There is also ascribed to him on doubtful authority the maxim, "Whatever God doeth He doeth for the best."

There is a mystic note throughout his teachings; mark the following:

"Everything is given in pledge ... the office is open, the broker gives credit; there is the ledger and the hand writes; whoever wishes to borrow may borrow, but the bailiffs daily exact; the judgment is fair; and everything is prepared for the Banquet."

In the spirit of Hillel's Golden Rule he regarded the greatest principle of Judaism the law "Thou shalt love thy neighbor as thyself."

He was always entrusted with tasks of delicacy and consideration—the notification to R. Gamaliel that he had been impeached, to R. Eliezar that he had been excommunicated. To the latter he broke the disagreeable news in these words: "It seems your brethren turn away from you."

Law and Faith.

Akiba established an Academy at Bene Barak. There was a wonderful fascination about the man that attracted hundreds of students to him— tradition says thousands. That was in part due to the enthusiasm of his *faith*. An instance of his faith is illustrated in his visit to Rome, with some of his colleagues, to intercede on behalf of his people. They burst into tears at beholding Rome's splendor, mentally contrasting it with Jerusalem's desolation. He met their tears with a hopeful smile: "The present ruined condition of our beloved land foretold by the Prophets, only assures me of the fulfilment of their brighter prophecies of our ultimate triumph."

Alas, even faith may have its drawbacks! Akiba's deep conviction that the restoration of Judea's independence was at hand, to be effected by the advent of the Messiah, induced him to encourage the revolt that was quietly but steadily spreading among his disaffected brethren.

Hadrian, little understanding the spirit of this people, reported to the Senate after making a circuit through the Roman provinces, that all was peace. He was both foolish and cruel enough to display his absolute power and Israel's complete subjection, not only by altogether withdrawing permission to rebuild the Jewish Temple, but by ordering a heathen shrine to be reared on its site, thus completely to paganize Jerusalem.

This was the last straw. The aged Rabbi Joshua went to implore the emperor to desist from this wanton project, but in vain. It was one of the last acts of the Patriarch's life. When he died it was said good counsel ceased in Israel. Like Antiochus of old, Hadrian wished to obliterate Judaism—and Christianity, too, for that matter,—and make the idolatrous worship of Serapis universal.

NOTES AND REFERENCES.

Masora is the technical term for the notes on the traditional Scripture text by the Fathers of the Synagogue. The original text has been thus preserved intact in these scrupulous and reverent hands. See article, "Masora," Isidore Harris, *Jewish Quarterly Review*, Vol. i.

The blessing that charity brings to the giver was a favorite idea of Akiba— a *Mitzvah*!

Simon b. Shetach was called the "Restorer of the Law"; Hillel the "Regenerator of the Law"; Akiba the "Father of Rabbinic Judaism."

In deciding the Canon of Scripture (p. 22), Akiba's influence kept *Song of Songs* and *Esther* in the Bible, but unfortunately kept *Ecclesiasticus* out of it.

***Theme for discussion*:**

Should Akiba's method of law deduction be called casuistic?

CHAPTER XXIX.

LAST STRUGGLE FOR LIBERTY.

Bar Cochba.

Preparations for rebellion had been carefully planned for some years. Arms had been stored in caves. Akiba was the inspiration of the revolt, its Deborah, let us say. But who was to be its Barak? The times created the man. A hero appeared to lead the forces of Israel whom the multitude in admiration called Bar Cochba (son of a star). This title may have been suggested by the name of his birthplace, Koziba, but chiefly also because he was regarded by the enthusiasts as the long-looked-for Messiah. This man, of colossal strength and strategic resources, was going to make Rome feel the power of a scorned people. Reinforcements came fast to the banner of the supposed Messiah, scion of David's house, who was to throw off the yoke of Rome and restore the throne of Judah. Soon he had half a million men at his back.

The Roman governor, Tinnius Rufus, who is the Talmud's archetype of cruelty, fled with his garrison. In the first year of the war fifty fortresses and a thousand towns capitulated before the advancing arms of Bar Cochba; for the presence of the beloved Akiba gave confidence to all. We might say of him as was written of Moses, "When Akiba raised his hand, Israel prevailed."

Hadrian, who first slighted the insurrection, had soon reason to fear it. His best generals were dispatched to Judea only to be repulsed. Already Bar Cochba was having coins struck with his insignia. Alas the act was premature. King Ahab once said, "Let not him boast who putteth on his armor as he who taketh it off." In the meantime Roman prisoners of war were treated with great forbearance; indeed some heathens, impressed with the enthusiasm of the Jews, had joined their ranks.

General Severus.

Eventually, after Bar Cochba had held sway for two years without cavalry and had repulsed every Roman army, Hadrian, alarmed, summoned the great general, Julius Severus, from distant Britain. The Jewish focus of operations was at Bethar, south of Caesarea, and one mile from the Mediterranean, and fortifications had been placed north, west and east to hold control of the country. Jezreel commanded the centre.

Like Vespasian, the great general Severus, decided on siege rather than attack. So he steadily cut off supplies and provisions and also barbarously put to death all prisoners of war. There was no Josephus to give us vivid details of this campaign, so we only know its general result. The three great outlying fortresses on the frontier were first mastered. The next battle took place on the field of Jezreel. One by one the Jewish fortresses fell. The whole Judean army was now concentrated in Bethar where the decisive battle must be waged. It was the Jerusalem of this war. Severus resolved to starve it out. For one year the Jews bravely held out against the finest army of the age. At last some Romans found a way into Bethar through a subterranean passage which some Samaritans, it is said, betrayed. Then followed an awful carnage in which Roman horses "waded to the nostrils in Jewish blood." More than half a million souls were slain and thousands more perished by fire and hunger. Yet so great were also the Roman losses that Hadrian in his message of the campaign to the Roman senate, significantly omitted the formula, "I and the army are well."

In the year 135 Bethar fell and tradition places it on the same date so disastrous in Jewish annals—the 9th of Ab. The Roman soldiers kept up a war of extermination against the scattered bands that still held out. Many who had taken refuge in caves were brutally massacred. All the Jews throughout the Roman Empire were made to feel the weight of Hadrian's anger in heavy taxation. As though wantonly to mark its complete desolation, the plow was passed over Jerusalem. North of it was built a Roman city—Aelia Capitolina. On the Temple Mount was erected a shrine dedicated to Jupiter, with the vindictive purpose of obliterating the very name of Jerusalem. (And it *was* forgotten—for one hundred and fifty years.) No Jew dared enter that city under penalty of death. But all this was but preliminary to his real punishment of those who were called rebels only because they failed. Keener sighted than Vespasian, who blotted out the Nation but tolerated the Faith, Hadrian saw that there was only one way to crush the Jew; that was by crushing his religion. To that abortive purpose he now devoted himself with all the inhumanity of a Pharaoh. To the cruel but cowardly Tinnius Rufus, who had fled at the first alarm, that task was entrusted. Judaism was proscribed. Obedience to its Law was declared a capital crime. Should they commit physical or spiritual suicide was the dilemma that now faced Israel. Was ever a people reduced to such straits?

Law and Life.

A few were ready for ignoble acquiescence and called it submitting to the inevitable, forgetting that "inevitable" is an elastic term that varies with our moral determination. Meeting secretly in a garret, the Rabbis considered the momentous question of the religious policy of this critical hour. They decided that while this terrible decree lasted the people might disregard Jewish observances under duress, since the Law was given, not that they should die, but live by it. But fearing that their lenient proclamation might be mistakenly applied to the fundamentals of religion and morals, they made this safeguard: Even to save his life, no Jew must commit the sins of *idolatry*, *adultery*, or *murder*. This vitally important declaration, involving the all-compelling sanction of the second, sixth and seventh commandments, became an abiding principle in Judaism.

But many of the Rabbis themselves refused to take advantage of the leniency they were willing to grant to others, and determined to obey every injunction of Judaism. In particular they determined to teach the Law to their disciples, on which the continuance of the Jewish tradition depended—though they knew that death would be the penalty of discovery. Roman spies were everywhere ready to pounce upon any who committed the "crime" of fulfilling the precepts of Judaism in obedience to the dictates of conscience. Some were only fined, but others were put to death with tortures too cruel to tell.

Martyrdom.

There were ten famous martyrs among the teachers of the Law. One of these, Chananyah ben Teradion, had the scroll of the Law he was expounding, wound round him and was burnt in its flames—wet wool being placed on his heart to prolong his agony. His executioner, inspired by such lofty example of faith and courage, sought death with him on the same pyre.

Another, Rabbi Judah ben Baba, gathered some of his disciples about him in a lonely spot, to ordain them as rabbis by the rite of *Semicha*, already explained. Roman soldiers discovered him. He bade his pupils fly. They refused to obey until he pointed out that having learnt from him important decisions of the Law, it was their duty to live and teach them to others. Later they found him pierced with three hundred lances.

Rabbi Akiba was among the martyrs and would not avail himself of the temporary suspension of the ceremonial Law. Reproached for exposing his life by teaching the Law he answered in a parable that has since become famous, that of "The Fox and the Fishes." Seeing the frightened fish swimming from nets set to entrap them, a crafty fox on the bank called out, "Come up on land and escape the snares of the sea." "Nay," advised the counsellor among the fish, "far wiser will it be to remain in the water, your native element, even though made perilous by the nets of men." Was not Judaism the *native element* of the Jew?

Soon this noble teacher was seized and cast into prison. Rufus ordered him to be flayed to death by iron pincers. But religion cannot be killed in that way. In the midst of his agonies, a seraphic smile illuminated his face. "Daily," said he, "I have recited the *Shema*, 'Love God with heart and soul and might,' and now I understand its last phrase—'with all thy might,'—that is even though He ask thy life; here I give Him my life." With this wondrous recital of Israel's prayer, this sweet soul, whose opinions may have brought him some opponents, but whose character all loved, passed away. His parable of "The Fox and the Fishes" contained a profound truth exemplified in himself; for, dying in his native element, the Law, he lives immortally in the Jewish heart; aye, through the inspiration of his death and that of others like him, does Israel abide to-day. Here was another application of the "suffering servant" in Isaiah's fifty-third chapter.

Thus ended Israel's last struggle for liberty. It severed, too, the last link that yet united the Jewish Christians to the parent Jewish body. For they said, "Why hold further relation with a community completely crushed and discredited in the eyes of all the world?" They believed that Judaism's collapse and disappearance was at hand.

NOTE.

Rome first despised the Judean revolt and then had to send its greatest general to quell it. Compare the similar experience of Britain with the Boers.

Theme for discussion:

What degree of pain or peril justifies disregard of ceremonial law?

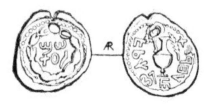

COIN OF THE SECOND REVOLT OF BAR COCHBA, 132-135 C. E.

(Nearly all the illustrations of coins used in this book have been taken from Madden's "Coins of the Jews," London: Trübner & Co.)

CHAPTER XXX.

R. JUDAH, "THE SAINT," AND HIS TIMES.

Sorrowfully the Jews now took up the burden of life once more. In spite of dreadful devastation and dreary outlook the faith and spirit of the majority remained unbroken. Hadrian had tried to eradicate Judaism, but he had failed. The defeated were still the victors. In the year 138 Hadrian was succeeded by the more humane Antoninus Pius. The religious persecution was stopped, Rome's normal toleration of Judaism was resumed. The Sanhedrin was reopened at Oosha, the Presidency being still retained in the family of Hillel. Rabbi Simon, the Nasi, was the author of the maxim, "The world rests on three pillars—Truth, Justice and Peace." Compare the "world's three pillars" of Simon the Just. (p. 30).

Mair and Beruriah.

Rabbi Mair was a unique figure of this time. He is said to have given one-third of his means to support poor students. Not at first recognized because of his youth, he gave expression to the maxim, "Look not at the vessel, but at that which it contains; for there are new flasks full of old wine and old flasks which contain not even new wine." Did not Rabbi Joshua express a similar sentiment?

Rabbi Mair was a broad man who gladly gathered knowledge from all, Jew and non-Jew alike. Mark this bit of wisdom: "Who studies the Law for its own sake is worth the whole world and is loved by God and man." Is not the study of the Law *for its own sake* the very essence of religion? He would illustrate his lessons by fables in the portrayal of which he was wonderfully gifted.

His wife, Beruria, is the most renowned—or perhaps the only renowned—woman in Talmudic annals. We might compare her to the Shunamite (II Kings, iv.), whom the Bible calls a "great" woman. Great was Beruria in strength of character, in dignity and withal in motherly affection. She was indeed a helpmeet to her husband and to many of her people in a time of storm and stress. Her own parents had been martyrs in the Hadrianic war. She was a scholar too. Her keen penetration and at the same time her womanly tenderness are revealed in her interpretation of the text, "Let sinners be consumed out of the earth." (Psalms civ. 35). Not *sinners*, but *sin*. Then indeed will be fulfilled the hope at the conclusion of the text—"The wicked will be no more."

Her strength of character is perhaps best revealed in the pathetic story told of the consoling way in which she broke to her husband the terrible news of the death of their two sons. Some "jewels" had been entrusted to her, which she so highly prized that it was hard to give them up; what should she do? They must be returned said R. Mair. In this way fortifying him with consolation for the sorrow awaiting him in this double bereavement, she gently led him to the chamber where the dead children lay.

Judah ha-Nasi.

As the epoch of the Tannäim opened, so now it closed, with a remarkable man—Rabbi Judah, called *par excellence* The Nasi, i.e., greatest of all. And no Nasi before him had been permitted to exercise so much power over the Sanhedrin,—now located in Sepphoris in Galilee.

Like so many of his predecessors, he devoted much of his wealth to the maintenance of students of the Law, and fed the poor during a famine. He came to be known as "the Saint." His most valuable service was the complete codification of all the Halachoth that had been gradually accumulating since post-Biblical time. While similar collections had been made before his time, commenced by Hillel, amplified by Rabbi Akiba and revised by Rabbi Mair, his final editing of the previous work became the officially accepted condensation of the Oral Law—the Mishna, superseding all earlier collections.

It is treated in the following chapter.

Rabbi Judah, not only compiled the teachings of others, but he left valuable maxims of his own:

"Be as careful of the observance of a light precept as of a weighty one."

"Balance the material loss involved in the performance of a precept against its spiritual compensation and the present desirable fruits of a sinful deed against the injury to thine immortal soul."

"Know what is above thee: A seeing eye, a hearing ear, and that all thy actions are written in a book."

No Nasi received so much reverential regard from the people at large. While he was dying, they gathered around his house, declaring in the exaggeration of grief that they would slay the person who would dare announce his death. At length there came forward Bar Kappara, a man of broad scientific attainments and withal a man of delicate imagination. In fact, he was a poet too, as may be judged by the way in which he announced Rabbi Judah's death: "Angels and mortals contended for the ark of the covenant; the angels have conquered, the ark of the covenant is gone."

Other Famous Teachers.

Just a passing word on other great men of this epoch. Rabbi Jochanan showed his breadth of view in encouraging the study of Greek and opening up its great literature to Jewish youth, and particularly in his recommendation of it for girls. This urging of the cultivation of the female mind formed a pleasing contrast to the prevailing practice—the comparative neglect of the education of women—which practice survives in some of our communities to-day!

To this period also belonged that keen logician, Resh Lakish, likewise renowned for his colossal strength and his scrupulous honesty. He discerned that the Book of Job was not a history, but a life problem put in the form of a story. He also taught that Hell has no real existence. Not that he or his age altogether denied a future retribution for the wicked. But Hell never appealed strongly to the conviction of the Jew. Certainly the Synagogue does not teach the doctrine of "everlasting punishment" to-day.

Another teacher, Rabbi Simlai, searched the Scriptures and enumerated 613 ordinances of Judaism—365 negative and 248 affirmative precepts. He found them further reduced to eleven principles in the 15th Psalm; in Isaiah xxxiii. to six; in Micah vi. 8 to three; in Isaiah lvi. to two; and in Amos v.-4 to one: "Seek ye Me and ye shall live"; to one also in Habbakuk ii.-4. "The just shall live by his Faith."

Nor must we forget that group of rabbis who, investigating the religious and educational condition of various towns and finding in one place no teachers, asked the magistrate to present the guardians of the city. He marched forth the armed men. "No," said the rabbis, "these are not the guardians, but the destroyers of a city. Its true guardians are the teachers."

Let us mention in this group, too, Rabbi Abbahu, the last of the great men of the Palestinian schools, renowned not so much as an expert on the *Halacha* as a keen *Hagadist*. This is another way of saying that he was not so much a subtle jurist as a great *preacher*. He was a student of human nature. His keen insight on one occasion chose as the worthiest to pray for rain, a man bad by repute, but who, he had discerned, was noble in character.

NOTE AND REFERENCE.

For complete enumeration of the 613 precepts, see article "Commandments," *Jewish Encyclopedia*, vol. iv.

Theme for discussion:

Can the number of our duties be specified?

CHAPTER XXXI.

THE MISHNA.

All the supplementary laws that grew up around the *written* Codes of the Bible were called, by distinction, the *Oral Law*. These included the decisions of the Scribes (p. 19), the Pairs (pp. 87-8) and the Tannäim (p. 186). Rabbi Judah the Nasi made a compilation of all of these and called it The Mishna. Derived from the Hebrew verb *shanah*, to learn or repeat, the Mishna is popularly known as the Second Law. It became the recognized code for all legal decisions, and the authorized text-book in all the schools.

It now took its place beside the Law of the Pentateuch, and just as that first Law was a text for further development, so too we shall see that this Second Law, containing Halachoth of the *Sopherim*, the *Pairs* and the *Tannäim*, became the parent of a vast growth of precepts and prohibitions in the interpreting hands of the generations now to follow.

The Mishna is divided into six groups (Sedarim) containing sixty subdivisions (Mesechtas), as follows:

I. SEEDS: AGRICULTURAL LAWS.

1, Introductory chapter on "Prayers"; 2, "Corners" of fields for the poor (Levit. xix., 9-10); 3, Doubtful produce (whether tithed or untithed); 4, Illegal mixtures (Deut. xxii. 9-11); 5, Sabbatic Year; 6, Priests' Tithes; 7, Levites' Tithes; 8, Secondary Tithes; 9, Dough offerings (Numbers xv., 17-21); 10, Prohibited fruits of first three years (Levit. xix., 23-25); 11, First fruits.

II. FESTIVALS.

1, Sabbath; 2, Uniting localities to extend limit of Sabbath walk; 3, Passover; 4, Half-shekel tax (Ex. xxx., 11-16); 5, Day of Atonement; 6, Tabernacles; 7, Festival regulations; 8, New Year; 9, Fasts; 10, Purim; 11, Middle days of the Festivals; 12, Festival Pilgrimage to Jerusalem.

III. WOMEN

1, Levirate marriage (Deut. xxv., 5-10); 2, Marriage contracts; 3, Vows; 4, Nazarites (Numb. vi, and xxx); 5, The suspected sinner; 6, Divorce; 7,

Betrothal.

IV. DAMAGES: CIVIL AND CRIMINAL LAW.

1, First division—general; 2, Second division—Suits between master and servant, etc; 3, Third Division—Municipal and social regulations; 4, The Sanhedrin and Criminal Law; 5, Punishment by flogging; 6, Oaths; 7, Decisions between opposing traditions; 8, Idolatry (crime as well as sin); 9, Ethics of the Fathers; 10, Accidental Offences.

V. SACRED THINGS.

1, Sacrifices; 2, Meat offerings; 3, Slaughtered animals for food only; 4, The first born sacrifice; 5 and 6, Redemption and Exchange (see Levit. xxii); 7, Excommunication; 8, Profanation; 9, Temple sacrificial services; 10, Temple arrangements; 11, Offerings of poor (Levit. v, 1-10, and xii, 8).

VI. PURIFICATION.

1, Household furniture; 2, Tents and houses; 3, Leprosy; 4, The "Red Heifer" purification (Numb. xix.); 5, Lesser defilements; 6, Washing; 7, Periodic defilement; 8, Conditional impurities; 9, Open wounds; 10, Personal purification; 11, Washing of the hands; 12, Defilement of fruits.

About 150 authorities are quoted in the Mishna, involving about two thousand statements. Here are a few specimen sentences:

"From what time should we begin to read evening prayers (Shema)? From the hour when the priests enter to partake of their offering till the end of the first watch, according to R. Eleazer; (other) sages say till midnight. Rabban Gamaliel says, till dawn. Once it happened that his sons returned (late) from a feast. They said to him, 'We have not yet recited (the Shema).' He replied, 'If it is not yet dawn, the obligation to read it still abides; nay further, where the sages have said, 'till midnight,' their injunction extends it till dawn."—Opening paragraph of *Mishna*.

R. Nechunjah b. Hakanah was accustomed to offer a short prayer on entering and leaving the Academy. His (disciples) asked the appropriateness of such prayer. He replied: "On entering I pray that no harm should happen through me, on departing I give thanks for my lot."

"It is man's duty to offer a prayer at the occurrence of evil, just as he prays at good fortune; for Scripture says, 'Thou shalt love the Lord thy

God, with all thy heart, with all thy soul and with all thy might,' 'With all thy heart'—with thy two inclinations of good and evil. 'With all thy soul' (life)—even though He (God) take thy life. 'With all thy might'—with all thy substance."—*Prayers*, i, 1.

"On New Year all who enter the world, pass before Him (God) like sheep to be judged, as Scripture says: He fashioneth their hearts alike, He understandeth all their doings."

"On six (different) months messengers are sent forth (to report on the occurrence of the New Moon); On Nisan on account of the Passover; on Ab, on account of the Fast (ninth); on Ellul, on account of New Year; on Tishri, to adjust the Festivals; on Kislev, on account of Hannukah; on Adar, on account of Purim. In the days when the temple stood they (the messengers) also went forth on Iyar, on account of Minor Passover" (see Numb. ix, 10-12).

The following are prohibited from testifying:—he who gambles with dice, he who lends money on usury, he who trains doves for racing purposes, he who traffics in the produce of the seventh year and slaves. —*New Year*, ii, 8.

Here is a specimen piece from Sanhedrin, with accompanying notes, translated for a forthcoming work, *Library of Post-biblical Hebrew Literature*:

They (the Judges[1]) examined them (the witnesses) with seven searching questions: "In what sabbatical year? In what year? In what month? What date of the month? What day? What hour? What place?" R. Jose said, "What day. What hour? What place? Did you know him? Did you warn him?[2] In a case of idolatry, whom did he serve? And with what did he serve?"

The more searching a judge is in his examinations, the more praiseworthy he is. It happened that the son of Zaccai examined (even) concerning the stems of the figs.[3] And what difference is there between investigations and examinations? In investigations if one should say, "I don't know," his testimony is worthless. In examinations, if one should say, "I don't know," and even two should say, "We don't know," their testimony stands. Whether in investigations or examinations, when they contradict each other, their testimony is worthless.

One witness said, "on the second of the month," and another witness said, "the third of the month," their testimony stands; because one knows of the intercalary month, and another does not know of the intercalary

159

month.[4] One said, "on the third," and another said, "on the fifth," their testimony is worthless. R. Judah said "it stands." One said, "on the fifth," and another said, "on the seventh," their testimony is worthless, because at the fifth (hour) the sun is in the east, and at the seventh the sun is in the west.

And afterwards they introduce the second (witness[5]) and examine him. If both their statements agree, they open the case for the defense. If one witness says, "I possess information to clear him," or one of the disciples (of the Sanhedrin) says: "I possess information to condemn," they are ordered to keep silence. If one of the disciples says, "I possess information to clear him," they bring him up, and seat him between the judges, and he does not go down during the whole day.[6] If there be substantial information, they give him a hearing. And even when he (the accused) says, "I possess information for clearing myself," the judges give him a hearing; only there must be substantial information in his words. If the judges find him not guilty, they release him, but if not, they defer his verdict to the next day.[7]

FOOTNOTES:

[1] Criminal cases were judged by a regularly constituted court of three-and-twenty qualified members.

[2] No punishment could be inflicted if the culprit had not been warned that he was charged with a crime and forewarned as to its consequences.

[3] The witnesses testified that the crime has been committed under a fig tree.

[4] i. e., one knew that the preceding month was what is called a complete month, counting thirty days, and the days of the celebration of the New Moon (Rosh Hodesh) belonged to the following month; while the other believed that the preceding month was what is called a defective month, counting only twenty-nine days, and that the semi-holyday of the new moon was observed on two days, the first of which belonged to the preceding month.

[5] It was forbidden to examine a witness in the presence of another one.

[6] Even if his information is worthless, he remains seated besides the Judges, the whole day, in order not to degrade him before the public.

[7] A verdict of guilty cannot be pronounced on the same day as that on which the trial was held.

While the Mishna is strictly a code only, still its underlying structure is religious. The moral is everywhere impressed. One of its sections is a Book of Morals called Ethics of the Fathers, iv. 9, from which rabbinic sayings have already been quoted. A complete translation of this section will be found in the Sabbath Afternoon Service of the Prayer Book.

We find no system of doctrines in the Mishna and no formulated creed. A bad life is summed up in the general term—*epicurean*, which probably meant sensual self-indulgence and scoffing scepticism. The Jew is not asked to believe in God's existence. That is taken for granted; atheism hardly came within his ken. He is asked rather to shun anything that tends to polytheism. Revelation and Resurrection are regarded as fundamental beliefs. He who denies them will be deprived of future life. To withhold immortality from him who disbelieves it we might call poetic justice.

While the ceremonial law was rigorous, its observance was saved from being mechanical by the importance laid on sincerity of intention and on inner devotion. Not the brazen serpent but the repentant heart cured afflicted Israel in the wilderness, the Mishna reminds us, pointing its moral with the quotation from the prophet Joel, "Rend your hearts, not your garments." To go beyond the Law in the keeping of one's word merits the highest praise. Many prohibitions were imposed against actions not wrong in themselves, as barriers against possible wrong. These formed a "fence around the Law."

Amoraim.

The acceptance of the Mishna as the Canon of Jewish Law curtailed— theoretically at least—the freedom of the rabbis who now followed, in the evolving of new Law. This later group of teachers was henceforth at liberty only to *expound* the Mishna. They are therefore called *Amoräim*, expounders, to distinguish them from the Tannäim, that class of teachers who interpreted direct from the Scriptures and whose work closed with the Mishna.

The Mishna tended still further to emphasize the legal character of Judaism (p. 19). While it may have robbed the individual of spontaneity of religious action, it strengthened the bulwarks of moral law.

Notes and References.

Another collection similar to the Mishna and arranged on the same plan, was called *Tosephta* (addenda). This contains for the most part commentaries on Scripture and much of what has been called Agada (p. 187).

Read article "Prof. Schürer on Life Under the Law," by Israel Abrahams in *Jewish Quarterly Review*, vol. xi., and "The Law and Recent Criticism," Schechter, vol. iii.

"The Mishna is for the most part, free from the blemishes of the Roman code. There are fewer contradictory laws, fewer repetitions, fewer interpolations than in the digests: ... as regards a certain outspokenness in bodily things ... its language is infinitely purer than that of the mediaeval casuists."—E. DEUTSCH, *The Talmud*, J. P. S. A.

Theme for discussion:

What is Revelation, and how did the sages apply it to the Oral Law? (See "Ethics of the Fathers," ch. i), Sabbath Afternoon Service, Prayer Book.)

Chronological Table.

Emperors of Rome.	Rabbis of the Academies.	
Antoninus Pius	138 Rabbi Mair and Simon b. Yochai flourished	140
Marcus Aurelius	161 Jehuda ha-Nasi, Pres. of Sanhedrin	165
Commodus	180 Jehuda ha-Nasi compiles Mishna	189
Alexander Severus	222-235 Rab opens Academy at Sora	220
Diocletian	284 Mar Samuel, Judge at Nehardea, about	225
Constantine	320 Academy of Pumbaditha	247
Constantius	337-363 Rab Huna dies	297

Neo-Persian Dynasty   226

Constantine's anti-Jewish decrees   315

Council of Nicea widens gulf between Judaism and Christianity   325

CHAPTER XXXII.

BABYLONIA AND ITS SCHOOLS.

Ever since the Bar Cochba war, the numerical centre of gravity of the Jews had shifted to Babylonia, and soon after the compilation of the Mishna in Palestine, Babylonia became the religious centre too.

This fertile country, in which history began, lay between the Euphrates and Tigris, with the Persian Gulf at the south. The name Babylon is sometimes used in Jewish annals to include the surrounding lands, with a southwestern boundary, as far as the Arabian Desert. This second "Land of Israel" had been a home for the Jews since the first forced exile there in the year 600 B. C. E., in the days of Jeremiah and Ezekiel. From Babylon came both Ezra and Hillel, though in the four centuries intervening between these two men, we hear nothing of Jewish life in Babylon.

Babylon's Varied Rulers.

This land had varied fortunes. The home of the Babylonians—one of the most important of the Semitic families and one of the most ancient civilizations—it was conquered by Cyrus the Persian, about 540 B. C. E. About the year 330 it was taken by Alexander in his triumphant march through Asia and became part of the Seleucidan Empire, (see p. 28). This brought into it something of a Greek atmosphere. In the year 160 B. C. E. it was conquered by Parthia—an Asiatic nation dwelling south of the Caspian Sea. This regime continued for four centuries, though the Parthians exercised no influence whatever on the Jews. In the year 226 A. C. E. a Neo-Persian dynasty was re-established. This continued till the coming of the Arabs in the seventh century —a later story.

During all these changes in the controlling power, the Jews continued in Babylonia undisturbed. When Judea fell, in the year 70, almost an annihilating catastrophe to those at hand, their life went on without a break, except that it brought to the new home a large number of Jewish refugees. So that by the second century after the Christian era, Babylon had become the centre of greatest Jewish influence and activity. Trajan had tried to conquer the land, but failed (p. 203). So Babylonian Jews remained out of the reach of the Roman grasp.

Resh Galutha.

What was their status here? Since the time of Cyrus the government had been Persian. Given almost complete political independence, the Jews simply paid taxes to the ruling power. As Persia had granted to the Jews the privilege of administering their own affairs in Judea so, naturally, the same permission was granted in Babylonia. There was this important difference. The head of the Judean community had been the High Priest; those were the days when the Temple stood. When we turn to Babylon in the century following Jerusalem's overthrow, we find the governor of the Jewish community was called Exilarch or *Resh Galutha*, Head of the Exile. *Galuth* was a word freighted with emotional meaning to our fathers.

The Resh Galutha, as distinct from the High Priest of an earlier day, was entirely a civil functionary, and the office carried more power. As Exilarch he was recognized by the government and occupied a place among the Persian nobility. At first but collectors of revenue, these officials were later treated as princes—perhaps as a mark of gratitude for the Jewish support when Parthia was fighting Rome. A good deal of pomp came to be associated with the office. These Exilarchs were all chosen from the House of David, and so represented a quasi-royalty. The line continued unbroken till the eleventh century. They exercised complete judicial authority among their own people. Unlike the Patriarch or Nasi of Judea, with whom we may also compare them, they were not necessarily learned in the Law.

The Jews of Babylonia were for the most part engaged in agriculture, commerce and handicrafts, and even in work on the canals. Fortunate indeed were they to have again secured a home beyond Rome's cruel control, where, undisturbed, they might live their own life. In the study of the Law they found inexhaustible material for intellectual and religious activity. But how was religion taught and the continuity of Judaism maintained in Babylonia?

At first they were entirely dependent on the Palestinian Academies established in Jamnia and Lydda and other places after the fall of Jerusalem, and were altogether subject to the Judean Sanhedrin. Many students traveled to Palestine to study at its schools. But after a time the community grew strong enough intellectually to establish academies of its own. The heads of the Academies corresponded to the Judean Patriarchs, only that all civil power was vested in the Resh Galutha, above mentioned.

Step by step the Babylonian students increased in learning; and, acquiring confidence, came to feel less the need of the guidance of the parent authority. Soon this settlement further east claimed independent jurisdiction. This was bitterly resented in Palestine. The removal of the Sanhedrin to Jamnia had been the first wrench. The second was the removal of the central authority from the Holy Land altogether, to distant Babylonia. But Palestine could not stem the tide. As the fortunes of the Jews declined there, its schools declined with them. Steadily waned, too, the authority of the Patriarch.

Rab and Samuel.

Babylonian schools also produced great scholars, some as renowned as those of Palestine. For reasons given on p. 227 they are all *Amoräim*, not *Tannäim*. Let us mention first *Abba Areka*, popularly called by his many disciples Rab (Rabbi), "*the* teacher," who flourished in Babylonia a few years after the Mishna had been compiled in Palestine. Apart from his duties as expounder of the Law, the Resh Galutha appointed him to the position of supervisor of weights and measures. Occasioned by this occupation to travel in outlying districts, he discovered the ignorance of the remoter congregations. This led to his establishment of the Academy of Sora about the year 220. It continued a seat of Jewish study for eight hundred years. Hundreds of pupils flocked to Rab's Academy. Some he maintained from his own purse. At the same time the study hours were arranged to give pupils the opportunity of earning their living. Some lectures were delivered to the public at large. An Academy almost as famous was established at Pumbeditha; another at Nehardea.

It was not only in the expounding of ritual and civil law to which Rab devoted his energies, but also to raising the ethical standard of the people. For the austere simplicity and purity of Jewish life had sadly degenerated in Babylonia. Wonderfully salutary and effective was the influence of Rab in his moral crusade. He made the betrothal and marriage laws more strict and more decorous. He also strengthened the authority of the Courts of Justice by resort to excommunication of refractory persons. Deservedly was this modest man called the Hillel of his day.

Usually associated with the name of Rab was the versatile *Mar Samuel*, his contemporary. He was essentially the rationalist of his age who discouraged with his hard common sense the dreamers who were awaiting the speedy and miraculous coming of the Messiah. In Jewish Law his ability chiefly was directed toward the interpretation of civil jurisprudence, for which he was especially fitted. As judge of the Court of Nehardea, he made a brilliant record. His most famous decision and that which most affected the Jews, was expressed in the phrase, *dina d'malchuthah dina,*—"The law of the land is the law for us." This means that it is our duty as Jews to obey the laws of the countries in which we live. This principle tended to reconcile our fathers to the lands of their exile, taught them their true relation to them, and was in the spirit of the message of Jeremiah to the very first exiles in Babylon—"Seek the peace of the country whither ye are exiled and pray to the Lord for its welfare." The ultimate result of Samuel's dictum was that the better the Jew, the better the patriot.

Samuel had the courage of his convictions. For when the Persian king, Shabur I (under whose rule the Babylonian Jews were living), was engaged in war against Asia Minor, many Jews fell, who were fighting in the ranks on the opposing side. Yet he would not countenance mourning for his fallen coreligionists since they had fought against his king!

Babylonia, with its broad unbroken plains that gave such wide survey of the heavens, had early become the cradle of astronomy, and Babylonian Jews were expert in this science. So versed was Samuel in the course of the stars that he once said, "The tracks of the heavens are as familiar to me as the streets of Nehardea." His astronomical knowledge enabled him to arrange a fixed calendar and made Babylon further independent of Judea in deciding the dates of the festivals. As already stated (p. 186) these had previously been decided by the appearance of the New Moon in Palestine. Samuel was also a renowned physician and applied rational remedies, when the world of his day clung to superstitious nostrums. But medicine and astronomy were characteristic accomplishments of the Jewish rabbis. Samuel did not scorn to learn from the Persian sages. While greatly esteemed, not all of his contemporaries realized how profound a scholar he was. For in a sense he was a man in advance of his time. We understand him better to-day.

With all his intellectual gifts, he was modest, self-denying and wonderfully tender-hearted. He had many laws passed to safeguard the interests of the poor and helpless, and, decided that the Court must take orphans under its fatherly protection.

In the patriotic incident above mentioned, it was seen that he practised what he preached. Here is another instance. He had laws passed against exorbitant prices. When grain he had purchased cheaply, rose in price, he still sold it cheaply to the poor. What a needed lesson for our times! Here are two of his maxims:—

"Deceive neither Jew nor pagan."
"Respect the man in the slave."

Zoroastrism.

What was the religion of Israel's Babylonian neighbors? The Parthians were inclined toward Hellenism and exercised no religious influence on the Jews. But when the Persians again gained control of Babylonia (226 C. E.,) they brought with them their own religion—Zoroastrism. Zoroaster or

Zarathustra was a great religious genius who flourished about 800 B.C.E. He reformed the old cult of the *Magi*, i. e., a caste of Persian priests and sages. His teachings are contained in the Parsee bible—the *Avesta*. The cardinal doctrine of this faith was dualism; that is, it explained the existence of evil in the world as the persistent conflict of two great spirits—Ormuzd, spirit of light and good (God), and Ahriman (devil), spirit of darkness and evil. In the process of ages Ormuzd and good will prevail. The sun is the visible representation of Ormuzd and fire the expression of his energy. So Ormuzd was worshipped under the symbol of fire. This worship spread over a large part of Asia. It did not deserve to be classed with the idolatries of the heathen world that brought so many immoralities in their train, for we see even while we must disagree with its recognition of a devil, that it expressed exalted ideas and urged its followers to live moral lives. But the rise of this Neo-Persian dynasty, awakening new religious energy, led later to a passing persecution of all non-fire-worshippers.

At the opening of the sixth century, Mazdak, a new zealot for the religion of the Magi in Babylonia, tried to impose on all under his rule certain dangerous doctrines of his own that tended to undermine the moral foundations of society. Naturally the Jews, always normally a chaste people, stoutly resisted. This meant fight. Again must they lay down the book for the sword, or rather, take up the sword for the cause of the Book. Led by the Resh Galutha Mar Zutra II, they actually succeeded in throwing off the Persian yoke altogether for some seven years; but they were, of course, ultimately brought into subjection, and consequently many martyrs were added to the Jewish roll of honor.

Babylonian Schools.

This incident carries us ahead of our narrative. To return:

The Babylonian schools—*Metibta*, as each was called (*Yeshiba*, Hebrew), continued to grow until they drew far more students than had been reached in Palestine, many of whom became great Amoraim. Babylon, in fact, was now a very large Jewish colony regulated by the laws of the Bible and Mishna as interpreted in the Academies. Even the Resh Galutha was in later times often a Jewish scholar, as for example, Mar Ukba. In addition to the *Resh Metibta* —head of the School—there was a *Resh Kallah*, President of the General Assembly—an institution not found in the Palestinian Academies. These were for the benefit of visiting students and met twice a year in the months of Adar and Elul.

Most renowned of Rab's successors was Rab Huna, who died in 297.

Following the recognized precedent, not to use the Law as a spade, he earned his living by farming.

Reverence was shown to Judea now only in so far that the pious desired to be buried there. Later persecutions in Roman provinces, of which Judea was one, brought still more refugees to Babylonia.

The next generation of scholars we must pass over rapidly with just a word. In Pumbeditha we may mention Rabba, who believed in the saving sense of humor, and also set himself the more serious occupation of classifying the Halachoth accumulated since the Mishna had been compiled. He gave to his students this fine principle,—"He who does good for reasons other than the good itself, it were better he had never been born." The method of deduction as taught in the Babylonian Schools was more subtle than that of Judea. Its hair-splitting tendency in the next generation of Amoräim occasionally degenerated into casuistry. But even that was the fault of a virtue.

NOTES AND REFERENCES.

Patriotism and Judaism.

Mar Samuel's theory and practice best answered the query of the anti-Semite, Goldwin Smith, "Can Jews be Patriots?" The American Jews had to face this problem in the Civil War of 1861, when they fought in both the Union and the Confederate ranks.

Read Dr. Mielziner's *Introduction to the Talmud*, (Bloch Publ. Co.), chap. iv.

This book is particularly recommended in connection with the chapters on Mishna, Talmud and the Academies.

Read Article "Babylonia," *Jewish Encyclopedia*, vol. ii.

Theme for discussion:

Is the Jew's first duty to his countryman or to his coreligionist?

CHAPTER XXXIII.

CHRISTIANITY THE STATE CHURCH OF ROME.

Rome's Decline.

Now we must turn our glance westward again—to Rome. At the death of Antoninus Pius in 161, two emperors reigned conjointly—Varus, a degenerate, and Marcus Aurelius, a philosopher. The Roman Empire was becoming steadily demoralized. It was at the mercy of a series of degraded creatures who engaged in scandalous conflicts for the bauble of royal power. At times the purple was offered to the highest bidder.

But in 222 the throne came into the hands of the high-minded Alexander Severus. Unlike most of his predecessors, he respected Judaism, and Hillel's Golden Rule was inscribed on the walls of his palace. So his reign meant thirteen pleasant years for the Jews—a little break of sunshine through the lowering clouds.

After the death of Severus, degeneracy again set in and usurper after usurper seized the throne. Rarely was the monotony of upstart emperors broken by a better type of man such as Diocletian. The demoralized condition of the State was reflected in the people at large. Paganism, even at its best, had failed as a scheme of life. Roman society was hopelessly corrupt and on the eve of collapse. The people no longer believed in the supposed divinities Jupiter and Apollo. The philosophers tried to explain them away as abstract ideas. The ceremonies of the temple became mummeries. The augurs (priests who were supposed to indicate the nature of events by the flight and cries of birds) could not look each other in the face without laughing.

The more earnest prayed for something better. Had Judaism not been discredited and under a ban and its observers spurned as an alien race, it might have been more largely sought—though its ceremonial code was exacting, its moral code severe, and its sole spiritual God seemed abstract and aloof to worshippers of divinities that could be seen. Judaism made not an iota of concession to win a single pagan to the fold. As it was, in spite of discouraging conditions, many would-be proselytes knocked at the doors of the Synagogue.

Why Christianity Appealed to Romans.

But for many reasons, Christianity was in a better condition to make converts. Most of its adherents had come through conversion, and proselytism was a cardinal item in its program. The eagerness of the Christians to bring a religious message to the heathen, deserves high praise and must not be underrated, though they betrayed weakness in being too ready to make concessions to pagan nations for the sake of winning converts. The semi-idolatrous idea that Jesus was at once man and God was a familiar conception to the pagan mind. The dramatic picture of his dying on the cross to save mankind appealed to their emotions. The treatment of the Hebrew expression "holy spirit," as a being—a separate divinity, introduced a third element into the God-idea—the "Holy Ghost," (old English: spirit.) This made the Christian divinity a Trinity: God, the Father, Jesus the Son, and the Holy Ghost. But a three-headed God, so revolting to Jewish ideas, was quite a recognized theological notion in the heathen world.

With these additions, so alluring to the pagan mind, the nobler Jewish teachings, which were Christianity's ethical foundations, were more readily accepted. Christianity became popular in Rome. Its adherents were found in all ranks. When they were a small and feeble group, the Roman emperors had persecuted them. But now, they were in the majority. The tables were turned. Only minorities are persecuted. Alas the Jews remained a minority.

Constantine.

Thus it was that an emperor named Constantine decided first to give toleration to all cults and ultimately to adopt Christianity—"partly from a genuine moral sympathy, yet doubtless far more in the well-grounded belief that he had more to gain from the zealous sympathy of its professors than to lose by the aversion of those who still cultivated a languid paganism." This act made it the religion of the empire. But since Rome was mistress of half the civilized world, this acquisition of power and numbers at once gave to the new Faith an eminence it has never lost. The effect of this promotion was profound and lasting and vitally affected the destiny of Israel.

Judaism and Christianity Contrasted.

The attitude of enthroned Christianity was at once inimical to the parent Faith. At first sight it would seem that it might be more kindly disposed to a religion to which it owed so much and to which it was so closely related. Alas to confess it—for such is human nature—the very closeness of the relationship was the cause of its enmity. It regarded the very persistence of Judaism as a denial of its theories and as a challenge to its claims. Christianity declared the law abrogated; Judaism called it religion's keystone. Christianity declared that the Messiah had come; Judaism maintained he had not. Christians called Jesus a divinity—Son of God; the Jews spurned this as blasphemy. The Church taught a Trinity; the Synagogue made the indivisible Unity of God its cardinal principle. Spiritual monotheism became for the Jew a passion.

The first act by which Christianity exercised its new power was to prohibit Jews from making converts to Judaism and to reward those who deserted it. Thus it conspired for the gradual elimination of the Jewish Faith.

As its ranks rapidly swelled, Christianity continued to make consciously and unconsciously more and more concessions to the heathen beliefs and customs that were deeply rooted in the hearts of people, who accepted the new creed more or less superficially. The original Essene ideas from which it had sprung were completely lost to view. Taking the imperial government as its model, the Church reproduced Roman administration in its systematic organization, even to its despotic demand of sole sway. It enforced a rigid uniformity of doctrine; it organized a hierarchy of patriarchs and bishops whose power was enforced by the State and whose provinces corresponded with the administrative divisions of the Empire, the emperor being head of the Church. In the year 325 a Council was called at Nicæa (Asia Minor) to draw up the official creed of Christianity. For it laid great stress on *belief*. This marked another distinction from Judaism, which, so far, had formulated no creed and had no particular theory of salvation. The Nicæan Council condemned the doctrines of the followers of Arius, a Christian whose idea of God was closer to Judaism, and declared the equal eternity and divinity of the three persons of the Trinity, with more decided emphasis. So the Arians were henceforth regarded as heretics. It further decided, that the Festival of Easter (which was the Jewish Passover readapted to commemorate the resurrection of Jesus) should now be arranged independently of the Jewish calendar.

The policy of suppression directed against Judaism commenced by Constantine was continued with greater ardor by his son, Constantius. He forbade intermarriage and imposed the penalty of death on Jews who made proselytes of Christian slaves. He even prohibited their converting heathen slaves. Further prohibitive acts followed. This hostile attitude was continued for centuries.

Thus the Jews in the Roman Empire were transferred from a heathen to a Christian regime. Quietly they continued on the even tenor of their way and prayed with greater fervency for the restoration of their ancestral home and for the speedy coming of the Messiah; it meant for them the coming of light and liberty.

The Calendar.

It became necessary for Hillel II., Palestinian Patriarch, in 359, to establish a fixed calendar based on that of Samuel of Babylon, (p. 234) to guide the people as to the time of celebrating New Moon and Festivals, as in these troublous times they could not always transmit the news obtained by observing the heavens. But the "second" day of the Festivals, for lands outside of Palestine, now no longer needed, was maintained as a matter of sentiment and is maintained still in conservative Judaism.

This planning of a Jewish calendar by which the Festivals were computed perpetually and yet kept in their natural seasons, was a wonderful piece of astronomical and arithmetical ingenuity. For a lunar year of twelve months is shorter than a solar year of three-hundred and sixty-five and a quarter days. To average the difference and thus prevent, for example, Passover eventually occurring in Autumn and Tabernacles in Spring, an additional month (second Adar) was added seven times in every nineteen years. Further, the calendar had to be so devised that certain Festivals should not fall on undesirable days —for example to prevent the Day of Atonement falling on Friday or Sunday. This ancient calendar is still our guide for the Jewish year.

CHAPTER XXXIV.

THE DIVISION OF THE ROMAN EMPIRE.

Julian.

But a brief check was made on Christian advance and its pitiless attempt to suppress Judaism in the coming to the throne of Julian in 361. For this emperor did not endorse the new religion, but accepted the old Roman cult of the Pantheon, though in its most idealized form, preferring to purify instead of abolishing it. But it was too late; it had been weighed in the balance and found wanting.

Julian, whom the Church styled "the Apostate," was both tolerant and philanthropic, and a man who fostered learning. As between Christianity and Judaism, though bred in the former, to which he continued to grant perfect freedom of observance, his inclination turned rather toward the latter, and he held it in high esteem. He removed the restrictive laws and special taxes against Judaism, imposed by his predecessors. He even took steps for the rebuilding of the Temple at Jerusalem. The Jews were transported with delight and began at once sending contributions toward its erection with greater zeal than was even shown, according to Scripture, by that generation in the wilderness in their gifts toward the Tabernacle. The Christians looked on with consternation, and regarded every unfavorable interruption as the miraculous intervention of heaven. Not a supposed miracle however, but a real event, brought the project to nought. Julian died on the battlefield.

Two Roman Empires.

In the meantime Rome was failing fast. The conflict for the throne on the death of each new emperor, showed that the Empire was crumbling from within. Long before the days of Constantine armies were electing their generals to the imperial dignity all over the empire. The throne was propped up a little longer by gaudy trappings, but this meant heavier taxation and further slavery. Finally the overgrown and undermined body split in twain, each half maintaining a separate existence. Byzantium, afterwards called Constantinople, was the capital of the Roman Empire of the East, while the city of Rome remained the centre of the Western half. The division was finally completed in the year 395. Although both were Christian, the duel empires were menaced by too many enemies from without to have the leisure to renew the anti-Jewish laws—for a time.

Huns, Goths and Vandals.

The influx of "barbarians," as all people outside of Rome were called, now came thick and fast. While some were absorbed in a friendly way, impressed with Rome's grandeur, and even served in its army, younger and healthier peoples looked contemptuously upon the decaying Empire and sought to absorb it rather than be absorbed. Even before the division, Julian had to keep off the incursions of the Franks and Alemanni (Germans). Theodosius, called the Great, bravely resisted the inflowing races, but he fought against destiny and therefore fought in vain. Driven by the Huns, a Scythian people from Tartary, under the leadership of Attila, the Goths crossed the Danube into the Roman territory as refugees; but cruelly treated, became enemies and began devastating the Western division of the empire. Alaric in 410 had sacked the imperial city itself. The Goths, to whom after much fighting, Rome granted important concessions, also—like Rome—fell into two divisions—the Ostragoths (Eastern), who settled on the Black Sea, and the Visigoths (Western), who occupied Dacia from the Dnieper to the Danube.

These details make dry reading; but the break-up of the Roman Empire after occupying the centre of the world's stage for four hundred years, marks the transition from antiquity to the Middle Ages. This change of his environment was in a measure to change the Jew.

Let us complete this general survey. Already hordes of Suevi, Burgundians, Alemanni and Vandals had invaded Gaul and set up a Vandal Empire in Spain, where they contended with the Visigoths for control. Genseric, called the scourge of God, invaded Africa in 429 and devastated the coast from Gibraltar to Carthage. It was he, by the way, who seized the Temple vessels that Titus had taken from Jerusalem. They had passed, like their first owners, through many vicissitudes. Next, the Huns began laying waste the Western Empire, though finally defeated by the Gothic king, Theodoric. At last Odoacer, in 476, at the head of barbarian mercenaries, dethroned the last emperor, and the Roman Empire of the West came to an end in that year.

Persecution of the Jews.

In the meantime Christianity held the reins of power in the surviving eastern half of the Roman Empire. Its Church Fathers began to regard it as a part of their function to preach against Judaism. The people at large followed by burning synagogues or turning them into churches. But the Emperor

Theodosius I. protected the Jews. Later, Bishop Cyril cruelly drove them out of Alexandria where they had had such an illustrious career since the days of Alexander the Great. No redress was made to them for loss of home and property. His disciples, following this barbarous precedent, seized the cultured Hypatia, a teacher of Platonic philosophy, whose rare learning had made her home a gathering place for students and scholars,—and the fanatic crowd rent her limb from limb.

But it was a bigoted and savage age. In mentioning the cruelly fanatic bishops, let us not forget the kind ones—Bishop Hilary of Poictiers in Gaul, at whose funeral the sympathetic Jews expressed their sorrow in the recital of Hebrew Psalms.

With Theodosius II, emperor of the eastern division of the Roman Empire, who came to this Byzantine throne in 408, began the systematic restraint of Judaism—the harsh discrimination against Jews before the law. They were prohibited from building new synagogues, from exercising jurisdiction between Christian and Jew, and from owning Christian slaves. The bishops and clergy began fomenting attacks in different localities, forcing baptism on some by threat. Ultimately the Patriarchate of Judea, the office of Nasi, was abolished in 425, after the Hillel family had enjoyed this dignity for three and a half centuries.

Israel suffered, too, at the hands of Christian ascetics who went to grotesque extremes and imposed absurd privations upon themselves to express religious zeal. Some condemned themselves to stand on pillars— hence called "pillar saints"; some to live as hermits in the desert. But with them all Jewish persecution was deemed a kind of piety, the logic being that Jewish beliefs were opposed to the truth and the Jews were the enemies of God. The most famous of these pillar saints was Simeon, surnamed Stylites, meaning pillar. As long as the Roman Empire of the West lasted, Jews were excluded from most public offices. The monies hitherto voluntarily contributed to maintain the Patriarchate were, now that this Palestinian official was deposed, demanded perforce to continue as a Jewish tax to aid a hostile State. Thus did Christian Rome follow the precedent of pagan Rome. This was the kind of treatment that they were now to meet in all Christian lands, marking the beginning of the Jewish *Middle Ages*.

Still Christian divines were glad enough to sit at the feet of Jewish scholars and learn from them the Hebrew tongue. In this way Jerome was enabled to make from the Hebrew a new translation of the Bible into Latin. It was called the *Vulgate* (Latin Vulgata, for public use). It has remained the authorized translation of the Catholic Church to this day.

The Holy Roman Empire, Bryce; chapter ii and iii. (Burt, New York.)

Hypatia, Kingsley.

On the Emperor Julian's relations with the Jews, especially with regard to his proposition of rebuilding the Temple, see two articles in the *Jewish Quarterly Review* vols. v. and x.

Theme for discussion:

What right had the *Eastern* (Byzantine) Empire to the title "Roman?"

Chronological Table.

JEWRY.		ROME.	
Hillel II Introduces fixed		Emperor Julian	361
Calendar into Palestine	359		
Completion of Palestinian		Division of Roman Empire	395
Talmud	409		
Extinction of Palestinian		Rome sacked	410
Patriarchate	425		
Death of Rabbana Ashi,			
editor of Talmud	427	Fall of Western Roman	
Completion of Babylonian		Empire	476
Talmud	500		
Persecution of Jews by			
Mazdak, the Persia	500		

CHAPTER XXXV.

THE TALMUD.

The times were becoming so uncertain in Babylonia as well as in Palestine that the Jews felt it necessary now to collect and *write down* their varied traditions and laws to insure their preservation. The sages could no longer trust the transmission by word of mouth; they could no longer rely on their memories, marvelous though these were. So they were reluctantly compelled to overcome their sentimental objection to writing down these traditions—which, as the very title, *Oral* Law showed, should be transmitted from mouth to mouth, inscribed, as it were, only on the tablets of the mind. Perhaps, too, they felt that writing would crystallize the *Halachoth* at the point where they were transcribed, into unchangeable decisions and prevent their further development. For while unwritten, they were fluid and could be modified from age to age. As a matter of fact, the writing down of the laws *did* tend to crystallize them, and thus retarded the progressive growth of Jewish Law.

The Gemara.

The work of codifying and writing down the Oral Law was commenced by Rabbana Ashi about the year 400. Placed at the head of the declining Academy of Sora, he breathed new life into it. His knowledge won him both esteem and authority such as had been granted to Rabbi Judah ha-Nasi, compiler of the Mishna in Palestine about two hundred years earlier. But Rabbana Ashi's was a vaster task—the compiling of all supplementary laws that had grown out of the Mishna proper and from all the Mishna collections in the course of two hundred years. It included, too, the discussion and incidental material that developed from every legal or moral problem, together with all the logical steps that led to the final deduction. This vast after-growth or commentary was called *Gemara*, which means completion. Together with the Mishna, which formed the text, it was called the Talmud. This commentary, Gemara, is far bulkier than the Mishna. Sometimes a few lines of Mishna would call for pages and pages of Gemara.

For about half a century Rabbana Ashi and his disciples, particularly Rabina, labored on this gigantic task. The completed work was called the *Talmud Babli* (Babylonian), as it was not only written in Babylonia, but contained largely the decisions attained in the Babylonian schools. Though do not forget that its Mishna text was written in Palestine. The final touches were made about the year 500. It contains twelve folio volumes or 2,947 leaves.

A similar work had been done in Palestine about the year 400. This Mishna commentary was called the Palestinian Talmud. Whether it originally contained commentary on all the Mishna we cannot say; but in the copies now extant there is only commentary to the first four of the six sections of the Mishna and to a few additional chapters. For this reason it is a less important work than the Babylonian Talmud and but a quarter of its size. Indeed, when we speak of the Talmud, we usually mean the Talmud Babli.

The Contents.

The two great divisions of *Halacha* and *Agadd* have already been explained in the chapter on the Mishna (xxxi). These same two classes of material, the legal and the narrative, characterize the Gemara. It will be understood at once then that the Talmud is not merely a code of laws for Jewish guidance, though primarily that is its purpose. It gives us also, though incidentally, an insight into the manners and customs of the Jews, their theological views and general reflections on life; their hopes and their sufferings for a period of some six hundred years—"A work in which a whole people had deposited its feelings, its beliefs, its soul." We have fragments of biography of Jewish scholars, bits of inner history under Roman and Persian rule, homely philosophy of the sages; glimpses too of their weaknesses and occasionally of their superstitions —all the more reliable because unconsciously portrayed. Interspersed between their legal discussions will be found an anecdote, an abstract thought of the rabbi whose decision is quoted, a bit of humor, a picture of Oriental civilization. As direct outgrowth of many of their ritual arguments, we are introduced to their science; astronomy and mathematics in the drawing up of their calendar; botany in their agricultural laws; hygiene, anatomy and physiology in the *shechita laws* (slaughtering animals for food); and natural history and medicine in various laws. There is, of course, very unequal value in their data, and naturally they shared some of the errors of their age.

The legal discussions in themselves reveal keen mental acumen, subtle logic, "deductive reasoning raised to the highest power;" they display a vivid sense of justice and philanthropy; and, touches of harshness too—wrung from a patient and forgiving people in the hour of agony.

The study of the Talmud was to become the chief occupation of the Jews for many centuries. It was a world in itself in which they lived, and in which they could forget the cruel world without. Its study reacted on their character. First the Jew made the Talmud, then the Talmud made the Jew.

Talmudic Literature.

Like the Bible, the Talmud produced a literature still vaster than itself. While the *Gemara* is a commentary, it needed later commentaries to explain it to the student—for although so diffuse in treatment, its language is terse. Frequently a letter stands for a word and a word for a sentence. Therefore in editions of the Talmud to-day, Mishna and Gemara together form the text and are printed in the centre of each page, while commentaries in smaller type are grouped around it. Since the days of printing all editions are paged alike.

Saboraim.

After the completion of the Talmud, the work of the Academies became preservative rather than creative. While not adding to the laws now gathered in the Talmud, the rabbis reviewed them and formulated from them complete codes for practical application. This tended to give a finality to the laws so far evolved, which had both its good and bad side. This undertaking gave to this next school of commentators the name of *Saboräim*—revisers or critics—the third group of law expounders. (For first group, *Tannäim*, see p. 186; for second group, *Amoräim*, see page 228). They edited the Talmud and amplified it with *agadistic* material and finally brought it down into the form in which we have it to-day.

NOTES AND REFERENCES.

Language of the Talmud:

The Mishna is written in Hebrew, and so too are some of the older quotations in the Gemara. Many Greek words are adopted, of which *Sanhedrin* is one; some Latin words too. But the bulk of both Gemaras is written in a dialect of Aramaic—we might say Jüdisch-Aramaic just as we speak of Jüdisch-Deutsch to-day.

A knowledge of grammar was brought to Persia (Babylonia) from Greece, which resulted in the important service of introducing vowel points and accents. This tended to simplify the study of Hebrew Scriptures and made the text more certain.

Ethics of Talmud:

The ethics of the Talmud have been touched upon incidentally in preceding chapters, and at length in the two following. For a systematic treatment, read Part iv., Outlines of Talmudic Ethics, in Mielziner's *Introduction to the Talmud*. See also *Ethics of Judaism*, Lazarus (translation), J. P. S. A.

Read "On the Study of the Talmud," *Studies in Judaism*, S. Schechter, J. P. S. A. 1908, for rabbinic parallels with New Testament teachings.

The Law of the Talmud:

In a note on the Mishna it was pointed out that it was free from some defects of Roman law. This does not exclude the fact that the rabbinic *halacha* was largely indebted to Roman law. On this Darmesteter says:

"Certain departments of legislation, such as the laws on slavery and prescription ... are almost entirely inspired by Roman legislation. But all they borrow takes on modifications under the manipulation of the rabbis. The Jewish mind transformed the alien elements by impressing upon them its peculiar character. And from this vast crucible in which three centuries had melted down materials of diverse origin gathered by the schools, was to emerge the essentially uniform and homogeneous work of Talmudic legislation."—*The Talmud*, translated by Henrietta Szold, J. P. S. A.

Themes for Discussion:

(a) Compare Bible and Talmud as literatures.

(b) In what sense can it be said that "the Talmud made the Jew?"

CHAPTER XXXVI.

SAYINGS AND STORIES OF THE SAGES OF THE TALMUD.

"Let me make the ballads of a people and I care not who makes the laws."

The maxims with which the rabbis occasionally endorsed their decisions and the bits of humor with which they relieved the tension of argument, may give a deeper insight into their character than their laws. These morsels of homely philosophy and casual reflections on human experience best reveal, too, their outlook on the world and on life. So in its way the *Agada* is quite as precious a legacy from the Fathers as the *Halacha*.

The writing of parables of which some of the rabbis were masters, is almost a lost art; it seems to have died out in literature. But no moral is pointed so aptly as through a tale and no teaching impressed so lastingly as through a story.

Many a Hebrew philosopher like Socrates, the Greek, and the yet earlier prophet (*nabi*) would make the highway his school-house and the passing crowd his disciples. Darmesteter suggests that the lesson might have been conveyed in somewhat in the following way:

"Who wishes to live long," cries an *Agadist* in the open street; "who wishes to buy happiness?" The original questions attract a crowd demanding to know the orator's secret. "Thou desirest to live many days," he answers, "thou wishest to enjoy peace and happiness? Keep thy tongue from evil and thy lips from speaking guile. Seek peace and pursue it. Depart from the evil and do good." And paraphrasing these words of the Psalmist (Ps. xxxiv, 13-15), he developed his ideas in the midst of the attentive crowd.

The parables and maxims that follow have been gathered promiscuously and are classified here under appropriate heads.

God.

"Show me your omnipresent God," said the Emperor Trajan to R. Joshua. "He cannot be seen, but let us try to look at one of his ambassadors," replied the rabbi, pointing to the midday sun. "I cannot," said Trojan, "the light dazzles me." "Can you then expect to gaze upon the resplendent glory of the Creator?"

A Roman philosopher asked: "If your God dislikes idolatry, why does he not destroy the idols?" Quickly came the wise reply: "Shall He destroy the sun and the moon because the foolish worship them and thus injure the innocent also?"

"Who denies idolatry may be called a Jew."

"He who possesses knowledge of God's law without fear of Him, the Lawgiver, is like one to whom the inner keys of a treasury have been given, but the outer ones withheld."

"God rejoiceth not at the fall of the wicked." When the angels were about to chant their morning hymn on the day the Egyptians were drowning, God stayed them: "The works of My hands are sinking in the deep and would you sing a song?"

"Without God's law there would be neither heaven nor earth."

"The aim of creation is man's fulfilment of God's will."

"The consciousness of God's presence is the great teaching of religion."

"In all God's creation there is not a single object without a purpose."

Providence.

"Man should ever say: Whatever the All-merciful doeth is for the best."

"Who hath bread for to-day and feareth for the morrow, is a man of little faith."

"God adjusts the burden to the camel."

"We cannot comprehend either the prosperity of the wicked or the suffering of the righteous."

Rabbi Akiba was alone in the wilderness at night with but a lamp to study the Law, a rooster to waken him, and an ass to carry him. He was inhospitably driven from a village in which he asked shelter, and had to camp in the open fields. A wind blew out his light so that he could not study; a wolf destroyed his rooster; a lion devoured his ass. But at the occurrence of each calamity, he still said: "Praised be God, whate'er He does is for the best." Entering the village next morning, he found its inhabitants slain by robbers.

Complete the providential application.

There is no mediator between Israel and God.

"If misfortune befalls a man, let him not cry to Michael or Gabriel, but let him come unto Me: everyone who calls on the name of the Lord shall be saved."

God scattered Israel through the world that the Gentile might learn the purity of Jewish teaching.

Prayer.

"Prayer without devotion is body without breath."

"Better little prayer with devotion than much, without."

"He who asks God for his neighbor what he needs for himself, his own wants will be first answered."

"Blessed be the mother who sends her children to the House of Prayer."

(See prayer and sacrifice, page 188.)

Righteousness.

"Who gains the approval of good men, may hope for that of Heaven."

"One should conduct himself as carefully before man as before God."

"What shall man do to live; kill his (lower) self. What shall man do to die; sustain his (lower) self."

"The righteous are greater in death than in life."

"A good man lost to his age is like a lost pearl. The pearl remains a pearl wherever it may be; only the owner feels its loss."

"Alas for him who mistakes branch for tree, shadow for substance."

"To him who lacks nobility of heart, nobility of blood is of no avail."

"Good men promise little and do much; wicked men promise much and no nothing."

"There are three classes of friends of God; the wronged who seek not revenge; workers for the love of God; cheerful sufferers."

"The righteous need no monuments, their deeds are their monuments."

"Three names are given to a man: the first by his parents, the second by the world, the third by his works."

"The best preacher is the heart, the best teacher time, the best book the world, the best friend God."

"The greatest of heroes is he who turneth an enemy into a friend."

The Study of the law.

"Study is more meritorious than sacrifice."

"A scholar is greater than a prophet."

"The soul of man is the lamp of the Lord; the law is light. God's light (the Law), is in man's hands: man's light (the soul), is in God's hands. Respect His light and he will respect thine."

"The Gentile who studies the Law is as a High Priest."

"Who studies the Law in private, it will proclaim him in public."

"Scholars increase the world's peace. They are called builders for they are engaged in upbuilding the world."

"I have learnt much from my teachers, more from my fellow students, most from my pupils."

"The wise learn from all."

"He only is free who engages in the study of the Law."

"The aim of learning is moral perfection."

Education in General.

In the days when the Temple was still standing, education of the young formed an important part in the life of the Jewish people. They had schools in and out of Judea. Ignorance was despised. "A fool cannot be pious," 'twas said. The studies to be undertaken in accordance with the age of the children, the previous home preparation, the number to a class, were all carefully planned. The curriculum comprised law and morals deduced from Scripture and rabbinic teaching, history, grammar, languages, according to the time,

Aramaic, Persian, Greek or Latin. Also to older scholars—medicine, hygiene, astronomy, botany, zoology.

All Scriptural quotation of flowers were applied to children and schools. "Teacher" was the highest title.

"The world depends on the children in the school."

"A city without school-children will be destroyed."

"Touch not mine anointed." These are the school-children. "And to my prophets do no harm." These are the disciples of the wise.

"You should revere your teacher even more than your father. The latter only brought you into this world; the former points the way to the next. But blessed is the son who has learnt from his father, and the father who has instructed his son."

"Who does not educate his children is their enemy and his own."

"Who is best taught? He who has learnt from his mother."

"Who acquires knowledge without imparting it is like a myrtle in a desert."

"Who are you whose prayer has alone been answered?" "I am a teacher of little children."

"Bestow most care on the children of the poor, for from them will go forth the Law."

"Pride is a sign of ignorance."

"A single coin in a jar makes the most noise."

"The rivalry of scholars advances science."

"If thou acquireth knowledge what canst thou lack; if thou lackest knowledge what canst thou acquire!"

Parents and Children.

"Three share a man: God, father and mother. When one honors mother and father, God says He dwells among them; and in honoring them one honors Him."

"Blessed is the generation in which the old listen to the young; doubly blessed when the young listen to the old."

"Do not threaten children with punishment you do not intend to inflict."

"Only when a parent induces a child to commit sin, is disobedience justifiable."

"Do not limit your children to your knowledge, for they were born in another age."

Rabbi Eliezar pointed out to his disciples the example of Damah. His mother often abused him, yet all he would say on such occasions was: 'Enough, dear mother, enough.' Once the priests came to him to purchase a jewel. Finding his father resting against the casket in which it lay, he asked them to come later. They offered him a larger price. He replied, 'I would not disturb my father's rest for all the wealth of the world.' They waited. When his father woke he brought the jewel; they tendered him the larger sum offered the second time. He declined it, saying: 'I will not barter the satisfaction of having done by duty, for gold; give me what you first offered and I will be content.'

Albini allowed none of his five children to open the door for their grandfather or attend his wants. That privilege must be his. Once his father asked for water. On returning he found the old man asleep. So there he remained, glass in hand, until his father awakened.

"Reverence mother and father by neither sitting in their seats nor standing in their places, by not interrupting their speech nor criticising their arguments and by giving heed to their wishes."

"Support the aged without reference to religion, and the learned without reference to age."

Woman.

The exalted place given to woman in Jewish teaching is in pleasing and remarkable contrast with her inferior position in the orient and throughout antiquity generally. In some respects she is made subordinate in the Jewish law, and is given a comparatively passive place in religious life; but on the whole the sages of the Talmudic era nobly resisted the example of their environment, in the reverence they paid to womanhood.

"God gave more understanding to woman than to man."

"All blessing in the household comes through the wife; therefore should her husband honor her."

"Man should consult his wife, treating her as a companion not a plaything; making her what God intended, a help-meet for him."

"Be careful not to cause woman to cry, for God counts her tears."

"He who loves his wife as himself and honors her more than himself, will train his children rightly."

Rab Jose: "I never call my wife *wife*, but *home*."

"He who dependeth on his wife's earnings will be deprived of blessing."

"Who is rich? Who has a good wife."

"Culture in woman is better than gold."

"Woman's sense of shame is deeper than man's."

"He who has no wife is not a complete man."

"Israel was redeemed from Egypt on account of the virtue of its women."

CHAPTER XXXVII.

SAYINGS AND STORIES OF THE SAGES.

(CONTINUED)

Work.

"Work dignifies the worker."

"He enjoys life who lives by the work of his hands."

"Work is more pleasing in God's sight than ancestral merit."

"Strip a carcass in the street and take pay for it, and say not: 'I am a priest or a great man and this work is beneath me.'"

The Fourth Commandment makes rest conditional on work.

"God did not dwell in the midst of Israel till they had built a sanctuary."

"Work must not be neglected for study."

"He who says 'I have toiled and not found,' believe him not; he who says 'I have not toiled yet have I found,' believe him not."

"Who does not bring his son up to a trade teaches him to be a robber."

"It is well to add a trade to your studies to be free from sin."

"Position cannot honor the man; the man must honor the position."

"Famine passes by the workman's door."

"Artisans need not interrupt their labors to rise before the passing scholars."

"Rather be a menial than a dependent."

Here is a characteristic bit of rabbinic *midrash* on a Bible text: "The dove returned ... and in her mouth an olive leaf" (Gen. viii, 11):—

"She said to the Holy One: 'Rather let my food be as bitter as the olive, but received from Thy hands, than honey-sweet but dependent on the hand of man.'"

"It is one's duty to support a slave crippled in his employ."

"O, River Euphrates, why is thy current not heard? My deeds testify for me; what is sown at my shores will bloom in thirty days."

"Judge by deeds not works."

"Say little, do much."

"Like a tree, man is known by his fruit."

"Say not, 'I will do nothing,' because thou canst not do everything."

"One good deed leadeth to another."

"Thy works commend thee; thy works repel thee."

"He who makes another perform a deed, is greater than the doer."

"A worthy action done in this world anticipates and leads the doer to the world to come."

"When God said to Adam, 'Thorns and thistles shall it (the earth) bring forth for thee,' Adam wept and said: 'Lord of the world, shall I and my ass eat from the same crib?' But when God further said, 'by the sweat of thy brow shalt thou eat bread,' Adam was cheered and comforted."

Truth.

"Truth is the seal of God."

"Jerusalem was destroyed because of the lack of truth-telling people."

"Who breaks his word is as one who worships an idol."

"Thus is the liar punished: even when he speaks the truth, none hearken."

"Truth is heavy, therefore few carry it."

Justice and Honesty.

"Let justice pierce the mountain."

"The judge who renders a true judgment for but one brief hour, is deemed as though he shared with God in the work of creation."

"Judge every man in the scale of merit."

"Judge not your neighbor till you stand in his place."

"Woe to the generation whose judges must be judged."

"Rabbi Phineas hospitably received two strangers. On departing they accidentally left behind them a few measures of barley. They returned a year later. 'Presumably our barley is spoilt by this time: never mind.' 'Nay,' said Phineas, leading them to his barn. He gave them five hundred measures of barley, the product of their few measures, which he had sown in his fields."

He who lends on usury is compared to a shedder of blood.

"Thy neighbor's honor and his possessions should be as dear to thee as thine own."

"Be honest in trade: if goods are damaged, acknowledge it."

"Credit and mutual trust should be the foundations of commerce."

A prince once made a law that a receiver of stolen property should be hanged and the thief go free.

"Not the mouse but the hole is the thief."

"An Israelite must not deceive even an idolater."

"Go to sleep without supper, but rise without debt."

"Rabbi Simon bought a camel of an Ishmaelite and later discovered diamonds under its saddle. 'The blessing of God maketh rich,' said his overjoyed servant. 'Nay,' rebuked the rabbi: 'Return those diamonds; I bought a camel, not precious stones.'"

Alexander, the world conqueror, came across a simple people in Africa who knew not war. He lingered to learn their ways. Two citizens appeared before the chief with this point of dispute. One had bought a piece of land and discovered a treasure in it; he claimed that this belonged to the seller and wished to return it. The seller, on the other hand, declared that he sold the land with all it might contain. So he refused to accept the treasure. The chief, turning to the buyer, said: "Thou hast a son?" "Yes." And addressing the seller: "Thou hast a daughter?" "Yes." "Marry one to the other and make the treasure their marriage portion." They left content. "In my country," said the surprised Alexander, "the disputants would have been imprisoned and the treasure confiscated for the king." "Is your country blessed by sun and rain?" asked the chief. "Yes," replied Alexander. "Does it contain cattle?" "Yes." "Then it must be for the sake of these innocent animals that the sun shines upon it; surely its people are unworthy of such blessing."

Kindness.

"Whoever showeth compassion is as the seed of Abraham."

"Remove from the highway what might endanger the property of others."

"To deserve mercy, practice it."

A sage, meeting Elijah in the thoroughfare, asked him to reveal the worthiest in the passing throng. First he singled out a turnkey. "He was kind to his prisoners." Next he pointed out two tradesmen. The sage ran to them and said, "Tell me your saving works." They were surprised. "We are only poor workmen, said to be cheerful and good-natured; we sympathize with people in sorrow and we try to reconcile friends who have quarreled. That is all."

"Be not cruel to inferiors."

"Rather be thrown into a fiery furnace than bring anyone to public shame."

"He who declines to tend the sick and he who hateth his neighbor, are as though they shed blood."

"Even though thy left hand pushes from thee, let thy right hand draw towards thee."

"Hospitality is a form of divine worship."

"Cast no stone in the well from which thou hast drunk."

"One should not partake of his own meal until his animals are first provided for."

"He who has no mercy on dumb animals should himself suffer pain."

While Moses was tending the flock of Jethro he noticed a lamb stray from the fold. He followed it; it did not stop until it reached a pool and there its slaked its thirst. "Thou dear innocent creature," said Moses, "had I but known thy wishes, I myself would have borne thee in my arms to the water." So he gently carried it back to the flock. Then was a voice heard from heaven exclaiming: "Moses, thou hast shown such compassion for the dumb sheep, thou art indeed worthy to be the shepherd of the flock of Israel."

"Give me your blessing," said R. Nachman to R. Isaac. He replied, "Thy request reminds me of the story of a weary traveler, who, after the day's exhaustion reached a well-watered date tree. Refreshed by its fruit and rested in its shade, he gratefully desired to bestow upon it a blessing. 'What can I wish thee; thou already hast foliage, shade, fruit, water; I can but pray that thy offshoots may flourish like thee,' 'Now, R. Nachman, thou already hast learning, wealth, children; I can only wish that thy descendants may be blessed like thee.'"

Charity.

"Charity (righteousness) delivereth from death."

"Charity is the salt of wealth."

"He gives little who gives much with a frown, he gives much who gives little with a smile."

"The truly beneficent seek out the poor."

"He who closes the door on the poor may have to open it to the physician."

"Charity is greater than alms-giving; alms-giving is a duty to the poor only; charity both to rich and poor."

"He who gives charity in secret is greater than Moses."

"A miser is as wicked as an idolater."

"Even he who depends on charity should practise it."

Aben-Judah was the most generous of givers to the needy. But storm and pestilence swept away his wealth. There was left but a single field. In contented faith he maintained his family upon that. He only felt the pangs of poverty when the collectors of the poor called and he had nought to give. Then he and his wife decided to sell half their remaining field and hand the proceeds to the charity collectors. "May the Lord restore thee to thy former prosperity," said they and departed. Turning more assiduously than ever to the plough, that very day he unearthed a treasure. When the collectors called the next year he made up the deficiency of the year preceding. On receiving it they said: "Though many exceeded thy donation then, yet we had placed thee at the top of the list, knowing that thy small gift came from want of means, not from inclination."

King Monobases (the son of Helen of Adiabene, who became a proselyte to Judaism, see p. 139), unlocked his ancestral treasures at a time of famine, and distributed them among the poor. His ministers rebuked him saying, "Thy fathers amassed, thou dost squander." "Nay," said the benevolent king, "they preserved earthly, but I, heavenly treasures; theirs could be stolen, mine are beyond reach; theirs were barren, mine are fruitful; they preserved money, I have preserved lives."

Said R. Akiba to the not very charitable Tarphon: "Let me profitably invest some money for you." Tarphon handed his four thousand golden denars. Akiba distributed them among the poor, with the scriptural explanation, "He hath given to the needy, his righteousness endureth forever" (Ps. cxii, 9).

Humility and Patience.

"Teach thy tongue to say: I do not know."

"Meekness is better than sacrifice."

"God teaches us humility. He chose but a low mount, Sinai, from which to promulgate the Decalogue; in a humble bush He revealed himself to Moses; to Elijah, in a still small voice."

"Greatness flees from him who seeks it, and seeks him who flees it."

"Rather be persecuted than persecutor."

"An aged man, whom Abraham hospitably invited to his tent, refused to join him in prayer to the one spiritual God! Learning that he was a fire-worshipper, Abraham drove him from his door. That night God appeared to Abraham in a vision and said: I have borne with that ignorant man for seventy years; could you not have patiently suffered him one night?"

"Seeking the highest good to bestow on Israel, God found nothing better than affliction." ("Sufferance is the badge of all our tribe,"— Shakespeare.)

Rabbi Joshua always advised patience and submission, even under provocation (see pp. 193, 205.) Once he pointed his advice with the apologue of The Lion and the Crane: While devouring prey, the lion got a bone in his throat. He offered a great reward to whomever would remove it. The crane came forward, inserted his long neck down the lion's throat and extracted the bone. He then demanded his reward. "Reward indeed," said the lion; "was it not sufficient reward that I permitted your neck to escape my sacred jaws?"

Make the application to Israel.

A lover, called from the side of his plighted wife, sent letters to her, faithfully promising to return. Long she waited and many mocked and taunted her. But each time she read her lover's letters, her waning faith was strengthened.

Suffering Israel is the maiden; the unseen God her faithful lover; and the Scriptural promises of redemption are His letters.

(Compare Akiba story p. 209).

Sin.

"Put not yourself in the way of temptation, for even David could not resist it."

"What the sages have forbidden on account of appearances, is forbidden even in one's innermost chamber."

"Commit a sin twice and you will think it sin no more." The first step counts.

"Evil passion is at first like a cobweb, and at last like a rope."

"The only indication of the Messiah's advent will be the disappearance of oppression."

"Beware of evil's small beginnings; Jacob's favoritism towards Joseph led to Israel's Egyptian captivity."

"What is the idol man carries within him—his evil passion."

"Sinful thoughts are worse than sin."

"A sinner is foolish as well as wicked."

"The end does not justify the means."

"He who deceives his neighbor would deceive God."

"He who denies his guilt doubles his guilt."

"Sin begets sin."

"Ill weeds grow apace; neglect is their gardener."

"Slander is a species of murder."

"Arrogance is a kingdom without a crown."

"The usurer will have no share in the future life."

"He who can testify in his neighbor's behalf and does not, is a transgressor."

"It is sinful to hate but noble to forgive."

"Say not 'sin cometh from God.' He giveth free choice of life and death."

"The wicked, even while living, are called dead."

R. Simeon said: The whole community must bear the blame of the individual sinner, emphasizing his lesson with this illustration:—Here is a boat-load of passengers. One proceeds to bore a hole through his seat, saying, "I am only piercing my own place." What happens? (Draw the inference.)

Repentance.

"There is no repentance without reparation."

"Better is an hour in repentance and good deeds in this world than all the world to come; though better is an hour of the world to come than the whole of this world."

"Even when the gates of prayer are closed, the gates of tears are open."

"When a man has turned from sin, reproach him no more."

"One who has sinned and repented stands higher in God's favor than the completely righteous."

"Repent one day before thy death." i.e. repent every day.

"Improve thyself and then improve others."

"Love those that reprove thee, hate those that flatter thee."

"The love that shirks from reproof is no love."

"He who does a worthy deed acquires an advocate."

"As the ocean never freezes, so the gate of repentance is never closed."

"If you wish your fast to be acceptable to God let it be accompanied by acts of charity and good-will." (see Isaiah lviii.)

"He who says 'I will sin and repent, I will sin again and repent again,' will ultimately lose power to repent."

A ship once anchored at a beautiful island waiting for a favorable wind. An opportunity was offered the passengers to go ashore. Some thought it safer not to leave the ship at all; the wind might rise, the anchor be raised and they would be left stranded. Others went to the island for a while to explore it, eat of its fruits and enjoy its beauties and returned to the ship refreshed and enlightened by the experience. A third group lingered rather long and scurried back as the ship was departing; but they lost their choice places on the boat for the rest of the journey. A fourth party indulged so freely in the island's pleasures, that it was hard to stir them when the ship rang its bell. "There is no hurry," so they lingered. Only after the last warning they made a wild rush, and had to clamber up the ship's sides; so they reached it, bruised and maimed; nor were their wounds quite healed at the close of the voyage. There was a fifth group alas, who drank so deeply and reveled so wildly that they heard neither bell nor warning. The ship started without them and at night-fall wild beasts emerged from their lairs and destroyed them.

Develop the analogy as a story of life.

Death and Immortality.

"Weep for the living mourners, not for the dead."

"Attempt not to comfort one when his dead lie before him."

"None are responsible for their words in time of grief."

"Trust not thyself till the day of thy death."

"This world is the vestibule; the world to come the palace."

To a denier of resurrection R. Gabiha said: "If what never before existed, exists, why may not that which once existed, exist again?"

"The longest life is insufficient for the fulfilment of half man's desire."

"One hour may win future life."

"He who makes the sorrowful rejoice will partake of life everlasting."

"After death one is not accompanied by his gold or his jewels but by his knowledge (Torah) and his good deeds." (see note on Immortality p. 44.)

Alexander reached the gate of Paradise. "Who is there," asked the guardian angel. "Alexander the Great." "We know him not, only the righteous enter here." Then he more humbly asked for a proof that he had reached the heavenly gate, and a piece of a skull was given to him! Alexander's sages proceeded to test it and finally placed it in one scale as a balance. They poured gold in the other scale, but the small bone weighed heavier. Alexander added his crown-jewels and diadem. The bone out-weighed them all. Then a sage placed a few grains of dust on the bone; up flew the scale! The bone was the setting of the eye. It is never satisfied until covered by the dust of the grave.

Wit and Humor.

"When the wine is in, the secret is out."

"A man's character may be tested in his portion (generosity), in his potion (wine-cup), and in his passion."

"If thou tellest thy secret to three persons, ten know it."

"A light for one is a light for a hundred."

"The sun will set without thy assistance."

"The soldiers fight; the kings are heroes."

"Life is lent, death is the creditor."

"If speech in season is worth one piece of silver, silence in season is worth two."

"Silence is good for wise men; how much more for fools."

"Wisdom increaseth with age,—so does folly."

"The poor who owe nought are rich; the old without ailment are young; the learned without religion are foolish."

"Thy yesterday is thy past; thy to-day is thy future; thy to-morrow—is a secret."

"Sufficient for the hour is its trouble."

"Use thy best vase to-day; to-morrow it may be broken."

Said an Athenian to a Hebrew lad:

"Here is a *Pruta* (a tiny coin); buy me something of which I may eat enough, leave some for my host and carry some home to my family." The boy brought *salt*.

A would-be wit took an iron mortar to a tailor, saying: "Put a patch upon it." "I will, if you will make me some thread of this sand."

R. Gamaliel bade his servant bring him something good from the market. He brought—a tongue. To test his judgment, he was next asked to bring something bad; he brought—a tongue. "If good there is nothing better; if bad there is nothing worse."

"Life and death are in the power of the tongue."

"Why should I be slave," said the serpent's tail to its head; "let me lead." "Lead on." First it dragged the body into a miry ditch; no sooner did it emerge than it became entangled in a thicket. Bruised and torn the serpent was extricated only finally to be led into a furnace.

"When the pitcher falls upon the stone, woe to the pitcher; when the stone falls upon the pitcher, woe to the pitcher; whatever mishap, woe to the pitcher."

"Money, lacking for necessity, is found for superfluity."

"Peace is the wisp of straw that bindeth the sheaf of blessings."

"Discord is the cistern-leak whence drop by drop all the water escapes."

R. Joshua met a little girl by the way and asked for some water. She handed him her pitcher, saying: "I will also draw some for the beast on which thou ridest." Quenching his thirst he said: "Daughter of Israel, thou hast followed the worthy example of Rebecca." "Rabbi," said she archly, "Thou hast not imitated the example of Eleazar" (Gen. xxiv 22).

NOTES AND REFERENCES.

All the Agada material scattered through the Talmud has been gathered into one book called "The Eye of Jacob" (after the name of its author). But popular collections more or less complete have been made in modern tongues. Among these may be mentioned:—*Rabbinische* Blumenlese by Leopold Dukes; *Parabeln, Legenden und Gedanken aus dem Talmud*, by Ludwig Seligman; *Stories and Sayings from the Talmud*, Katie Magnus; *Gems from the Talmud* by Isidore Myers, the quotations given in the original and translated into English verse: *Hebrew Tales*, Hyman Hurwitz; *600 Talmudic Sayings*, Henry Cohen; *Selections from the Talmud*, H. Polano.

———————

Immortality of the Soul: Zillah. H. L. Harris.

BOOK V.

SHEM AND JAPHETH.

CHAPTER XXXVIII.

BEGINNING OF THE JEWISH MIDDLE AGES.

In the Byzantine Empire.

To turn again to the history proper. The production of the Talmud is part of the story of Babylonian Israel. Except that fanatic outbreak about the year 500 (p. 236) little occurred to disturb the even tenor of their way. They were "happy" because they "had no history."

But life was going hard for their brethren elsewhere. Many were settled in the lands of the Eastern half of the Roman Empire known as the Byzantine. It included all ancient Rome's conquests in Asia, Eastern Europe and Northern Africa. Our present Turkey forms the bulk of it.

Yes, the status of the Jew was growing still more precarious. In many Palestinian towns, notably Cæsarea and Antioch, insurrections broke out, usually during the circus races. Ravages against the Jews were actually endorsed by the emperor Zeno. Churches were everywhere replacing synagogues in the land which had once been theirs, and Jerusalem became an archbishopric where Jews were not even *admitted*. Such are the changes of time!

Laws of Justinian.

Under Justinian, anti-Jewish legislation was systematized. He was the emperor who became famous because of the Digest of Roman law, accomplished in his reign, in the year 541. His theory was—"one religion, one law, one state." Against the fulfilment of such an ideal the Jews stood, so to speak, as an obstacle. Therefore the laws of this Digest (or rather of his later Novellae) that concern them, are severe. Among these, was the provision that Jewish witnesses could not testify against Christians. Justinian, who further made them bear the expense of the magistrate office without its privileges, also forbade their celebrating Passover prior to Easter! He even went so far as to prohibit the recital of the *Shema* since he regarded its declaration "God is one" as a protest against the Trinity! This meddlesome intruder, furthermore, tried so to modify the Synagogue service that it might encourage Christian ideas.

Altogether there was almost an unbroken monotony of suffering under

Byzantine rule. Judaism was made to cost its followers dear. But their deep faith that Providence would ultimately usher in a glorious dawn if they were but patiently loyal, saved them from despair. Under the Byzantine rule at its best they were left contemptuously to themselves and were granted a certain autonomy in the management of their communal affairs.

Jews again Involved in War.

In the early part of the sixth century, Persia tried to wrest Palestine from the Byzantine Empire. Jews must look on while others fought for the country that was once theirs. Since Byzantium was treating them so badly and Persia (which included Babylonia), was treating their brethren humanely, the Jews settled in Palestine, decided to support Persia with its arms. If successful, they could live secure under its more tolerant sway. So under the leadership of one Benjamin, Jews mustered an army once more.

The Persians, however, were ungrateful to these allies, and when victory seemed to be theirs, not only refused to cede Jerusalem according to promise and for which the Jews had so longingly hoped, but even imposed oppressive taxes upon them, thus going back upon their own record. How cruel the world is to minorities! Further ill-treatment induced many to enlist under the banner of the Byzantine emperor Heraclius in 627. By solemn treaty he promised them immunity from all punishment for having taken up arms against him.

Fortune turned in his favor. Persia withdrew. The monks now urged the triumphant emperor to extirpate the Jews from Palestine. He reminded them of his solemn promise of protection made to them. They told him that a promise to Jews need not be kept; and, that to slay them would be an act of piety! Thus sanctioned, he began a severe massacre. Further, those old edicts of Hadrian and Constantine forbidding Jews to enter Jerusalem were once more enforced in 628. But Judea was not long to remain in Christian hands.

Rome's Successors.

As already stated in chapter xxxiv, the Western half of the Roman Empire had succumbed to Northern tribes by the year 476. The Ostrogoths, led by Theodoric, became masters of Italy, the Visigoths of Spain, the Franks and Burgundians of Gaul—the Gaul that had been great Caesar's pride to conquer. Here we see the beginning of the formation of the nations of Europe. They all accepted the Roman system of law and government to a modified extent, and also that which now became the Roman religion—Christianity. So the victors became the disciples of the vanquished—a not unusual experience in history.

In each of these lands and under each of these peoples, Israel was pretty well represented by the beginning of the sixth century, and in each it had a distinct history. So, in continuing our story we shall have to follow many strands. They were treated better in these new European countries than in Byzantine lands—at least at first.

Italy.

The Ostrogoths, the new rulers in Italy, were *Arians*. (p. 243.) The other group of Christians—the orthodox—called themselves Roman Catholics. Catholic means universal. Christianity claimed to be a universal Church and Rome had once claimed a universal Empire. This religious monopoly, the theory that this church offered the only saving creed, did sad mischief in the coming centuries. These Arian Ostrogoths were kinder to the Jews than were the catholics. The greater tolerance of the Arians may perhaps have been due to the fact that their idea of God was a little closer to that of the Jewish. But Arian Christians, always a small minority, soon disappeared, just as in the early days of the church, Jewish Christians were absorbed by pagan Christians. But as long as these two divisions of Christendom lasted, they were very bitter against each other. When a Byzantine army threatened the Ostrogoths, the Jews loyally stood by those who, if they had not treated them generously, had treated them justly. Later we find the Jews defending the seacoast of Naples for the Ostrogoths in 536. Only when overwhelmed by superior numbers did they at last surrender. Thus Italy, once the country of which Rome was the capital, was becoming the sport of nations. From the Ostrogoths it passed to the Byzantine Empire. Then in 589 it was seized by a tribe from the Elbe called Lombards. Its later story is told in the sequel to this book (*History of the Mediaeval Jews*).

The Popes.

But through all these changes, the city of Rome remained the religious centre of the Church as Jerusalem had been the religious centre of Judaism.

The Roman *bishop* (overseer) acquired power over all bishops in other Christian centres, and became the head of the Church with the title *pope* (Greek-father). In the course of time these popes exercised immense power, and we shall see kings trembling before them. For they came to be regarded as the representatives of God on earth. Whoever dared oppose their will was excommunicated, i.e., cut off. Then all shrunk from the person thus put under the ban as from a person smitten with leprosy; for the superstitious age regarded him as accursed and doomed. Very terrible was it when this dangerous power was in the hands of an unscrupulous pope, which not infrequently happened. But there were many good popes, too, and the Jews found among them, as we shall see, friends as well as foes.

Gregory I, one of the earliest and also one of the greatest, would not allow his bishops to molest the Jews, "whom God had found worthy to be bearers of His truth"; though he offered the bribe of remission of taxes for their conversion!

Slavery and Trade.

Slavery was still a recognized institution of society, due in part to constant warfare, the daily business of life and to the custom of enslaving prisoners of war. So slaves were in nearly every household and in the fields, taking the place of the humble toilers of to-day.

So we find Jews holding them likewise. They often converted them to Judaism and in all cases were kinder to them than most masters. But Gregory vigorously objected—not to slavery, but to the enslaving of Christians, and particularly to the possession of Christian slaves by Jews. The Church greatly feared that by proselytizing their slaves the Jews might increase their numbers. This was to be prevented at any cost.

If the question were asked why Jews came to trade in slaves, the answer would be because they were becoming traders in general, and traffic in slaves was part of the commerce of the age. It is then part of a larger question—how came the Jews to seek trade as a means of livelihood? *First*, by the law of necessity. Most other avenues of activity were being closed to them. Not permitted to own lands, they could hardly be agriculturists. Gradually the army, the public service and most of the professions were forbidden to Jews.

Secondly, on account of their dispersion through the world, which had its compensating advantages. United to their brethren by close fraternal ties, speaking a common tongue and moving frequently from place to place, the exchange of commodities was facilitated. Then having smaller opportunities of expenditure, and in any case of moderate tastes, they naturally possessed ready means.

Lastly, their hard fate in lands of exile, the growing precariousness of their position under fanatic powers, quickened their wits in the life struggle and endowed them with the capacities that earn success in trade. (We are not therefore surprised to learn that the Jews invented bills of exchange.)

This is all there was to justify the medieval belief in the colossal wealth of the Jews and the fantastic notions as to its acquisition.

The humanity of the Hebrew slave laws is one of the commonplaces of history. See Exodus xxi and Deut. xxiii.

The Slave Trade, chapter vi in *Jewish Life in the Middle Ages*, Abrahams, J. P. S. A.

Theme for discussion:

In what respect did medieval slavery differ from Russian serfdom and from the bond service in the early colonial era of America?

CHAPTER XXXIX.

IN THE SPANISH PENINSULA.

Gaul and the Franks.

The "wanderings of the Jews" have begun. The drift of the migration is westward. They are gradually leaving the Orient and finding homes in European lands. In Gaul, the land that is largely France to-day, Jewish merchants from Asia Minor had found their way long before the Christian era. After the fall of Judea, many Jewish prisoners and slaves were brought thither. The first places of settlement were Arles, Narbonne, Marseilles, Orleans and Paris. We find them in Belgium too.

The successors of Rome in Gaul were Franks. The Franks (free men) were a confederacy formed about 240 C. E. of tribes dwelling on the lower Rhine and the Weser. The Frankish Empire, which extended far, was not one central government, but was subdivided into several monarchies. Under nearly all, the Jews enjoyed the rights of Roman citizenship.

We find the Jewish industries varied, including agriculture and all kinds of commerce (still in its infancy); in medicine they had been early distinguished. Some were soldiers too, for the restraints of the Church had not yet reached Western Europe. Even when Christianity was first introduced by the warrior Clovis, Jews and Christians mingled freely and held cordial relations; though the Jewish dietary laws occasionally caused embarrassment and ill-will when Jews sat at Christian tables. It was only the *higher* clergy who began to look upon these cordial relations with misgivings and to discourage them. In this way hatred was *artificially fostered* by the Church. Not till the beginning of the sixth century did a Christian king of Burgundy begin to discriminate unfavorably against the Jews, and to break off kindly relations by forbidding Christians to sit at Jewish tables. Soon the Church Councils began to issue severe anti-Jewish edicts. So in different provinces and towns within the Frankish empire we find restrictions such as these gradually introduced: Jews must not make proselytes; they must not "insult" Christians by showing themselves in the streets on Easter; they must not be permitted to serve as judges or as tax-farmers.

Their worst enemy at this early day was Bishop Avitus. He first tried to convert the Jews by preaching Church doctrines to them. Persuasion failing, he resorted to violence and incited a mob to burn their synagogues. This was in the year 576. Their fanaticism once fed, the masses fell upon the Jews and massacre began. Baptism was accepted by several in order to save their lives —others escaped to Marseilles.

Vicissitudes in Spain.

So far Gaul. Let us now turn to Spain or rather to the Peninsula, for Portugal was not yet a separate kingdom, and what is now the south of France was also included in the Roman territory taken by the Visigoths. Where the Jews were early settled in the lands of southern Europe, in very remote antiquity—too early even to trace—they were brought there as slaves in considerable numbers after the Judean War with Rome in 70, and were soon redeemed by their sympathizing brethren. As in Gaul, so here, the Visigoths, being of the broader Arian school, regarded the Jews with cordiality and esteem, and their superior knowledge gained for them public positions of honor and trust.

So we find the public-spirited Jews gratefully defending the passes of the Pyrenees against the inroads of the Franks and Burgundians, and winning distinction by their courage and trustworthiness. How patriotic the Jew always becomes when given the barest tolerance, we shall see right through his history!

Nor did they forget their religion, but became faithful disciples of teachers sent them from the Babylonian schools. For their well-wishing neighbors did not interfere with their complete observance of the precepts of Judaism.

But as soon as the orthodox Christians—i.e., the Roman Catholics— obtained the upper hand, the higher clergy, behaving identically like those in Gaul, began to sow the seeds of mistrust in the hearts of the people, and forbade close intercourse with Jews, as sin. Anti-Jewish legislation soon followed, the unfair discrimination to handicap the Jews in the race of life. They were deprived of their public posts. How Jewish history repeats itself!

Their height of misery was reached when one Sisebut came to the throne in 612. Jews were now prohibited from holding slaves, though slaves were held by all others and formed a necessary class in the restricted civilization of the age. The climax was reached when he offered them the alternative of baptism or expulsion. Very many preferred exile to apostasy. Some found the sacrifice of land, home and possessions too great, and *externally* submitted to a Faith that cruel experience had taught them to abhor. Under his successor, Swintilla, who repealed the harsh laws, the exiles returned to the land and the apostates to Judaism. But the Church Council re-enacted the unnatural command of forced baptism and the returned converts were compelled to become

Christians again. What sort of Christians could they become under such conditions? But most cruel enactment of all—to think that a religious council should have proposed it—their children were torn from them and placed in monasteries to become completely estranged from both their Faith and their kindred. This hard law was mitigated however by the opposition of the powerful Visigothic nobles.

The next king who occupied the throne offered the remaining Jews the same alternative of exile or baptism. Again they submitted to banishment. Once more they were allowed to return though under many restrictions. But the forced converts were held in the Church with an iron grip, while, strange contradiction, they had yet to pay the Jewish tax! In secret and peril they still continued to observe the Jewish festivals. But the spies of the Church soon discovered this double life and compelled them to spend Jewish and Christian holidays away from their homes and in the presence of the clergy. After a few years in which this cruel vigilance was relaxed, King Erwig won over the clergy to his support by reinstating this Jewish persecution with more violence than all his predecessors. Now baptism was demanded, with confiscation, mutilation and exile as the penalties of its rejection. The Jewish Christians who had secretly clung to Judaism right through, were placed under complete clerical espionage. These abortive edicts were passed in 681. The next king, Egica, "bettered the instruction" of his predecessor. Jews were now forbidden to hold landed property, to trade with the Continent, or to do business with Christians. In their despair, the Jews of Spain entered into a conspiracy against this barbaric government. They were discovered, and nearly all reduced to slavery.

But relief was to come from an unexpected source. A new religion, Mohammedanism, had been brought to life and was becoming a great power in the world. It was destined to change for centuries the fate of the Jews of the Peninsula and transform an iron into a golden age. But to understand this movement, we must turn to Asia once more and look into the life of a new people—the Arabians.

NOTE.

This age produced nothing of a literary character except polemic replies in Latin to works written at this time to prove Christianity from the Jewish Scriptures.

Theme for discussion:

Why do you suppose the higher clergy opposed the mingling of Jews and

Christians and the lower, favored it?

CHAPTER XL.

ARABIA.

The Land and the People.

The Peninsula of Arabia is bounded on the southwest by the Red Sea, on the southeast by the Indian Ocean, on the northeast by the Persian Gulf, and on the north touches the mainland of Palestine and Syria, reaching to the Euphrates (see second map). So that we might say it lies between three continents. It is divided by geographers into three parts: 1. Arabia Felix (fortunate)—the largest—all the land between the three seas. 2. Arabia Petraea (stony)—the end adjoining the Peninsula of Sinai. 3. Arabia Deserta —the desert between Palestine and the Euphrates. The old Ishmaelites used to dwell in Arabia Deserta—a land scorched by burning sands, with scant vegetation and brackish water. These Bedouins were brave, hardy, and of simple habits, but restless and rapacious. The description of the wild ass in the thirty-ninth chapter of Job well fits their character.

The nature of the land made the building of cities and organized society impossible. Conditions encouraged a lawless life, and necessity, rather than choice, tempted the Bedouins to attack merchant caravans. A French proverb runs, "To know all is to excuse all." While not endorsing this dangerous maxim, we can see that their home largely decided their character. We are all influenced by surroundings in some degree. Yet some make the most of even hard conditions and barren soil. Not so the Bedouins. They never rose to greatness religiously—satisfied to worship stars and stones and to gratify the wants of the hour. So they have not advanced. But of the Arabs of central and southern Arabia we have a better story to tell.

Arabian Jews.

Long before the fall of the second Temple—probably before the fall of the first—Jews found their way to Arabia. By the time they made their presence felt there, we find them established in separate groups or tribes.

There were many points of kinship between Jews and Arabians. The Bible hints this in making Abraham the father of both peoples through Isaac and Ishmael (Gen. xvii, 18-20). This tradition the Arabs accepted from their Jewish neighbors. They certainly both belonged to the same race—the

Semitic. The Semites included Assyrians, Chaldeans, Babylonians, Syrians, Phoenicians, Hebrews, Arabs and Ethiopians. In spite of the religious divergence, the Jews adapted themselves—externally at least—to the Arabian mode of life. (It is a nice question in how far Jews should assimilate with their surroundings and in how far stand aloof.) So, while the Jews of southern Arabia engaged in commerce, those of the less civilized north were agriculturists and wandering shepherds like their Bedouin neighbors. Like them, too, some even formed robber bands; yet here at least we meet a favorable variation in that the Jews were more humane to their enemies. Further, the Jews adopted the patriarchal status of society of their Arabian surroundings—not so dissimilar to the social life depicted in Genesis—i.e., each group of families lived under the guidance of one patriarch or Sheik; such were Abraham and Jacob. The Sheik was a kind of king and his will was obeyed as law by the particular group under his sway. For there was no central government. In unsettled districts, hospitality becomes the greatest virtue, because it represents the greatest need, and its violation, the gravest crime. This is well illustrated in the Genesis story (chapters xviii and xix) of the contrasted behavior of Abraham and the people of Sodom.

The religious ideas of the Arabians while not gross were primitive. They had a Holy City, later known as Mecca, near the Red Sea border, in the centre of which was a black stone preserved in a Temple called the Kaaba. This they no doubt worshipped as an idol. Indeed three hundred idols were associated with this place. While fierce in warfare, in which they frequently engaged, and remorseless in revenge, they mitigated these rough tendencies by the institution of four holy months, during which the taking of life was avoided.

The Jews as such were better educated than the Arabs, and may have taught them writing, and were altogether looked up to as the intellectual superiors of the Arabs. Far from interfering with the religion of the Jews, the Arabs were rather prepared to take the position of disciples. They adopted some Jewish rites and accepted their calendar; moreover, the Jewish teaching exercised a salutary influence on their character. Many converts came to Judaism unsought, and when a Sheik accepted Judaism, the clan followed. Naturally, under such favorable auspices the Arabian Jews lived up to their religion with ardor and zeal, that is, as best as they understood it. They were students of Jewish law and turned for guidance probably both to Judea and Babylonia. They had their school too at Yathrib, later called Medina—north of Mecca, near the Red Sea. But the Bible was taught in Midrashic paraphrase, rather than in the original Hebrew text.

Jussuf the Proselyte.

The most important convert to Judaism was Jussuf, the powerful king of Yemen, in the southwestern quarter of the Peninsula—about the year 500 A. C. E. The Jewish sages were invited to teach Judaism to the people at large. The enthusiastic but unwise King Jussuf, hearing that Jews were persecuted in the Byzantine Empire (p. 281), put to death some of its merchants. This only paralyzed trade and brought on war. So the Jews were hardly fortunate in their ally, for he did not grasp the spirit of Judaism and tried to impose it by force —i.e., by the sword. This recalls the forced conversions of John Hyrcanus (p. 78). Yussuf stirred up enemies against himself and the Jews in many surrounding lands; his foes at last completely crushed him. Thus ended the ill-starred Jewish kingdom. Israel might well exclaim, "heaven save us from our friends." No, Judaism was not destined to spread in that way. "Not by force, not by power, but by my spirit, saith the Lord."

Samuel the Chivalrous.

Like the Arabs, the Jews cultivated poetry and held it in high esteem. Most renowned of these Jewish poets was Samuel Ibn Adiya. His life is perhaps more interesting than his poetry, for it shows how this stimulating environment at its best encouraged a fine spirit of chivalry among the Jews.

For Samuel was also a powerful Sheik in whom the weak and persecuted always confidently sought protection. One day a famous Arabian poet and prince pursued by his enemies, sought refuge in his castle. Going forth to seek the aid of the Byzantine emperor, Justinian, he entrusted to Samuel his daughter and his arms. No sooner had he gone than his enemies hastened to the castle, demanding the arms from Samuel. But Samuel would not break his promise, so the castle was besieged. Obtaining possession of one of his sons, the savage enemies threatened to slay him unless the father gave up the arms. It was an agonizing alternative to the father, but he did not falter. "Do what you will, the brothers of my son will avenge this deed." So at that awful cost, the trust was kept. What wonder that an Arabian maxim should run "Faithful as Samuel." Other poets sang his praise.

But we must pass quickly over the rest of this epoch till we reach the end of the sixth century. By this time Judaism had widely spread and Jewish colonies were found along the whole northwestern coast. In Medina their numbers were particularly large—consisting of three great tribes. They had built their own villages and fortified strongholds.

It was in the year 570 that a man was born whose name, Mohammed, was to ring through all Asia, and whom all broad minds now recognize as one of the great religious teachers of mankind. Closely was his fate linked to Israel's, for again was Judaism to inspire a prophet and give birth to another world-religion.

NOTE.

Carlyle, in his *Heroes and Hero Worship*, says of the wild Bedouin:—"He welcomes the stranger to his tent as one having right to all that is there; were it his worst enemy he will slay his foal to treat him, will serve him with sacred hospitality for three days, will set him fairly on his way; and then, by another law as sacred, kill him if he can."

Theme for discussion:

Win did Judaism not succeed as a proselytizing religion?

CHAPTER XLI.

MOHAMMED.

Mohammed, to name him by the title that he afterwards acquired, was born in Mecca, five years after the Byzantine emperor Justinian, and belonged to a branch of the powerful Koreish tribe. He began life as a shepherd. At twenty-five he married Kedija, who had employed him as camel-driver. Traveling extensively for her, he found his fellow-countrymen in a condition of religious neglect. The old star-worship and fetichism were losing their force, just as in more classic lands the divinities of Olympus had lost their meaning, some half dozen centuries earlier. Mohammed, given much to solitary contemplation, yearned for something better. He became filled with fine aspirations to uplift his fellowmen. For a period he led an ascetic life, spending much time in prayer. In the solitudes of the wilderness he experienced at times a strange exaltation. Others, like himself, groping for religious truth, were brought in contact with Jewish and Christian colonies in Syria and Babylonia. But the idea of one sole God, *Allah* (Arabic), he learned from Jewish teachers. A highly nervous nature, he "dreamed dreams and saw visions," and gave vent to his emotions in violent outbursts.

It was in about his fortieth year that he felt the divine call to preach God to his benighted Arabian brethren after the manner of the Hebrew Prophets, whose words had moved him deeply. He began to feel that perhaps he was the ordained Messiah whom the Jews awaited. He had learnt the Hebrew Scriptures in the more highly colored *Midrashic* form. From what he thus learned and from what he gathered from some hermits and from a group of ascetic Arabians, together with his own religious experience, he gradually evolved a religion for his people that came to bear his name.

He did not reach these convictions without much anguish of soul his spirit torn by doubt—the true experience of every deep religious nature. First Kedijah, then his family, then a small circle of adherents gathered about him, convinced of his divine mission. His vigorous personality attracted many more. At first his purpose was not to teach a new religion, but to reinforce the great truths recognized by the noblest natures in all times, his own enthusiasm contributing the only new element. The humbler classes were first attracted, the higher holding aloof. Is that not always so? Guided by his first teachers, the Jews, he saw the worthlessness of idolatry and preached a strict monotheism. He also adopted many Jewish rules, among them some of the dietary laws.

But gradually he made *himself* the centre of his message. He had some allies, but many opponents, especially as he denounced the idols of the Kaaba and rode roughshod over many of the cherished traditions and superstitions of the Arabians. Partly for this reason and partly because the success of his preaching meant the withdrawal of rich revenues derived from the pilgrims who came to the "holy city" of Mecca, its people began to persecute him. His life was full of peril. A breach with the Arabians was a breach with the world —a living death. So, for a moment he temporized and was prepared to make a quasi acknowledgment of the old divinities. But with the conversion of his uncle and one Omar—a man like himself of great force of character—he took a rigid stand again. He was put under interdict by the Koreish, his own family tribe.

The Hegira

In the meantime he suffered much privation. Among the people of Medina however, his preaching, in which he referred to the Jewish Scripture for endorsement, received more kindly recognition; for among them, Jewish teaching had, as it were, prepared the way. This meant new converts. So in the year 622 Mohammed bade all his followers emigrate with him to Medina. This was called the famous *Hegira* (flight), and marked the turning point in the movement. Medina became a commonwealth and Mohammed its chief and judge. All disputes, hitherto decided by combat, were now brought to him for decision. Thus he began to build up a system of law and justice. Here then he founded a religious settlement, and its whole social tone was raised. He preached particularly against greed and injustice. The bitter blood feuds were modified, property rights were respected, and the position of woman elevated. He had long since condemned the barbaric Bedouin practice of putting to death newly born daughters. The whole life of the people of his community was ordered with a kind of military precision in which the battle cry was, "No God but one God."

Unfortunately he also proclaimed, "Who is not for me is against me." This meant war against all outside his adherents.

The cardinal precepts of the New Faith were: 1. Confession of unity of God; 2. Stated times of prayer; 3. Alms giving.

His most daring act perhaps was breaking with that fundamental principle of Arabian life—blood relationship. The old Arabian ethics had concentrated all duty within tribal boundaries. These were now to be disregarded and a new brotherhood built up, that of *Islam* (submission)—a religious brotherhood that could disregard even the holiest ties outside of it. Yet to ask his followers to exchange kinship for faith was an unnatural demand. This long meant bitter resistance; but Mohammed's determination prevailed.

His followers now became an army and a remorseless conflict was waged with all who refused to come within the fold. This, brought his arms against the Jews. Their strongly fortified castles were taken one by one. Completely to break with the old regime he even ordered his followers to attack the caravans in the "holy month of truce, Ramadhan." This was a severe test of their faith. Victory steadily followed his aggressions and brought him many converts; many deputations came in voluntarily, dazzled into conviction by his success.

In 630 he had conquered Mecca. This was called "The Conquest." Although he compelled the inhabitants to give up their idols he compromised so far as to retain the Kaaba and the Festival of Mecca and to reinstate Mecca as a holy city. Abraham, now styled an Arabian, was said to have worshipped the Kaaba stone and was credited with being the father of the ritual. Fascinated by the glamor of Mohammed's remarkable triumphs, adherents came to him from all sides. What other creeds have taken centuries to attain, he achieved in his lifetime. This too rapid success is one of the defects of his movement. It grew too fast for excellence. So some of his successes were failures, for to obtain them the spiritual was occasionally sacrificed to the worldly.

As each new province came under his sway, its submission was to be exemplified by proclamation of the *Mueddin* for prayer, payment of alms-tax and acceptance of the Moslem law. But in each instance the internal tribal affairs were left untouched. In 632, in the eleventh year of the Hegira, Mohammed died. But not till Arabia was at his feet. He had founded a religion and a State.

NOTE.

Islam, the name given to this religion, and *Moslem*, to its followers, are both derived from a word meaning 'submission' (to God). *Musselman* is another variant.

A Jew, *Waraka Ibn Naufel*, is said to have been Mohammed's chief teacher and one of his strongest supporters.

Theme for discussion:

Should Mohammed be called a prophet?

CHAPTER XLII.

ISLAM AND THE JEWS.

Mohammed never forgave the Jews for their refusal to accept him as "The Prophet" of God, superseding all others. He had accepted so much from them —the fundamental idea of monotheism, the chief points of the Calendar, the Sabbath, the Day of Atonement, much of the Scripture and Midrashic narrative, and many details of the ceremonial law. He asked of them so little —it seemed—to regard him as God's chosen and supreme messenger to man, to all intents and purposes the Messiah, whose advent was foretold in their own Scriptures, and to whom they should henceforth look for the interpretation of their Faith. But that "little" they could not conscientiously give. For not even Moses, their only recognized lawgiver, "greatest of their prophets," were they prepared to regard quite in the way in which Mohammed asked allegiance. Their hearts told them that this man was not sent by God on a mission to them, however much he may have been sent to the Arabians. He was not *their* Messiah. So to accept him would be traitorous to their traditions and to the teachings of the Scripture (Deut. xviii, 15-22). For the acceptance of Mohammed would have ultimately meant the stultification of their religion and its submergence in a new cult of which he would be the founder. At that rejection, his regard for them turned to hate, and instead of allies, he chose to look upon them as rivals, as enemies of the true Faith, Their endorsement was the one thing needed for the complete confirmation of his mission. Therefore, forgetting how much he owed to their spiritual treasures, he became their persecutor.

Christianity and Islam.

How history was repeating itself! Was not this identically Israel's experience with that other creed to which its religion had given birth— Christianity? Its adherents likewise said to the Jews, "We accept your Scriptures, ethics and divinity. Accept only from us this individual Jesus, *greatest of all prophets*, the Messiah, in whom all your prophesies have been fulfilled, who represents God's new covenant with man." And because they refused, they were hated and spurned.

From endeavoring to pattern his religion as closely as possible after the Jewish example he now in sullen resentment sought by arbitrary changes to emphasize its differences. Instead of turning to Jerusalem in prayer,

Mohammedans were told to turn to Mecca. He changed the Jewish Yom Kippur (Ashura), which he had adopted, for the holy month of Ramadhan. He altered the Sabbath from Saturday to Friday, making it a day of worship, but not of rest. Here again was an attitude towards Israel parallel with its experience with Christianity; for after three hundred years the Church had changed the Sabbath to Sunday and rearranged its calendar to make Easter independent of Passover. Then like Christianity, too, he inserted in *his* Scripture—the Koran—unkind things and calumnies about the Jews. Yet, on the whole, the Koran holds up many Bible characters as exemplars.

There was a third parallel between these two daughters of Judaism. Just as Christianity, to win the heathen to the fold, accepted into its theology many heathen rites and even beliefs, so now Mohammed, to win the allegiance of the heathen Arabs, accepted many of their most cherished traditions. The Kaaba Stone—an idol—was still to be regarded reverently in the new Faith. Lastly, Islam, like the Church, also claimed to be the one true and universal Faith, (See pp. 198-9). Judaism that had given birth to both, never made such claim.

Mohammed's conception of the future life was not as spiritual as that of Jews or Christians. In promising gross pleasure in the realm beyond, he unconsciously gratified the expectations of sensual natures.

The Koran or the Sword.

Let us hasten over the sad conflicts between Mohammed and the Jews—his wars against their chiefs, until he had succeeded in crippling their once powerful clans. The "Battle of the Foss," 627, is one of the unfortunate blots on the reputation of this really great man. Seven hundred Jews were gathered in the market-place and offered the alternative of "the Koran or the sword." But the Jews had been inured to martyrdom. There was no hesitancy in their choice. The grim warrior-prophet carried out his savage threat against them. They were all slain and the surviving women were sold.

All through Arabia this religious crusade was waged against them. Thus fell the city of Chaibar, but no such ruthless massacre was repeated. Many of the defeated Jews were even left in possession of their lands. They continued their losing fight but little longer against the triumphant advance of Mohammed. By the year 628, all the Jewish tribes had lost their independence; the sword was taken from them. So that era of arms and chivalry was now closed for the Jews of Arabia.

A Jewish woman, Zainab, who won Mohammed's favor, tried to be a Judith to her people and attempted to poison him. The dish was hardly tasted by him, so the plot failed and she paid for her daring with her life.

Spread of Islam.

Mohammed must be studied from the political side as founder of a great State as well as from the religious side as founder of a great creed. Indeed, he was a greater statesman than prophet. His followers believed in him intensely and were united to him by ties that death could no longer break. His fiery words embodied in the Koran became their inspired Scripture. With his name upon their lips, a crescent on their banner and the great watchword, "Allah is God, and Mohammed is his Prophet," these fearless warriors carried all before them. Islam became a great power in half a century, a power that had come to stay. It is accepted by nearly two hundred million souls to-day. Here was surely a great message—lifting the Arab from the slough. We see here, as in the rise of Christianity, the hand of Providence bringing light to the Gentiles.

Under Mohammed's successor Abu Bekr, there was a momentary falling-off, but the movement rallied under the leadership of Omar who followed the master's policy of spreading the new Faith by conquest. At the head of the Mosque, (the Church of Islam) was now an emperor—a caliph. Not so many years after Mohammed's death not only was most of Arabia Moslem, but the sway of Islam had reached Persia, conquered the land and superseded Zoroastrism. Syria and Egypt were next wrestled from the Byzantian or Eastern Roman Empire. Palestine had been taken from Persia by the Byzantines in 628 only to be lost again in 638 and in both wars the long-suffering Jews who saw their old home tossed from one conqueror to another, had looked to the incoming enemies as deliverers, (pp. 282-3).

What changes had Jerusalem seen! When the Jewish Temple was destroyed, it became a heathen capital—Aelia Capitolina, adorned with a heathen shrine. In its Christian era it became a bishopric. Under the Mohammedans a mosque held the place of honor. Such it remains to-day.

Islam was now accepted in Asia, as Christianity had been accepted in Europe, not by individuals, but by whole nations. Somewhat intolerant at first against opposing creeds—some of the Mussulmen were fanatics—it became later renowned for its breadth and enlightenment. Very soon the Jews found the Mohammedans their friends, against whom they had nothing to fear. Jewish poets began to hail their advent. Even in Babylonia the Moslem sway was more liberal than had been that of the Persian Magi in the latter years. The political, social and religious status of the Jews was to remain undisturbed; the same secular official was to be at their head (pp. 231, 233).

220

In fact, the Resh Galutha was given even heartier endorsement, and was treated as a prince by the government, with his civil and judicial powers increased, making the Jewish community in Babylonia almost a State in itself. It was the Caliph Omar who, in 638 raised Bostonai, a descendant of the House of David, to the post of Resh Galutha (Exilarch). The academies at Sora and Pumbeditha were continued without a break; their heads, called *Geonim* (Illustrious) had also certain powers and took equal rank with the Resh Galutha. The Jews became loyal subjects of the Mohammedan rulers, and when Caliph Ali's successor was deposed by a rival house (for Islam had also now split into two wings), the Jews came gallantly to his support. Here and there Moslem law in its freshest and noblest expression reacted favorably even on Jewish law. New religious movements in early stages of enthusiasm always reach high moral levels. It will be borne in mind that the Jews in all their past experience were necessarily influenced to a degree by their environment, while remaining loyal in all essentials to the traditional conception of Jewish life.

The ceremony of the inauguration of a Resh Galutha was henceforth more impressive than ever. There was quite a little court about him. Likewise the official organization of the two Academies was very elaborate with their President, Chief Judge, Assembly of Teachers or Senate, and their Greater and Lesser Sanhedrin. Their administration left its lasting impress on all Jewish communities. All looked now to Babylonia as their religious centre and gladly sent contributions toward the maintenance of the Academies. The prestige of the Babylonian community steadily grew with the extension of Mohammedan sway.

Fall of Visigothic Spain.

It was the spread of this great power that was to bring relief to the Jews of Spain, persecuted almost unto death. Verily the Moslem was unto them as a savior—for his arrival brought liberty, light and peace. After having subjected a large part of Asia, the sway of Islam spread unresistingly westward. All the north coast of Africa was soon under both its temporal and spiritual control. Christendom was alarmed at the rise of this new star and the checking of the advancing hosts from making inroad into Europe became now the first duty of every Christian monarch. Any warrior who could throw them back from his country's border at once sprang into fame.

In the meantime, however, none could withstand them. Nearer and nearer they approached the borders of Spain. There the outrageously treated Jews (pp. 291-2) awaited their arrival as any besieged city at the mercy of a relentless foe awaits the coming of its army of release. Already across the narrow Straits of Gibraltar on the African side, they were making common cause with the Moslem and were prepared for the invasion of the Peninsula.

The destined hour arrived. In the year 711 a great battle was fought in Xeres, in which the last Visigothic king fell before the army of Tarik. City after city—Cordova, Granada, Malaga, Toledo—fell before them, the Jews rendering valuable aid from within. The Mohammedans found they could not entrust their conquered towns into more faithful hands than these Jewish allies. Thus the Jews were raised at once from degration and thraldom to liberty and prestige. A new light had dawned and under the broad and cultured regime of the Moors, as these Western Mohammedans were called, a golden age was now to dawn for the Jews of Spain.

NOTE.

The Koran:

The Moslem Scripture is called the *Koran*, meaning readings; compare the derivation of *Karaites*. The Koran was not written by Mohammed, who could not write, but it contains his teachings.

Theme for discussion:

Amplify the probable consequences of the acceptance of Mohammed by the Jews.